RIDERS OF THE NIGHT

EUGENE CUNNINGHAM

THORNDIKE
CHIVERS

This Large Print edition is published by Thorndike Press, Waterville, Maine, USA and by AudioGO Ltd, Bath, England.
Thorndike Press, a part of Gale, Cengage Learning.

LIBRARY OF CONGRESS CATALOGING-IN-PUBLICATION DATA

Cunningham, Eugene, 1896–1957.
  Riders of the night / by Eugene Cunningham. — Large print ed.
    p. cm. — (Thorndike Press large print western)
    ISBN-13: 978-1-4104-3730-3
    ISBN-10: 1-4104-3730-2
    1. Ranch life—Fiction. 2. Large type books. I. Title.
PS3505.U428R53 2011
813'.52—dc22   2011011164

BRITISH LIBRARY CATALOGUING-IN-PUBLICATION DATA AVAILABLE

Published in 2011 in the U.S. by arrangement with Golden West Literary Agency.
Published in 2011 in the U.K. by arrangement with Golden West Literary Agency.

U.K. Hardcover: 978 1 445 83788 8 (Chivers Large Print)
U.K. Softcover: 978 1 445 83789 5 (Camden Large Print)

Printed and bound in Great Britain by the MPG Books Group
1 2 3 4 5 6 7 15 14 13 12 11

CAST OF CHARACTERS

Burk Yates, wanted nothing to do with the Y Ranch — until someone tried to fleece him of his share.

Myra Yarborough, slim, blonde, and proud, was Yates's partner at the Y.

Turkey Adkins, the best bandy-legged cow-puncher in Yates County, was rarin' to fight again for the Y — provided Burk Yates gave the orders.

Chihuaha Joe, daredevil adventurer, signed up with Burk just for the hell of it.

Lance Gregg, handsome unscrupulous owner of the Wallop–8, found Burk Yates an obstacle to his underhanded schemes.

Frisco Fanny, gorgeous dance-hall queen, saved Burk's life a couple of times.

Barney Settels, dangerous small-time gambler, lost his head over Fanny.

Ed Freeman, thick-skulled sheriff of Yatesville, never knew anything was wrong in

Yatesville — even when the corpses piled up outside his door.

Chapter I

'Citizens — Be Aware!'

Yatesville was lit by three flickering, discouraged oil lamps. Where the yellowish glimmer of these was not, the county seat was pitchy dark. For there was no moon and the hour was three of the spring morning. There was no life anywhere on the streets. Even the gambling-houses had closed more than an hour before. Faraday, the lank marshal, had shambled home. Straggling cowboys found sleeping-quarters in rooming-house or livery corral.

The main street was merely an inky tunnel where the oil lamps did not palely dapple it. It was silent, too. But faintly from the west there sounded a muffled, deliberate pounding; horses' hoofs, thudding upon the soft dust of the county road beyond the limits of the town. The dull noise came nearer, but seemed scarcely louder — as if, the closer to Yatesville those riders came, the more cautiously they rode.

Five minutes passed. Ten minutes. Then, abruptly as a lantern-show's beginning, against the weathered gray of the adobe buildings which lined both sides of the main street there was silhouetted a cavalcade of perhaps a dozen horsemen, looming gigantic where the street-lamps flung their shadows.

There was occasional faint creaking of saddle leather, the low blowing of a horse, the tiny jingling of spur or bit chain. Coming farther upstreet at deliberate walk, the horses' hoofs fell almost silently upon the dust.

On they came, these riders. Past the First Chance Saloon; on to and by the Congress Saloon. They reached Judge Amblet's long general merchandise store, but made no halt there. Other stores, saloons, gambling-halls were also left on one hand or the other. Now, the square, two-story 'dobe that was the courthouse of Yates County loomed ahead. Beyond it was a livery corral with a wide gateway. The twin gateposts were connected and braced at the tops by a great section of cottonwood log.

Past the courthouse the riders came, with that same deliberate, steady fall of hoofs. In a solid body they approached the livery corral adjoining. One shadow separated itself from the mass — a rider moving up ahead, like a scout, into the gateway of the corral. He reined in his mount and sat moveless for a long minute. At last, he lifted his arm.

Slowly, the other riders halted in mid-street moved again. They came forward to the gate; halted again. From the mass of them a small group split off and joined the single rider in the gateway.

There was a period of near-silent business there beneath the cross-bar of the gate. Small sounds — creakings, the rasping of rope upon leather or rough bark, an odd panting — there were, but none of the cowboys sleeping back in the corral's stalls were awakened. Three or four minutes passed. Then a grim voice:

'All right!' it grunted.

Through the darkness, as softly, sinisterly, as it had come, the party rode back along the main street. At the First Chance Saloon that same grim voice barked, once again:

'Yo!'

The thud of the hoofs quickened, chains jingled, leather squeaked. The party moved at a long, hard trot; vanished.

The hours of darkness dragged on. Presently, in the eastern sky over the far crest of the rugged Crazy Horse Range showed the

9

faintest flush of rose and pearl. It deepened, widened, until every raw color of the spectrum writhed up and out, as if stroked flashingly upon the gray sky by gigantic, invisible brush. Then over Crazy Horse Peak itself peeped the rim of a disk that looked like molten brass. Light came to all the Crazy Horse country.

In Yatesville, men stirred from houses or corrals or wherever they had spent the night. They came out into the daylight to begin the day's business. From one end of the main street and the other, storekeepers and freighters and other early birds appeared. And in the cool light of early morning, swaying a little in the gentle dawn breeze, two strange, limp things dangled like bundles of rags from the cross-bar of the gate of the livery corral beyond the courthouse.

Men were drawn there as by a magnet. They clustered about the gateway. They gaped open-mouthed, some of them. Others — like Rufe Redden, the storekeeper who had first seen them — stared broodingly from under down-drawn brows, their mouths sullenly tight, their brown faces immobile.

For to all of those who came to look, the two strangled men hanging from lariat-ends there at the gatebeam were well known; very well known indeed over all the Crazy Horse Range.

Upon the breast of each man a paper was pinned to the shirt. It was not necessary to move up more closely than one fancied approaching a dead man, in order to read the legend upon those improvised placards. The wording was alike on each and printed in the same strong, steady hand:

Citizens! Be Aware!
Do not touch these scarecrows before nine today.

Someone pulled himself away from the grisly fascination of the spectacle for long enough to go after gangling Faraday, the city marshal.

Faraday came shambling up, snapping a suspender over bony shoulder, blinking sleepily, muttering. But at sight of the bodies he lost his drowsiness. He stood there under them like a man transfixed. One long hand remained motionless, gripping a suspender. His loose mouth moved buzzingly. He was reading the placards' curt warning slowly and painfully, for Faraday was much more the professional peace officer than the scholar — and plenty in Yates-

11

ville said that he was not much of a peace officer.

' *"One,"* ' he finished, reading the signature of the legends. 'One . . . Why — why, hell! The One-Gang done this-yere . . .'

He moved up closer and stared into the faces of the dead men, small head coming forward on buzzard-like neck, little eyes squinting painfully, as if he expected to find in those contorted features something that a policeman should know.

'Pedro Garcia — an' Shorty Willets from the Y . . . Yes, sir! Pedro Garcia, an' Shorty Willets! What d'y'know about that! I ain't seen Shorty for — it's more'n a week. But Pedro, I run into him just yesterday. He says he sold out that li'l' place o' his on Brushy Crick. He was headin' for New Mexico, last night, he says. To see that rich brother o' his at Las Cruces. But he never went . . . One-Gang got him . . .'

He stopped short. His small black eyes were very round as he stared from one to the other of the figures. He did not need to voice his thought; hardly a spectator there but had been impressed by the same oddity of this business, the coupling together here of that shady character, Pedro Garcia, who had last worked as *vaquero* on Lance Gregg's Wallop–8, with little old Shorty Willets, as good a cowhand as the Crazy Horse country knew, and lately foreman of the big Y outfit.

Absently, it seemed, Faraday's long hand went up, reaching toward Shorty Willets. It was brushing the stiff, sweat-warped leg of Shorty's old overalls when, from the men watching, there came a dry voice:

'My goodness! Yuh ain't forgittin' what the sign says, Faraday?'

The marshal jerked back his hand as from a red-hot stove. He recoiled from the bodies. Then his sallow, lantern-jawed face was flooded with angry blood. He whirled upon the grizzled, bandy-legged little cowboy who had so contemptuously drawled the question.

'I reckon I can do whutever I'm a mind to, Turkey Adkins!'

'Shore yuh can! An' she shore ain't a dam' thing to me!' Turkey Adkins nodded. 'I'm jist tryin' to git this straight in my mind, that's all. I was jist a-augurin' whether yuh was callin' the One-Gang's bluff or — jist forgittin' it. Now, go right ahead! If yuh cut 'em down, now, yuh're a brave man. For yuh're tellin' the One-Gang they can't bluff yuh none; tellin' 'em to go to hell! Go right ahead!'

Tight grins ran around the watchers. For

it was as Turkey had said. Perhaps there was no danger whatever in ignoring the brazen warning of the gang which was daily becoming more notorious for its rustling and robbing and killing across the country; and even more notorious — and impressive! — for the calm insolence and the daring displayed in everything it did. But — these two exhibits alone were enough to make thoughtful even so thoughtless a man as Faraday the marshal.

'Well — I'm marshal, I reckon!' Faraday blustered at last. 'Nobody can interfere with me when I'm a-carryin' out my duties. Nobody better try it, neither. So ——'

Up went his hand again. He touched the saddle-warped leg of Shorty Willets's overalls. Defiantly, then, he looked around the ring of quiet faces. Then he got out of a pocket a big jack-knife and opened its largest blade.

'Come on, somebody! Hold 'em up while I cut them lass-ropes!' he ordered. Then, after a moment of utter silence and movelessness: 'Come on! Y' expect me to do ever'thing!'

Still nobody moved. Turkey Adkins rolled his cigarette from one corner of his wide, thin-lipped mouth to the other, spat expertly through his teeth, and regarded the marshal with one squinting gray eye closed against up-wreathing smoke.

'Ol' cow die — mouth o' the branch.
   'Tain't goin' rain no mo'!
Them buzzards held a public dance.
   'Tain't goin' rain no mo'!'

Thus Mr. Turkey Adkins, singing absently and very softly — precisely as if he had not heard a word of the marshal's invitation to flout the One-Gang.

'By Gemini! I'll do it all by myself, then!' Faraday snarled loudly.

He jumped up to the top of a 'dobe wall that flanked the gate. He scrambled up a gatepost until he was sitting astraddle of the cross-bar. Then he inched along until he came to where Pedro Garcia's lariat was turned about the cottonwood log. He took the jack-knife from between his teeth.

Turkey Adkins turned from watching him, to stare across the street. On the opposite side from the corral gateway there were no buildings. Most of Yatesville — that part which fronted upon the main street — lay west of the courthouse. There was little or none at this end behind the main street. So Turkey, standing at the corral gate, looked straight out into the open greasewood and mesquite flats beyond Yatesville — straight out to a little rise in the land perhaps an eighth of a mile away.

He nodded to himself. Since he commanded a clear view of that brush-crowned rise, it seemed natural to believe that anyone upon it commanded equally clear view of the gateway. He turned back, to stare squintingly up at the marshal. But Faraday seemed to have no thought of such scientific and geographic details as these noticed by Turkey Adkins.

He was leaning forward, now. The jack-knife was in his long, lean hand. The edge of the blade had touched the turn of the lariat when, from somewhere over toward that little rise, a flat and vicious report sounded. Something struck the right-hand gatepost of the corral. Shreds of bark and a little puff of smoke-like dust went flying. Again that flat, faraway *whang!* It was a miss. But the third shot of this continuous string slapped the cross-bar immediately under the seat of the marshal's pants. He came off the cross-bar with a wild howl; came as a kingfisher dives from a limb, head-first and careless of how he landed. He looked spidery as he fell in the dust, all thrashing long arms and legs. He howled steadily as he rolled over and over toward cover.

The men about the gateway had achieved the effect of merely fading from the scene. Mostly, they had jumped the wall of the corral and were sheltered now behind its thick 'dobe bricks. But Turkey Adkins was not one uselessly to expend so much effort. He had slipped sideways along the wall the precise distance necessary to be protected from a shot across that cleared space — and not an inch farther. Now, he squatted and watched with one bright, calm gray eye, the other closed as usual under the spiral of smoke from his cigarette.

He studied the marshal's frantic rolling until it ended, and, on hands and feet, Faraday galloped up beside him. He said nothing as the marshal jerked himself gaspingly erect and glared wildly toward the source of the lead.

'Git that dam' bushwhacker!' Faraday yelled wildly. 'Make doll-rags out o' him!'

'Who? Me?' Turkey inquired. 'My motter is that grand ol' hailin' cry they use up in Arkansaw: Let ever' gent kill his own snakes! Nahsir! He wasn't doin' no shootin' at me, fella! He was dustin' the south end o' yo' breeches. So *you* go git him, yo'self. I ain't got a bit o' use for no part o' that fella. He

17

shoots a lot too en-tire-ly where he's a-aimin', for me!'

Faraday, being now sheltered, raced across the street to the corner of that building which bounded the gap across which the hidden rifleman had fired. He had his Colt in his hand. He reached blindly around the building's corner with it and emptied it in the general direction of the rise. Turkey, loafing across after him, sing-songed the spots:

'One — Miss! Two — Miss! Three — Double the Last! Four — Five — Miss! Miss! Yuh're certainly proud o' that hawglaig, now ain't yuh? Tell yuh what, Faraday! Yuh ought to ram two bullets down each ca'tridge an' try to shoot twicet as fur! Or do yuh figger he's got a weak heart an' yo' noise'll skeer him to death?'

The marshal ignored Turkey's remarks. He reloaded his pistol and when he turned back across the street he swaggered. But the effect was spoiled when a pebble, flung by Turkey, kicked up dust at his heels. He jumped forward and sideways with a howl like that which had marked his coming off the cross-bar. Turkey, his brown face somber, lip curling, followed him.

'It's too bad I never had a long gun!' Faraday was telling the reassembled group

18

at the gate. 'I'd have got that hairpin!'

'Knowed a man name' Mister Brown.
  'Tain't goin' rain no mo'.
Wore his hat on upside down.
  'Tain't goin' rain no mo'!'

Faraday glared at the singer. Turkey regarded him speculatively for a bit. Then:

'Well!' he drawled, stretching. 'Reckon I'll ramble down an' hunt me up a bite to gnaw on. I'll be back, Faraday. Don't yuh worry about me not comin'. Around nine, I'll sa'nter back. To watch yuh cut them pore devils down, yuh know."

'Y're mighty brave!' Faraday sneered. 'S'posin' y' cut 'em down y'self? Yah! Don't like the notion, huh?'

Turkey blew the cigarette-stub from a pursed underlip and shook his head.

'I'm skeered to!' he said. 'If a big, brave man, with a great big pistol, like — like you, Faraday, if he's skeered, I'm runnin' like hell. I'll be back at nine, sharp, though!'

CHAPTER II

'If only he was Yates kind!'

Judge Amblet looked thoughtfully at the

swinging bodies of Shorty Willets and Pedro Garcia. He was a tubby little man with round, expressionless face, clean-shaved on cheeks and upper lip. He stared with small, deepset, and round blue eyes at the bodies, tugging with fat hand at the paintbrush chin whisker. He jerked his head at the marshal.

'Cut 'em down, Faraday,' he ordered nasally. 'Help him, Tooley. Hold 'em up while he cuts 'em down.'

Faraday moved a thought deliberately toward the grisly figures. A smallish youngster of stupid yellow face, wearing a deputy sheriff's star upon red flannel shirt, clumped after him.

As he reached up toward the rope that suspended Shorty Willets, involuntarily Faraday's head came turning for a swift glance across the open at that crest in the flat from which he had been fired on. It was not yet nine ——

'I *wisht* I had a watch!' Turkey Adkins cried anxiously from the watchers. 'Awful thing if a mistake was made, now . . . jist when ever'thing seems all right. But that's the way things do go — jist when yuh think yuh're safe, yuh git piled. Bad enough in Yatesville as 'tis — with some part of a marshal. But to lose that part an' not have any ——'

20

'Go ahead! Cut 'em down!' Judge Amblet snapped irritably. 'You shut up, Turkey Adkins! This is official business an' I don't want any interference. You let Faraday alone.'

From that little rise came no more shots. Nobody really expected any. For a posse of wild-riding cowboys had burned the ground getting out there after the shooting. They had asked nothing more than a glimpse of something to shoot at — and had found nothing but the spot where a horse had stood waiting in an arroyo, the place where a man had sprawled comfortably with both elbows propped to hold his rifle the better to steady it, and — this was the telltale thing — two empty .44 shells and a third one, set very prominently upright near by, on a carefully smoothed circle in the dust.

'The One-Gang, all right!' the cowboys had said to each other. 'Yeh . . . That's the sign.'

But now, as gently the two dead men were lowered to the ground and carried into the justice-court, there was no further objection by the gang which had hung them there.

Doc' Stevens made an examination and reported to Judge Amblet, who nodded heavily. Rufe Redden was the first witness. He stood with big freckled paws clenched on his hipbones, red hair falling tousled over his forehead. Belligerently, he told of opening the front door of his store, diagonally opposite the corral gateway, and observing the bodies. Recognizing them instantly, too. Faraday testified concerning the attack made on him and snarled at Turkey Adkins when the bandy-legged little cowboy nodded grave approval of the account. One of the cowboys who had ridden out to the rifleman's ambush testified concerning the single shell stood upright in the dust.

'I reckon that's plenty,' Amblet nodded gravely. 'It's my verdict that the deceased — Shorty Willets an' Pedro Garcia — they came to their death by bein' strangled an' 'twas at the hands o' parties unknown to me personal but callin' theirselves the One-Gang. It's a mighty sad affair, folks. The authorities'll do all that's humanly possible to clear it up ——'

'I'm shore glad to hear that!' Rufe Redden growled. 'Because, with all the other things this sneakin', murderin', bushwhackin' gang's done, it does seem to me that the authorities is about due to try somethin' — or git clean off the driver's seat an' let in a new bunch o' office-holders that *can* do somethin'! By God! I'm sick an' tired o' this way o' doin'! The most o' you

22

people gi' me a big pain right where it hurts most! Looks like we can't git a grand jury that'll do more'n pass resolutions endorsin' the sanctity o' the home, or somethin'!'

He turned his angry red face upon the bench.

'Will you quit poundin' that gavel, Amblet? You said you was done. Well, me, I'm just beginnin'! I'm sick an' tired o' this dam' One-Gang! All o' you know that things is dam' bad an' gittin' a sight worse. Gittin' so a man can't call a cow or a horse or a dollar his own, no more — no! nor his woman, for that matter! I'm sick an' tired o' the way Yates County's bein' mismanaged. You know dam' well that if that lousy gang was to ride into this justice-court right now an' yell for your shirts an' the fillin's out o' your teeth, the bulk o' you'd let out a howl an' start beatin' your foreheads ag'inst the floor! Action's the thing this county needs. I want to see some!'

He whirled and stalked toward the door. Turkey Adkins, squatting in a corner with inevitable brown cigarette drooping from his mouth-corner, lifted his hat solemnly as Rufe passed him. The big red storekeeper stopped short.

'What the hell you tippin' your hat to me for?' he snarled.

'Dam' if I know,' Turkey shrugged. 'Do'no' if it's because yuh're a dam' brave man, Rufe — or because yuh're apt to mightily soon be a dead man!'

Judge Amblet took it upon himself to resent Rufe Redden's outburst — when Mr. Redden could be seen through the doorway, halfway across the street. He said that, as an official of the county, naturally he knew how hard all officers had worked on a very difficult case. This One-Gang was notorious for leaving never a bit of evidence that the authorities could twist into a clue — and into a noose. But, speaking for the county administration, even though he was but one of the humblest of elected officials, the sheriff's office and every other department of the county government was working diligently. If any man there felt as Rufe Redden seemed to feel, he had only to produce some evidence on which a warrant might be issued ——

He broke off, scowling at that corner in which a little group was talking and from which rose an annoying drawl that interfered with the judicial flow of eloquence. He stiffened angrily and asked that the last remark be repeated.

'I was jist a-sayin',' Turkey Adkins shrugged, 'that we shore had things different in Yates County when Ol' Burk Yates was alive . . . Yuh never hear o' any One-Gang business them days! Nahsir! Blame' good reason, too: Ol' Burk he never liked that sort o' doin's an' he never stood for it!'

There being no indication of anything of further interest here, Turkey got up from where he had been hunkering against the wall. As he went out at reeling horseman's gait, he whistled his favorite tune. He was well outside before Judge Amblet had marshaled a crushing rejoinder.

'Is that so?' the Judge flung after Turkey's back. 'Is *that* so!'

Turkey sauntered on with hat-rim low over his eyes, whistling dolorously. A buckboard, coming into town, drew quietly up behind him. Softly as the team's hoofs fell upon the dust, Turkey heard the noise. He turned, still whistling, as it stopped and his name was called.

'Why — hello, Myra,' he drawled tonelessly. 'How's ever' li'l' bitsy ol' thing, anyhow?'

'You know how everything is!' the slim girl in the buckboard said shakily. 'You know that everything's bad — and steadily getting worse. That is — if they could be worse than now!'

'Oh!' Turkey nodded. 'Sounds mightily

like yuh heerd about — Shorty . . .' He jerked his head mechanically toward the corral.

'God! I — I can't believe it, Turkey! I — I can't believe anyone would be so — cold-blooded, so cruel! To deliberately murder poor Shorty Willets, simply because he worked for us — I heard about it as I came in. The — inquest? It's been held?'

'*Umhmm!* Shore! Held an' done with. Settled ever'thing. Ol' Amblin' Amblet has done gone back to sellin' calico.'

He fished a sack of Duke's Mixture from one pocket of his brown duck jumper and hunted from another a book of brown 'saddle-blanket' cigarette papers. Carefully, as if it were a religious rite, he sifted tobacco into a paper held troughlike. He squinted critically down, put three grains back into the sack, and hard brown fingers flickered. He licked the edge of the paper and looked up at her as he thrust the cigarette into his mouth.

'What'd the blackbird say to the crow?
  'Tain't goin' rain no mo'!
'Tain't goin' hail — 'tain't goin' snow;
  'Tain't goin' rain no mo'!'

Myra Yarborough sat patiently, regarding

26

the little man steadily. She knew the bandy-legged, bristlingly independent cowboy very well. Very well, indeed! for he had demanded his pay just as she had been on the verge of flinging it into his face. But that had been six months ago. Six long months ago when Shorty Willets had been riding for the Y, capable, willing to handle the range-affairs. Now —— It was different, now!

'What do you mean by what you said? That they settled everything?' she asked slowly, turning sideways in the buckboard seat, a slender, blue-eyed girl with hair yellow as corn and a red, pretty, and self-willed mouth.

'Huh? Mean? Why, Amblin' Amblet give the matter due considerin' an' decided that the deed was done by parties unknowed to him personal an', o' course, the duly elected authorities'll bring in the dirty murderers — mebbe . . .'

'Don't start that infernal song again!' she exploded, recognizing the symptoms in the Y's ex-foreman. 'Turkey . . . I've been thinking . . . I — Do you think — I mean, will you ——'

Turkey's hand dropped from his cigarette and disappeared into a side pants-pocket. Ostentatiously, he drew out one silver dollar and sufficient fractional silver to make

27

seventy-five or eighty cents more.

'Nah . . .' he drawled. 'Nah! I got too much money. Too much money en-tire-ly!'

He separated the coins on his palm, leaving a silver dime isolated. He squinted with gray eye down at the lone coin.

'I could take an' th'ow away all but that much,' he said meditatively, 'an' still I'd have too much money to go back to work for the Y. Yuh know, Myra, I reckon that when I'm done with a place or a body, I git jist a li'l' bit doner than anybody yuh ever see! An' I shore was plumb done with yuh, the day I rolled my bed an' hightailed off the place.'

'I was going to fire you, anyway!' she flared. 'I'll have no back-talk from any of my ——'

'Servants,' Turkey supplied, with a small grin, but by no means a humorous grin. 'Yeh, I knowed right well yuh meant that. Funny! Reminds me o' somethin' I was oratin' to Judge Amblin' Amblet a spell back: It shore was different when Ol' Burk Yates was alive. Yes — ma'am! It shore was that!

'The Y them days, it was run like a cowfolks' cow-outfit. Wasn't run, then, accordin' to the last letter o' instructions from the head-wrangler up to Vas-sar nor yet at Culver. Burk Yates, he had a mind an' he could make it up without callin' in no outside help.

'Take this rustlin' business: When some Y stuff was stole, them days, we jist sort o' got together, an' counted noses an' seen that ever'body had plenty grub an' ca'tridges. Then, off we 'loped jist as pleasant as ary Sunday-School picnic ever yuh did see. We kept a-splittin' the breeze till we come up to the hairpins we needed — them that done the stealin'. We give 'em the cottonwood prance, if they was physical-able to stand her. Else we jist buried 'em without. Then we sa'ntered back home to work!'

'I take back my offer!' she said furiously. 'I don't want you on the Y. I don't want you working for me!'

'Then that makes two o' us with mightily like notions.' Turkey nodded impassively. 'Besides, yuh don't need nobody like me to rod that spread — when yuh git so much valuable help — free, gratus an' for nothin'! — out o' Lance Gregg an' the Wallop–8.

'What d' yuh hear from Burk, these days? Has he learned how to do that jiggle in the saddle — what d' they call it — postin'? — back East at Culver? An' how to lift his li'l' finger dainty-nice when he picks up his teacup? Well . . . I did figger it was a kind o' shame, about that boy. I sort o' figgered he

29

must have some amount o' whalebone an' whangleather in him, bein' Ol' Burk's git. But — shucks! Them colleges has ruint better'n Burk, I reckon — boys *an'* gals . . .'

Furiously, she lifted the lines from her lap. Then she stopped, cheeks still blazing red and blue eyes snapping. For a second buckboard was coming into town from the west — from the direction of the railroad at Cottonwood Crossing, a village of sorts nearly twenty miles over.

Turkey, too, stared at the other buckboard. Brown face tightened; sun-squinted gray eyes drew to narrow and shining slits. Then he was taken by a sour grin. He hummed quite audibly and Myra's yellow head jerked back to him. She frowned uncertainly.

'Who is that, in the buckboard?'

'That?' Turkey cried amazedly. 'Yuh mean to say yuh cain't read the brand? Well, if my ol' eyes ain't plumb gone back on me, that-there's the Last o' the Fightin' Yateses. Yes, sir! Mister Burk Yates, o' Yatesville, Yates County, Texas — an' Culver, Pennsylvania, o' course. Half-owner, along o' Miss Myra Yarborough, o' the one-time amount-to-somethin' Y Ranch. Watch him, will yuh! Watch him! Blamed if he ain't a-practicin' that postin' business in Froggy's buckboard seat! Shore is hell, now ain't it, what them

30

colleges do to country boys an' gals!'

But Myra had slapped the lines on the pintos' backs. She jerked away, and when the buckboard rolled down-street, Turkey loafed over to lean against the wall of the nearest building. He stared thoughtfully at Myra's buckboard while it drew up to Froggy's and stopped beside it. His weathered face was like a mask carved from brown stone, now. He ground the butt of his cigarette to rags and powder with flashing movement of his fingers.

Under his breath he swore furiously, a torrent of savage rangeland oaths. For all morning he had been under the bitterest of restraints, bottling up the killing rage that had come with sight of Shorty Willets dangling from that corral gate cross-bar with insolent, challenging placard upon his breast. Now, the sight of Young Burk Yates coming back to the range his father and Duke Yarborough had settled back to the county and the town Ol' Burk had founded and named, had power to snap the iron control Turkey Adkins had kept upon himself. For Shorty Willets had been his good friend; had been his very good friend.

'If only he was Yates kind, not jist Yates blood!' Turkey said helplessly to himself, when his fit of fury had passed. 'But his ma, she was one o' them elegant town-ladies, she was! I reckon there's a streak o' soft in his bacon. If he'd been worth a hoot in hell, he'd have stuck down here last year, when Ol' Burk cashed in, an' took up the work o' bossin' the Y, instead o' leavin' it to that crazy, mule-stubborn gal . . .

'Nah, Turkey Adkins! I reckon yuh'll jist have to play the li'l' ol' lone lobo this trip. Where yuh'll be ridin' — an' how — there'll be no postin' in a postage-stamp saddle that could lift the scalps none . . . Still — an' yet ——

'The last o' the Fightin' Yateses. Man! I shore *wisht* he was that!'

CHAPTER III

'They can't get away with this!'

The two buckboards stopped seat-to-seat. Burk Yates and Myra Yarborough sat with heads turned sideways, facing each other. Myra's clear, blonde head was raised as defiantly she met Burk's somewhat swollen, bloodshot, very sullen dark eyes. He towered on the seat there beside squat little Froggy, his driver. At twenty-two, he had Ol' Burk's six feet of height and, if he would never own his father's enormous shoulders, he had a

32

lean and powerful and athletic grace Ol'
Burk had never known.

He lowered across at the girl. There had
been an extended session in his Pullman
drawing-room ending only as he dropped
off at Cottonwood Siding, a mixed poker-
party of more than mere dampness. His
mouth was still dry and his head throbbed.

'Seems I can't leave a thing to you!' he
burst out. 'I thought I might expect you to
make some effort at management, until
term-end. But, no! I have to drop everything
——'

'A bottle! It must have been a bottle you
dropped, from the look of you!' she flared,
with equal bitterness. 'But I gathered from
your letters that you expected everything of
me. It seems to me that *you* might have
gathered, last year, that conditions in the
country aren't normal. Just to protect your
own share of the Y, you might have thought
of doing something!'

'Well, I'm here, now!' Burk said sullenly.
'I left everything to come down and see
what could be done to rescue the pieces of
the property. I was in a fair way to end a
beggar, it did seem. I'd been hoping I could
graduate before I had to come back, but
there's no use talking about that ——
What's to be the arrangement? Am I to

33

protect my share while you protect yours? You take Shorty Willets to handle yours, while I take Turkey Adkins? And is all the stock that's been stolen a debit against my account — because I wasn't here to watch over it?'

'That's not fair!' she cried. 'It's not so, either!'

There were angry tears in the blue eyes now, and her face was flaming.

'I — I've been working — trying to keep the ranch going — as it used to be — and you say that to me — and Shorty Willets — he ——'

Suddenly, she put face down upon her arm, on the back of the buckboard seat. She began to cry gaspingly. Burk's dark brows drew together frowningly. He leaned a little toward her, his hand coming up. Then he straightened with small shrug, lip curling. He waited grimly for her to lift her head.

It was coming to him that he had been long away from this Crazy Horse country — barring that flying trip of the year before. Even his vacations had been spent in the East — in Philadelphia or New York. They had been — naturally! — more pleasant than if spent down here under Ol' Burk's heavy thumb. If Ol' Burk had guessed how his son and heir had educated himself in the night life of those cities — Burk grinned sourly and returned to contemplation of Myra Yarborough.

He had almost forgotten what Myra must have grown into, he reflected. He recalled her most clearly as a hard-riding young daredevil in overalls and boots and man's Stetson, with yellow pigtails streaming. And for nearly two years, now, they had been quarreling peevishly by letter. He had asked the reason for the abrupt shrinkage of income from the place. She had written one irritable and irritating letter after another until he had grown sick of opening the envelopes to see the further tale of losses which seemed to be the only tale she had to tell.

'Shorty — Shorty's dead!' she gasped finally, half-lifting her face. 'Murdered! Lynched! Last night — here!'

Burk gaped at her unbelievingly.

'Lynched! In Yatesville! I —— Why, how could that have happened? What had Shorty Willets done? You mean that — that the people here lynched Shorty Willets?'

She told him chokingly of the finding of the two bodies — and of the grim warning of the One-Gang pinned to their shirts. Burk stared incredulously while in him rose a helpless sort of fury. He had been accustomed to think of this great scope of country here, between the Crazy Horse Range and the Tortugas, as in a way constituting his inheritance — and Myra Yarborough's, of course. Their fathers had been the pioneers of it all. The very county and town bore his father's name. Now, he, last of the Yateses, was in grave danger of becoming one of that class of ranchers of whom men said 'they used to be ——'

'By God!' he said between his teeth. 'They — they can't get away with this! They won't get away with it!'

Myra looked furtively up at his working face. His savage tone was so much like Ol' Burk's. Then a corner of her red mouth climbed unpleasantly.

'You sound *so* much like Uncle Burk . . . You even look somewhat like him . . .' She said very sweetly — too sweetly. 'If I didn't recall so vividly those letters you wrote from school — complaining, without knowing a thing about conditions, that the Y was mismanaged or this gang couldn't operate as it did, couldn't run off Y horses and cattle — I could take your likeness more seriously, Burk. But I'm afraid that whatever of Uncle Burk's about you is merely a reflection. School's spoiled you — school or — the vacation amusements that put the puffiness under your eyes! You don't know anything about this country any more — hardly more than if you were Eastern-born. But — what will you do?'

'Leaving aside the remarks about my vacation amusements and my personal appearance — neither of which is any affair of yours,' Burk said with dignity, 'I'm taking charge of the Y. I will do whatever seems necessary and best.'

'You mean you think you'll just run the Y to suit yourself?' she inquired, ruffling belligerently. 'Well — you'll please remember that I own a half-interest in the place. So, whatever is done on it will certainly be done with my approval — or it won't be done at all! You'll not come back after neglecting the place for these years and ride roughshod ——'

'Neglect! You're a fine one to talk of neglect — or of running the Y. You had your chance at that. You've been running things to suit yourself, and the direction you picked seems to have been right straight down into the ground!'

'Nevertheless,' she said, with chin up, 'you'll get my consent to anything affecting the management of the ranch.'

'I'll do whatever's best — in my opinion,' he snapped, sticking out his chin at her.

'What's a woman know about running a cow-outfit? Nothing! Or less!'

'Then I'll take legal steps!' she told him, mouth hard as his own.

'Say! One of us is going to leave the Y! I can see that! One of us is going to sell out!'

'I'm not going to sell! The Y is my home. More than it is yours — you'd rather live in the East, anyway. You've proved that. But my father put his life's work into the place the same as Uncle Burk did. I'm going to keep my half. But I'll buy you out! I'll give you a mortgage and pay you off annually.'

'Mortgage! With no income to meet the interest, even. If I sell, it'll be for cash. If I sell! Is Turkey Adkins in town? I want him to ——'

'Turkey isn't working for the Y, any more. He hasn't been, for six months,' she told him. There was a shade of uneasiness in her tone, now. 'He — I — he quit.'

'Quit! Turkey left the Y?' cried Burk, scowling. 'Why — Dad always said that Turkey was the best cowman in the State of Texas! Shorty Willets was a good man, of course. But he wasn't in Turkey's class. Say! What'd you do — to make him quit?'

'Do! I started to fire him, but he quit before I could. He was entirely too — independent and too — talkative! That's the trouble with employees in this country. They have entirely too much to say to their employers and ——'

'Myra,' Burk said incredulously, 'Texas-raised, as you were, do you mean to tell me that you brought back Vassar notions of the proper relations to Landed Gentry of the Lower Classes? Did you try to work Texas cowhands — such as your father and my father were in their beginnings — Eastern-style? As if they should tip their hats to the Master and Madam? Did you try to make Turkey wear livery? Oh — Lord!'

'I — I ——' Myra began furiously. But Turkey Adkins wandered up. He stopped at the wheel of Froggy's buckboard and squinted critically at Burk, then sadly shook his head.

'Hi, Burk!' Turkey offered gravely. *'Como 'sta?'*

'Bien! Bien! Y Ud.?' Burk grinned. Slipping into the familiar *pela'o* Spanish of the country was somehow pleasant — like pulling on a comfortable old pair of boots. Sight of Turkey's homely, grizzled face, known since childhood, was pleasant, too.

'Oh, I'm tol'able — tol'able — for a ol' wore-out, stove-up cow-wrastler. I seen yuh come in, Burk. In-ter-est-in', it was, too! Yuh was jigglin' up an' down on that buckboard seat like them Eastern folks jiggle in their mail-order saddles. So I 'lowed I'd drift down by yuh an' kind o' widen myself by lookin' at yuh!'

Myra's mouth twitched, and she stole a covert glance at Burk. She seemed to be setting herself for the explosion when Burk suddenly grinned.

'Reckon,' he said. 'But if you went back there, and they gave you a postage-stamp saddle with short leathers that set your knees under your chin, you'd post, too! You'd post or fall off! I'm glad to see you, though. Myra tells me you're no longer the chief and outstanding pillar of the Y . . .'

'Well,' Turkey said judicially, 'Myra has got her faults — plenty of 'em. Includin' some she wouldn't admit. But usual she tells the truth — as she sees it.'

'Now, listen to me, Turkey,' Burk said earnestly, leaning over the seat-arm. 'Things have got into a hell of a mess on the Y and you know it. This dam' One-Gang that's been stealing and murdering so blithely and gay has put us hubbing hell. So far as I'm concerned, there are two things to do — settle down to a war, or sell out! I don't 'specially want to sell ——'

'Who would yuh be sellin' to?' Turkey seemed to meditate aloud. 'To — Myra? Or to Lance Gregg? An' what'd yuh git?'

'To Myra — if she could raise at least half cash. But she can't! Now, if I stick and run the place, I've got to have a good foreman. Shorty's gone — not that he was ever one-two on a ten-count with Turkey Adkins. Suppose you get your hot roll, now, and bring it out and sling it in the foreman's bunk?'

Turkey looked far away, to the serrated crest of the Crazy Horse Range; looked down at his shabby boot-toes; looked swiftly up at Myra's hard-set red mouth.

'Gather up corn in a new silk hat.
  'Tain't goin' rain no mo';
Massa growl if yuh eat much o' that.
  'Tain't goin' rain no mo'!'

'Hundred an' fifty a month?' he demanded abruptly, squinting at Burk.

'Why — you blame' pirate! Seventy-five to a hundred is the most any foreman in this country ever got — and you know it! Tell you what, though; come out for a hundred and, the minute we see the country straightened out so we're making money, a hundred and fifty it'll be!'

'Nah, I reckon not,' Turkey drawled, staring at the mountains. 'Reckon I don't want to go to work, no how. But I always did want a chancet to turn down a hundred an' fifty a month.'

Burk grew red. But Turkey, with a spacious gesture that might have been taken for farewell, went drifting off. Burk shot an angry side-glance at Myra, whose mouth worked.

'Monkey, monkey, drink yo' beer.
  'Tain't goin' rain no mo';
How many monkeys yuh reckon's here?
  'Tain't goin' rain no mo'!'

'He's a — very peculiar person,' observed Myra. Burk glared at her. But a tall gentleman walking toward them hove into sight in time to replace the peculiar Mr. Adkins in Burk's mind.

'Isn't that Lance Gregg, the Wallop–8 fellow?' Burk inquired. Myra, with quick side-glance, nodded affirmation. She showed more than normal color, Burk thought. He looked again at the oncoming figure, then back once more at Myra. She, meeting the somewhat speculative narrowing of his dark eyes, grew rosier still and angry-looking — as if she resented her betrayal of emotion.

Lance Gregg — even Burk would admit

— was a figure to draw attention anywhere. He was big and perfectly proportioned, and he had a reckless, swaggering air about him.

He came lounging up to the side of Myra's buckboard, a strong hand at the well-kept brown mustache he wore. His white shirt was of silk and a blue silken neckerchief was knotted artfully about tanned throat smooth and thick as a column. His trousers were of a silvery whipcord stuff, thrust into half-boots of glossy alligator-hide that were heeled by McChesney 'girl leg' spurs glinting with gold and silver plate.

Burk looked him up and down, from fifty-dollar white Stetson to small feet. He observed that the open-topped holster sagging from Gregg's hand-stamped cartridge belt was empty. It was proof that Lance Gregg was a law-abiding citizen; for one did not openly wear a short gun within Yatesville's limits.

'H'lo, Myra,' Gregg smiled at the girl. She returned the greeting, if with a shade of constraint. Somewhat hurriedly, she indicated the sullenly quiet Burk.

'You met Mr. Yates last year — when he was home from school.'

'Probably did,' Gregg nodded carelessly, without looking at Burk. 'How's everything, young fellow?'

Burk took his time about answering. He was somehow very certain that Lance Gregg was never going to be a favorite of his.

'Not so good, Griggs,' he drawled, purposely distorting the name. 'But — perhaps they're due for an improvement. Soon, even.'

'That so?' Lance Gregg lifted his brows, troubling now to look directly at Burk. 'How's this improvement going to be worked — if that isn't part of a deep, dark secret?'

'Probably by a little of this and a little of that . . . Being in the right place at the right time; doing the right thing — old Y-style. Which reminds me: Wallop–8 lost much stuff to this marvelous One-Gang? Or has the Y been its only customer?'

'Nothing to speak of. They seem to have made up their minds to — round our corners. We're not fond of gentlemen with long ropes and sticky loops, on the Wallop–8. If they worried us — well! we'd have to worry them.'

He turned back to Myra.

'Having luncheon with me? I think we're due a little talk. Sorry about that bunch of cows being lifted right out of headquarters pasture. Perhaps you can tell me something that'll let me suggest something. We've got to find that hole in the fence. This business has got to stop. I'll think of something!'

Myra flashed a glance at the tight, narrow-eyed face of Burk. She seemed embarrassed. Burk looked thoughtfully at her before staring very calculatingly indeed at Lance Gregg. His smile was anything but pleasant as he waved his withdrawal from the scene.

'Go ahead!' he told Myra. 'I'll have some things to attend to. I'll be busy for quite a while. But I'll hunt you up, some time this afternoon. I'll take a lift in — *your* buckboard out to the ranch. If you don't mind, of course! Anyway, I'll see you later.'

Then, quite ignoring Lance Gregg, he grunted to the stolid and patient Froggy, who was sitting like a statue beside him; had hardly moved during the long stop.

'Take my traps up to the hotel — the Municipal — will you, Froggy? Just throw 'em on the porch where I can pick 'em up.'

He paid off the driver with a bill from what was getting to be a lean roll, touched hat rim to Myra and jumped down.

Chapter IV

'Stop the stealin', or ——'

'So!' Burk meditated, heading for the Blue

45

Front Mercantile Store of Rufe Redden. 'Mr. Lance Gregg's the Power behind the Throne on the Y, these days — the throne Myra's been talking as if *she* filled with much pain and unease of mind . . . That's evident when Mr. Gregg dismisses me — half-owner of the outfit — from his supervisory considerations. *He* will look into the matter of stuff lifted out of our headquarters pasture. *He* will decide the steps to be taken. Will he, now? I think something's due for a change — if there's any possibility of a change doing anything, accomplishing anything, at this late day . . .'

He fished in a coat-pocket for a cigarette. His hand brought out, with the package, something pink. A slow smile twisted his tight mouth as he looked down at the fluffy rosette. He stopped short and stared blindly at the false front of Redden's. Not the weathered planks of the Blue Front, but the hard, bright prettiness of a girl, he saw. Soundlessly, he shaped a name.

Elinor . . . She was a looker — and a lot of fun. She had helped a lot to enliven the long trip from the East; helped to soften the bitter resentment with which he had dropped his pleasant way of living at school, to come and see what pieces were left of his property. Good-looking . . . wise . . . played poker like a man . . . better than some men! For she had helped to thin that roll which was the last of his ready money. He could see her as she leaned from the observation platform there at Cottonwood Crossing, waving at him, smiling with something like promise, then bending quickly, lifting a shapely leg, to fling that garter to him . . .

'I like you lots, Big Boy! . . . And I'd *like* to like you lots better . . . I'll be in San Antonio, at the Gunter, for two weeks . . . Put a few cows in your pocket and come to see me . . .'

He shook his dark head vaguely and jerked his eyes down to look with distaste at Yatesville's main street. After all, what was there, particularly, to hold him here? The Y was going to hell, if it hadn't already gone! If he tried taking hold, there would be Myra, prompted by that big, too-good-looking sharpshooter, Lance Gregg . . . Bucking him at every turn; unpleasant to deal with . . . On the other hand, there was Elinor . . . and San Antone . . . plenty of other places . . . an easy, pleasant life, with for spending the amount of money he ought to get for his interest in the ranch, rundown as it was . . .

'I don't know why I have to be a cowman, simply because the old man was,' he told himself. 'And, what's worse, a busted cow-man! Which seems to be my fate if I stick here and don't pull out what I can from the wreckage . . .'

He turned on his heel and stared down-street to where the faded sign of Pinckney Lathrop announced dealings in ranch lands and city properties. He hesitated briefly. Even to think of cutting loose from the Y was a wrench. Then he stepped out with face set stubbornly. He walked briskly toward Lathrop's door and upon the thresh-old made no pause at all. He walked inside the long, dingy office and back to where Pinck' sat with hunched shoulders round-ing above folded papers with gilt seals, buzz-buzzing their contractual language to him-self like a country scholar in the first reader.

'Hello, Pinck'!' Burk greeted the agent.

Lathrop turned from the littered old roll-top desk, to peer suspiciously over rimless half-spectacles with small, marble-hard blue eyes. He nodded with recognition of Burk.

'Hello, young feller. Come home to go to work, huh? About time — if mebbe not time enough . . .'

Burk pulled up the wired kitchen chair to sit across from Pinck', straddling the seat, arms upon the back and chin on arms.

'Looks like that, huh? Well . . . Suppose it

looked to be — oh, too much work, for a man who's known something better?'

Pinck' stared at him fixedly. His pink, round face was far too small for his gigantic body, just as it was too small for his elephantine ears. But the almost hairless skull was large enough to hold the shrewdest brain in that wide scope of country. Burk knew that, both by hearsay and observation.

'Oh!' Pinck' grunted after a long silence. 'Oh! Thinkin' about sellin' out, huh? Who to — if you don't mind tellin'? If there's any money loose in this neighborhood, I would appreciate directions to it. *I* never seen times so hard around here. But, o' course, you got Eastern friends an' I hear they have got some money back there. I'll be glad to draw up the papers for you, Burk. I ain't made a dollar in six months.'

'I haven't got any prospects lined up,' Burk snapped impatiently. 'Myra would buy ____'

'Jawbone, huh?' Pinck' nodded contemptuously. 'Reckon she would have to jawbone me for the price o' transferrin' papers. An' you'd get paid — yeh! in pork!'

'That's the trouble,' Burk scowled. 'She's naturally due first chance — if I decide to sell at all. But what would be the use of sell-

49

ing, except to get money! You haven't got anybody on your lists? Of course, the Y's rundown to some extent, but hardly enough to cut the price of it — except on the stock. That's been eaten away, I know, while I was gone ——'

'Ha-ha! Ha-ha!' Pinck' barked unpleasantly, glaring at him. 'I reckon you ain't looked hard at the Y, lately! It ain't worth thirty per cent — no, not twenty per cent! — o' what it was one time. Ol' Burk an' Duke Yarborough could've sold out one time for a hundred thousand ——'

'A hundred and seventy-five thousand,' Burk corrected him. 'I have that tale by heart, you know, Pinck'. They asked two-twenty-five — and didn't really want to sell at that figure. So don't try hoorahing me. What could I get for my half, today?'

'Derned if I know,' Pinck' shrugged. ' 'Course, I'll act for you, Burk. I'll try to hunt up a buyer — that's my business. An' I'll try to sting him for all the hide'll stand — that's to my interest because it boosts my five per cent. But don't go off with no comical notions about what the Y's worth to a outsider. I don't want to hunt you up a buyer an' start dickerin' an' then have you howl about the price!'

'But what would you ask?' Burk snapped.

'I'm not going to give you *carte blanche* — a free hand — to sell me out at any figure you might set. I admit that the Y's rundown to a certain extent — but that doesn't affect the land and improvements. I'll tell you what I'll do . . . I'll take — sixty thousand for my interest, if you can get me a sizable chunk of cash. If *that's* not lowering my sights ——'

'Six-ty — thous-and!' Pinck' gasped. He shook his head until one temple of his spectacles came out from behind even his enormous ear. 'Why — you ain't got no more chance o' gettin' any such ridiculous figure than — than — I told you, Burk, you don't know what you're up ag'inst! Now, if you'd said "Twenty thousand" ——'

'Don't be silly! Forty thousand for the Y! I hate to tell you, Pinck', but you're right on the edge of giving me a pain in the neck!'

'I could ask fifty,' Pinck' said slowly. 'If you'd take thirty — providin' I could squeeze the feller up to that . . .'

He turned swiftly, reminding Burk of a snake writhing toward it's hole. From a pigeonhole of the desk he snatched a bunch of letters and hunted through the stack until he found one in a long envelope. Holding this so that Burk could not see the faces of the pages, he read deliberately. Then he

51

lifted his head and stared blankly at the fly-specked Winchester calendar on the wall. At last, he nodded as to himself.

'Burk! I got a man might be ribbed up to buyin'. He is — well, I ain't spillin' much about him, but I don't mind tellin' you he's a Englishman with plenty money. He wanted a ranch, but not one like the Y. Not a half-interest in one, neither. But mebbe I could iron that out . . . It'd be cash! All cash! If you'll take thirty thousand, you can have the money tomorrow! I will pay it to you an' take my chance on this Englishman! Now, what d' you say?'

Burk shook his head. In his mind's eye, he could see grim Ol' Burk Yates standing there beside Pinck' Lathrop. It was a vivid visualization. He could see that hard-handed pioneer swelling wrathfully, ready for one of his famous explosions. To sell the Yates name out of the famous Y . . . To sell at all was bad enough — his father would have thought. But to sell the sweat and the blood and the brains poured into the big ranch for a picayunish thirty thousand dollars ——

'No!' he said thickly. 'Hell, no!'

His hand went mechanically to coat-pocket. He fished out the limp cigarette pack and took from it the single remaining cigarette. He put hand to pocket again, hunting a match. His hand touched the garter, and Pinck', watching him, frowned slightly. For Burk's sullen face had altered. There was something of uncertainty about it, now.

'Thirty thousand . . .' Burk was thinking, abruptly. 'You can cover a lot of territory — have a tolerably full time — on thirty thousand, cash . . . Elinor . . . "Come get the other one . . ."'

'No!' he said again, explosively, jerking hand from pocket without the match. 'If your Englishman has plenty of money, then he can pay a fair price. I'll drop to fifty thousand, but not a dime less! And that's final, Pinck'!'

He stood up so suddenly that the old chair fell over. He picked it up and skated it back against the wall. He lowered at Pinck', whose smooth little face was infinitely calculating.

'It won't be thirty thousand — for either one o' you — in six months,' Pinck' said softly. 'Way things are goin' — if you could stick an 'work like hell, it'd take years to build back to anything like the old valuation, Burk. An' — mebbe you wouldn't get a chance to spend them years workin' . . . You heard about — Shorty Willets . . .'

'That's not bothering me!' Burk snarled.

'But I'm willing to sell out — to get out of this damned country — away from these damned people — if I can get a fair price! You tell your Englishman what I'm asking.'

'Not a bit o' use. With the conditions bein' different, anyway, from what he wants, he wouldn't pay no such price. But — Burk . . . I'll do all I can to sell for you. An' — don't talk to nobody about the deal bein' under way, huh?'

'Hell! I'm not proud of it!' Burk shrugged sulkily, over his shoulder. 'Unless you talk, nobody will.'

On the sidewalk he looked once more at Rufe Redden's. He wondered if Turkey Adkins would be around Rufe's. If anybody could hand out facts about conditions, it would be Turkey. Anything the grim, independent little rooster gave forth would be the simon-pure quill. He thought of Rufe Redden, too.

He had known the big, blustering storekeeper all his life. Rufe was fifteen years his senior, but he had always been friendly enough with Ol' Burk's son and heir. He went up the street and into the store. Rufe, standing well back behind the counter, looked up at him, stared steadily for a long minute, then nodded without cordiality.

'You back?' he grunted. 'School ain't out

already?'

'For me it is,' Burk said grimly. 'For all time. Rufe — it looks to me as if things around here had certainly got into a sweet mess! Funny — a salty population like the people in Yates County, letting a gang of sneaking thugs like this One-Gang buffalo 'em and ride roughshod over everybody and everything!'

'You been away at school, ain't you?' Rufe nodded expressionlessly. 'Seems like I heard you had. Pennsylvania . . . That is right smart of a way from Yatesville, ain't it?'

Burk reddened angrily. He could guess what Rufe was thinking; which would be what the majority of the oldtimers in the country were thinking — or had long thought: That with his father's death he should have forgotten such youthful things as going to school; should have stepped into the position left vacant by Ol' Burk's going; should have begun — in short — to act a man. Yates County found it hard to understand a man going to school. It branded him as a kid. Unreasonable, of course, but Ol' Burk, he knew, had owned pretty much the same notion.

'Don't rub that in!' he said irritably and uncomfortably. 'I only had until the end of this term, to finish. I naturally thought that,

55

with Turkey and Shorty to handle things, the Y'd rock along as well without me as with me. But with Myra's letter of a week or so ago, I began to see that conditions were a lot worse than I'd dreamed; that I'd better come back and try to protect the Y or — or do something.'

Rufe moved without answer up the inner side of the counter. From a shelf by the door he got his blackened corncob pipe and a package of tobacco. He rammed Mail Pouch into the bowl, staring out across the street with belligerent blue eyes angry under shaggy red brows. There was the flick of a match and the sucking sound of smoke drawn through dirty stem.

'Stop the stealin' or — sell out,' said Rufe at last.

Burk, moving mechanically up beside him, looking mechanically the way Rufe was looking, also saw the two standing before the Star Hotel across and down the street. His dark brows drew together slightly. Myra certainly seemed to have a case on that big swaggerer . . . He had her hand and she was smiling up at him. Of course, it was nothing in the world to him; Myra was nothing but his partner in the Y; that she happened to be a girl, instead of a man — well, it was nothing but accident; certainly, it changed nothing. He thought of Elinor's provocative face . . .

Lance Gregg lifted wide-rimmed Stetson with that air he managed to get into his every action. He left Myra and came swinging along, toward the store, but on the far side of the street.

'Sell out,' Rufe repeated slowly. 'To Lance Gregg, huh?'

'That's two of you to say that! Turkey said it, too. Now, what's the idea? What makes you think that Gregg wants the Y?'

'Who else'd buy?' Rufe drawled. 'For money, I mean. Myra ain't got a nickel.'

Burk scowled from the storekeeper to Gregg's big figure. Suddenly, his eyes narrowed. For Lance Gregg's course was straight for the office-door of Pinckney Lathrop. Burk thought rapidly and when Gregg turned into Lathrop's he made a small grunting sound.

'I — wonder!' he said aloud. 'It seemed funny' — he told himself after a moment — 'for Pinck' to offer to buy with just a vague prospect of selling to his "Englishman" . . . I do wonder!'

He turned again to Rufe and asked for smoking material.

'You'll have to go down to Judge Amblet's,' Rufe grunted, without looking at him. 'Me, I don't stock them tailor-made rolls o' E-gyptian camel-fodder Easterners got to have.'

'Who the hell asked you for tailor-mades!' Burk snarled, for some reason furious out of all proportion to the reason. 'You've got Durham, haven't you? Duke's Mixture, haven't you? Then don't be so dam' conversational to customers!'

Rufe threw back shaggy head and laughed until he must put big hands to his sides. He turned into the store and from the shelf got a sack of tobacco and book of brown saddle-blanket papers. Tears were in his eyes as he handed them over.

'That'n's on the house, Burk,' he gasped: 'I reckon mebbe that fool-school never spoiled you — en-tire.'

Burk grinned, a trifle shamefaced. He sifted tobacco into a paper, rolled it deftly, and put a match to it. Over the cloud of smoke, he looked thoughtfully at Rufe.

'What do you know about Lance Gregg? He told me that the Y was the only outfit the One-Gang dared bother. They didn't — for instance — trouble the Wallop–8. If they did, he'd settle them. How-come? Is he supposed to be bad medicine from the creek-forks, or something?'

'It's true enough that the Y pastures are

just a regular practice-ground for the dam'
thieves,' Rufe nodded. 'Ary time they ain't
got a safe to blow or a stage or a train to
hold up, they do mosey right down to the Y
an' wrap up a bunch o' hawses or cows or
whatever's handiest. They don't bother
other folks much. Mebbe they leave the
Wallop–8 plumb alone — I do'no'. I do'no'
much about Lance Gregg, neither. Except
he's dangerous.

'He come in around two year back.
Bought the Wallop–8 off the bank an'
started in smackin' folks that laughed at him
for a sucker. He killed Tony Vargas right
there on my porch. An' Tony, you know, he
was s'posed to be right smart of a gunman.
Nah . . . it wasn't bein' fast on the draw —
it was hawse-sense. Tony spread it all over
town that he was aimin' to collect Gregg.
But when they met, right there, Gregg had
a .41 Remington in the palm o' his hand.
He never made a move an' that fooled Tony.
I reckon he never did rightly sort out his
idees o' what happened till he woke up in
the middle o' Jordan River, with the water
leakin' into him through them two .41 holes
Gregg'd made in him.'

'You think, then, that his gunplay bluffed
the One-Gang?'

Rufe looked at him with a sort of wariness

59

in his face. Then he looked away again.

'Oh . . . mebbe . . . *Quien sabe?* Never can tell.'

Then, though Burk waited, he seemed to forget the topic. Burk thought he understood. Like the rest of the country, Rufe regarded him, not as the Last of the Fighting Yateses, but as a schoolboy — and, therefore, not worthy of any confidences. They put him down as a kid who had inherited more than he could hold. One to another, they said:

'Ol' Burk, *he* never would've stood for this One-Gang racket! He'd have tied their tails into Spanish knots an' piled 'em — a-bellerin' like bulls, too!'

Soberly, he looked at Rufe.

'You've got something up your sleeve that you don't figure to spill to me, Rufe. I know it, well enough. Maybe I can guess why, without any trouble, either! All right. That's your privilege. I don't know yet what I'm going to do. But if I stick here, maybe you won't mind talking straight out.'

'Can happen,' Rufe said inscrutably. 'Mebbe.'

CHAPTER V

'Garters or — Ca'tridges?'

Out on the street, he looked mechanically toward Pinckney Lathrop's. After all, he meditated, it was nothing to him who bought him out, if he got the money he wanted. Suppose Pinck' had been lying; suppose Lance Gregg had commissioned him to buy the Yates half of the Y. If he wanted to pay fifty thousand for it, let Myra worry about the change in partners!

'Shame, though, for as nice a kid as Myra to fall so hard for that big strutter,' he shrugged. 'She is a nice kid . . . and, if I'm not very much mistaken, she's ready to marry him — and wake up finding that he's a very different proposition as husband.'

It occurred to him that he was very ready for a drink. He had taken his last on the train, with Elinor and the drummers who had made up their poker-party. He grinned faintly at thought of those stern notions of Ol' Burk Yates, about the education and upbringing of sons. Not a saloon or gambling-house in town had ever seen his face. Ol' Burk had seen to that! He would have been 'fit to tie,' Burk thought, had he been able to see the episodes from his son's

61

between-terms amusements.

He drifted down to the Congress and in its long barroom looked about. He saw Turkey Adkins in a far corner, sitting with chair propped against the wall, boot-heels hooked in a round, hat-rim down over his eyes as if asleep. Then he saw Lance Gregg well down the bar. Staring at him, Burk felt the keenest dislike that he had ever known for a human being. He disliked everything about the Wallop–8 owner from his clothes to the way he wore them. The supercilious expression that seemed a very part of Gregg's handsome features roused in Burk a desire to put a fist against Gregg's mouth.

There was a bar-tender standing admiringly before Gregg. He was nodding like an automaton, grinning soapily. Yet he was not naturally a servile figure, either, being squatty and powerful, with the look of a broken-down prize-fighter about him. Whether Gregg noticed him, or not, Burk could not tell. But the bar-tender looked sidelong, grinned in entirely different fashion, and came briskly down the bar.

'Well, what'll it be, son?' he inquired. 'Sa'sp'riller? I got some nice lemon squash, too.'

Burk eyed him steadily. Unabashed, the bar-tender grinned at him, then turned, seemed to study the back-bar, shook his head regretfully and turned about. The drinkers — and those in the rear of Burk in the big room — grinned widely. Someone laughed when the bar-tender made an exaggerated, ladylike gesture with hairy, knobby-knuckled right hand.

'I'm awful sorry! But somehow, we jist let the mineral water run out. But if you'd come back in a few days, we'd ought to have some in by then.'

A bunch of cowboys roared. Burk thought that the bar-tender must have a reputation for clowning. And this was precisely the sort of comedy a cowtown saloon's audience would appreciate. But the laughing stopped with the flashing dart of Burk's hands over the bar-top. They caught the simpering bar-tender-chin and cauliflowered ear. Burk leaned backward with foot against bar-front. He jerked violently, and the bar-tender, yelling and thrashing his hands, was dragged up to the bar-top, then across it. Burk half-turned and the man of drinks continued past him, to land with a thud upon the splintered pine floor.

The impact was upon his face, and when he had slid thus forward for a yard, then rolled over, his features resembled nothing more vividly than a slab of raw beefsteak.

But he was a fighter! Over he rolled. He scrambled to his feet with big fists doubled. He blinked savagely — apparently preparatory to a bull-rush. But Burk had moved silently toward him and, before the bartender located him, he swung a pair of alternating hooks that carried each his hundred-eighty pounds behind. The bartender crashed again to the floor. This time he stayed there, limp, with mouth gaping.

Burk looked down at him, grinning faintly. Then, while the audience watched with frowningly intent eyes, he turned and went straight back to where Lance Gregg leaned upon the bar, grinning. Burk stopped there.

'Too bad you don't do your own fighting, Gregg!' he said contemptuously. 'But I suppose that's the way you've kept that pretty-boy face of yours unmarked, this long!'

'Are — are you talking to me?' Gregg cried. For once, the tolerantly superior expression was wiped from his face. He seemed shaken off-balance by this unexpected challenge.

'Don't act the baby!' Burk grinned — without humor. 'You know damned well I'm talking to you. Don't try to crawfish!'

'Taking August by surprise has sort of turned your head, it would seem,' Gregg snapped. 'But I'll give you one more chance:

You trot along home, sonny. Else you'll be badly hurt!'

Burk laughed in his face and stood watching him steadily. A sudden wave of red came up into Gregg's face. The long blue eyes were smoky, opaque.

'All right, then!' Gregg said thickly. 'All right! You asked for it! Now, see if you can stand it!'

With which he drove his fists in lightning alternation straight at Burk's chin. Burk weaved with the mechanical reaction of the trained boxer. One blow went over his shoulder, but the other he could not quite duck. Though it struck him only glancingly, it would have spun him halfway about but for the dragging weight of Gregg's other arm, across his shoulder. Burk shook his head, leaned forward, and held with left hand while he drove a short and torrid right to Gregg's stomach.

Gregg grunted despite himself with the impact of that one. But he slid sideways, away from the bar. Then, in the open, he rushed Burk, swinging furiously but not wildly.

He was perhaps fifteen pounds the heavier. He had an inch or so the advantage in reach. More than that, he had, to counterbalance Burk's speed and science, the hardness of maturity in his powerful body. He was no mere slugger, either! Burk admitted that as he slid away, bobbing, rolling, ducking, countering. Burk had been school heavyweight champion. He recognized scientific boxing when he saw it. Presently, he knew that he was a good deal the better boxer, but that his recent loafing and drinking had done him no good.

He was getting winded. So he tore in at the first opening he saw and with forehead against Gregg beat a two-handed tattoo on the bigger man that drove him back. But he came in again and Burk was very tired. He whipped up his energy and met Gregg in two-handed fighting. Neither troubled to guard. It was bang-bang-bang! wherever a knotted fist could land — to head or body.

'Can't stand much more of this!' Burk told himself grimly.

So he rushed Gregg the more furiously. He was gasping, now. He was short with a right to the jaw and stumbled. Gregg came at him like a charging cat. Artistically, if automatically, Burk ducked and weaved and side-stepped. For the first time, he could think of Elinor with something besides admiration . . . For he was fundamentally a man of his hands, Ol' Burk's son. He would have given anything in reason for the condition that would let him end this fight with Lance Gregg out on the floor.

Condition would have done it. He knew that. For he could outbox Gregg and he had hurt the Wallop–8 man time after time. Given good condition, he could wear him down and at the last make a chopping-block of Gregg. But not this time! He was all but nauseated and a swinging right to the heart helped him not at all. He wished fervently that he had never seen Elinor or those genial drummers and their liquor and cigars!

He went down to one knee with a terrific right hook to the side of his head. He came up again and tried to slug. He went down again without landing a blow. He came up and was immediately knocked flat upon his back. Instinctively, he rolled over, trying to suck in enough breath to relieve pumping lungs. He got one knee under him and Lance Gregg, his mouth open, too, rushed at him. It was more push than blow that landed, but Burk was driven sideways. He came up once more, squinting at Gregg, and this time made his feet. He flung both arms around Gregg and hung on desperately.

'Here! Here!' a raucous, somewhat nervous, voice cried. 'Gregg! Burk Yates! Now, y' all cut out that squabblin'!'

For answer to that, Lance tore himself loose and launched another looping swing at Burk. Burk was inside of it and it missed. He drove one at Gregg's stomach that didn't miss. But he took one to the chin that floored him again. As he scrambled up, Faraday, the lank city marshal, slid in between and began expostulating with Gregg:

'Now, that's plenty, Gregg! Y' whupped him plenty! Let it drop, now! He cain't stand up to y' —'

A haze was swimming before Burk's eyes. He got somehow to his feet and lurched down the bar, out the back door and through to the outdoors. He leaned against a building and for a while was very sick. A voice sounded at his elbow, presently. He looked blearily at Pinck' Lathrop.

'Say, Burk — what the devil you been doin', anyhow?'

'What do — you want?' Burk panted. 'Make it — short!'

'I just been thinkin' about our li'l' deal. You want to come down to the office an' talk about it?'

'No! I don't want to — talk about anything!'

'Sick, huh? Well, but this is important, Burk. I told you I'd buy the place — kind o' on spec' that I can talk that feller into takin' the half an' all — an' I'll hand you the money this very day, if you want it. Thirty thousand . . .'

'I'm not selling — for thirty thousand,' Burk grunted, straightening. He felt better, much better, if still weak.

'That's a lot o' money!' Pinck' cried aggrievedly. Then, when Burk was turning toward the Congress's back door again: 'I tell you what I'll do — bein' it's you, Burk. I'll give you thirty-two — inside thirty minutes!'

Burk put out a hand to brace himself against the saloon end-wall and looked at Pinck' Lathrop without pleasure.

'Pinck', it gives me great pleasure to tell you that you are a very artistic liar and actor — but you don't fool me a bit! I know that your "Englishman" is Yatesville-manufactured, wearing the P-L brand. I know that your client is Lance Gregg — wait a minute! Don't bother about looking injured and virtuous! I know that! I know that Gregg wants the Y and that' — which was purest inspiration — 'when I walked through your door, it was like an answer to your prayer! For Gregg had already told you that he wanted the Y. Now, I'll tell you something else!

69

'I'm not selling! I'm sticking! I've changed my mind about several things in the last little while — *por dios!* Lance Gregg will never get a foot of Y land' — then he thought of Myra, smiling up at Gregg . . . and changed the sentence — 'a foot of my half of the Y, until I'm dead enough to skin! Put that one in the pigeonhole along with that imaginary letter from the synthetic Englishman, Pinck'. But don't bother me any more!'

He went inside. Around the bar was clustered now a thick crowd of drinkers. They were talking in an excited gabble. They were gesticulating. They turned, grinning, with the fall of Burk's feet behind them. He looked for Gregg and failed to find him.

'Gregg's drifted,' Turkey Adkins explained, appearing at his elbow. 'Man! I never thought to see a man wear a look *so* s'prised as what Lance was wearin' toward the last, when yuh was takin' ever'thing he had on the shelf an' comin' in for more!'

Hard-handed punchers, cowmen, freighters, townsmen, they crowded around the white-faced Burk. He looked at them with some surprise. You might believe that he had licked Gregg! he thought. Quickly, he was made sure that he could have no more

70

well-wishers if he had put Gregg on the floor, instead of going there himself. But what he wanted, now, was to get away.

Turkey, though, had other ideas. He had Burk's arm, and he turned him toward the bar where August, a battered spectacle, looked out upon the world through swollen lids.

'M' young *compadre*, here, he'd like to know if yuh got anything in stock but them private drinks o' yo's, since he ask' yuh last time,' Turkey drawled.

August muttered viciously under breath, and Turkey smiled upon him sweetly.

'Goodness me!' he cried. 'Still belly-achin'? We got to drag yuh out into the open ag'in, before we can order? Fella! If I was yuh, I'd let Jordan roll!'

August whirled and snatched a bottle of Old Crow from the back-bar. He slapped it down on the bar and put glasses out. Turkey filled them and lifted his glass. Over it, he regarded Burk with humorous lifting of one tight mouth-corner.

'Here's to the dear ol' almy motto!' he drawled. 'Looks like they do learn a country boy *some* things that's useful.'

Presently, drifting side by side down the street toward the hotel, Turkey was moved to conversation:

'Yuh know, me, I'm likely the changeablest fella yuh ever see, Burk . . . I bet yuh I am that! Now, talkin' about that fo'man job we was augurin' about — I am broke enough to take it, now that I think the thing over ag'in.'

'Didn't want to work for a school-kid, huh?' Burk nodded.

'Well,' said Turkey judicially, 'I'll go so fur's to say I was wonderin' if the's any streakiness *to* yo' bacon . . . An', too, I wasn't certain yuh wouldn't decide to sell out an' hightail East where the's a lot o' high life an' the gals, they wear purty pink hobbles, an' when yuh buy 'em yuh git a lot for yo' money in looks an' lovin' kindness — long's yo' money holds out. I knowed Lance Gregg had put Pinck' onto buyin' yo' half in the Y — if he could git it for li'l' or nothin'. I was — right close when he made that dicker with Pinck'. So — all in all — I wasn't takin' cards in that game. The' mightn't have been fight in yuh!'

'Fight? You saw me get most thoroughly licked!'

'Yeh. Licked that time. But, hell! Gittin' licked is nothin'. We all o' us git licked now an' ag'in. It's how a man acts when he's gittin' licked interests me! Whether he climbs up ever' time he's knocked down an' tries for another swing. So — like I was sayin' — I'll take on that fo'man job. Make it seventy-five a month — an' ca'tridges, o' course! Lawdy! Lawdy! The ca'tridges we're goin' to use up, when we start after that One-Gang! Yuh can hang that pink hobble over the head o' yo' bed, Burk, an' ever' time yuh look at it, yuh can figger how much simpler it'd been, if yuh'd gone on down to Santone an' bought the other one . . .'

'How the devil did you know about that?' Burk snarled.

'Froggy, with three drinks into him, he's a mightily extended talker.' Turkey grinned seraphically. 'Well? Which'd yuh rather have? Garters or ca'tridges? Ca'tridges, huh!'

CHAPTER VI

'Like a dam' butcher block!'

Myra having come to the Star Hotel, Burk had had his luggage brought from the Municipal's porch to the Star. Now, he sat in a big cypress rocker at the end of the Star's porch. On the rail at his left, with back comfortably against the corner post, Turkey Adkins perched with one gray eye closed against his cigarette's upwreathing smoke. He looked half-asleep — an attitude that had deceived a good many persons.

'I take it,' Burk said slowly, 'that you haven't been exactly horsing around to find anything about this so-called One-Gang. Not since Myra fired you, anyway. But, while you were out at the ranch, did you see anything? Anything that'd serve us for a point of departure?'

'Reckon not,' Turkey shrugged. 'I know I got dam' sick an' tired o' Lance Gregg Wallop–8 in' the ol' Y all-time. Oh, no! I don't mean blottin' our brand. I mean he was always clutterin' up the landscape like yuh might say; ary which way a man'd look, the'd be Lance, a-goin' or a-comin' or a-settin'.

'An' advice! Burk, that hairpin'd make Sollermon look a modest li'l' violet, he would! He's fuller o' advice than ary human ever I see — an' I've knowed a lot o' preachers! Myra, she naturally figgered that a nice, polished-up fella like Lance, he's bound to know more'n her — uh — servants could. Ever' time a critter had a tick on it, she'd ask Lance what to do!'

Expertly, he rolled the stub of his cigarette from one side of wide, thin-lipped mouth to the other, then spat through his teeth.

'Like one time I'd found me a nice, neat

74

kind o' hole in the air, over at Brushy Crick
pasture — a hole that was all that was left
o' sixty head o' prime Long Twos. I kind o'
scally-hooted around till I found a bunch o'
hawse-tracks. Over an' on top the bunch
the' was the near hind-track o' somebody's
big hawse with a busted shoe. I got right
worked up over that track. Looked like the
firstest chance I'd got at them long-ropin'
sticky loopers.

'Well, I snooped around plenty. I found
this fella's hoofprints just ever'wheres —
down in the crick-bed where them steers
had been shoved along onto rocky ground;
all over a soft spot where they'd crossed
over, goin' towards the Tortugas. Yuh
couldn't make out much o' anything *but*
that dam' busted shoe. I trailed along a spell
till it petered out. So I hightailed for the
house an' — by Gemini! — I run across it
right in the dooryard! Over at the corrals I
found the hawse itself — Lance's big
Wallop–8 sorrel! I went inside fast an', shore
enough! the' was Lance an' Myra . . .'

He spat again through his teeth and made
a contemptuous sound in his throat. Burk
watched him narrowly as he got out
Durham and papers.

'Myra looked at me like I was somethin'
the cats'd drug in — somethin' that'd died

75

out on the range, yuh know — an' died a right smart while back. She wanted to know what I thought I wanted. I told her about the steers bein' gone an' about me trailin' that busted hawse-shoe over the country. An' I'm tellin' yuh, Burk! The ol' hawgleg was ridin' light in the holster! For right then I was suspicionin' that fella like 'twouldn't do to tell. I would've splattered him all over them new Navajo rugs o' Myra's on general principles, if he'd made one li'l' ol' bitsy eyebrow jiggle!

'They kept lookin' at each other an' grinnin' like — like I was about five year ol', yuh know, an' had just come runnin' to break the news that *all* the hawses had four laigs, not just some o' the *caballado.* Myra, then, she ask' me if that was all I wanted. Yes, sir! Like 'twasn't nothin' a-tall!

'Lance Gregg, he says I'm 'way behind-time, like always. Says he's already found the tracks an' follered 'em till they petered out an' come an' told Myra about it. He explains, then, to Myra, that his hawse has got a busted hind-shoe an' I been trailin' it an' I'm *so* disappointed because he ain't the king-rustler like I thought I'd found! An' he says he's mightily sorry he has to disappoint me when I'm expectin' to find a rustler settin' in the house waitin' for me.

'They both laughed fit to kill. Man! I was fit to tie! I went out right soft an' quiet before I killed me somebody. I ain't usual a bid fonder o' bein' made a dam' fool of than other folks is. But the's more to this, Burk: I keep wonderin' *which way* I'm bein' made a fool of, by Lance Gregg!'

The heavy brown paper ripped in his hands. The tobacco sifted down over Turkey. Burk lifted his brows at this sign of emotion — which was not betrayed by anything in Turkey Adkins's weather-carved brown face.

'Later on, when I'd cooled off some, I lit into Lance kind o' easy-goin'. I ask' him if he'd ever hear-tell about the right way to foller a trail — keepin' off the tracks, so's they wouldn't be messed up an' all that. He got mad, o' course. He 'lowed he knowed as much about trailin' an' likely more as I could. An' Myra come outside with her voice right off the ice. So I let it go at that. An' when I tried to git her to send to the Association for a stock-detective, she wouldn't. I done it myself, then. I know the president an' he knows me. I wrote him a letter an' I told him things was bad an' I was workin' for a dam' fool gal an' would he send up a man.'

'One come?' Burk asked curiously, watching the little man.

'Yeh . . . An' a Fargo detective was with him. An' — well, mostly, the Association has good men. But I do' no' what-for they ever hired Bud Burney. I have knowed him too long an' in-*tric*-ate to be took in by that gab o' his. Mebbe the Association ain't. Anyhow, he come into town an' inside an hour ever'body knowed he'd come to heel the One-Gang. Same for this Fargo detective. Now, how the hell yuh goin' to loop any body, when they know yuh from the back?

'I've seen a lot o' them two since I rolled my bed off the Y. They come in an' look an' talk as wise as ary thing on top the earth except a burro. They are a matched team o' the finest saloon-detectives ever I laid eyes on. They talk about investigatin' an' follerin' clues an' so on — an' the stage is stuck up inside ten mile o' where they're gassin'. That was last week. The two of 'em rode out, wavin' back to let us know they'd bring in the stage-robbers by supper time. They ain't back yet!'

Myra Yarborough came out of the wide center door from the hotel hallway. She had a letter in her hand which seemed to interest her — judging from her expression. She was so engrossed with it that she could not see — or did not care to see — Burk and

78

Turkey. Burk wondered which. She walked to the other end of the porch and sat down, to continue her reading.

Burk watched her idly, sitting with skinned hands locked behind his dark head. He found himself thinking that she had certainly grown up into a pretty girl. But spoiled! Lord, but she was spoiled by a little authority and money and education!

Then he shrugged the shoulders of his spirit. If she had been marked by Eastern schooling, hadn't he been also? If he were willing to put aside everything — he was very conscious of that bit of elastic and ribbon in his coat-pocket — and concentrate on ranch affairs, present problems, mightn't she be also? It seemed only fair to credit her with the intent.

'Any idea when you're going home?' he called to her.

She ignored the question — he thought that she could hardly help hearing it. She continued reading and Burk got up to move over and stand beside her.

'I'll ride out with you when you go — if you don't mind.'

'What?' she asked, lifting her yellow head jerkily from the study of her thick sheaf of letter-pages.

'What have you been doing?' she gasped.

79

'Your face!'

He had forgotten for the moment that he was bruised. Even washing had not removed the signs of battle. And his clothes were badly disheveled.

'Doing?' he said blankly. 'Oh! A small argument, with a hardly important personage . . .'

'He thought that he'd start his graduate-life by a row with me,' a voice drawled amusedly, from behind Burk. 'Which was, of course, merely continuation of education — if he'd known it. I had to demonstrate to him the folly of youthful impulses.'

Burk turned slowly, keeping careful grip on himself. He looked steadily at Lance Gregg.

'What you demonstrated was something that I knew . . . that several days on a train are very poor training for a fist-fight — even with a rather crude practitioner who fights foul. But, of course, you naturally wouldn't know how gentlemen fight . . .

'But, outside of that one point, I don't know of anything I noticed. If you're expecting any permanent effects from that little sparring-match — how disappointed you're going to be! For I'm staying on the Y. I told your Man Friday. Did Pinck' tell you?'

Lance Gregg's face darkened furiously

with the rush of blood and the long blue eyes went opaque again, as in the Congress bar-room before he swung his first furious blow. But this time his hand fumbled at the empty pistol-holster. Burk looked steadily, contemptuously, at the fumbling hand.

'Too bad! It's not there. But haven't you got a derringer palmed, this time?'

He shifted his feet slightly, ready for any move. But Myra, staring palely from one to the other of them jumped up.

'Lance! Burk! Are you trying to imitate drunken mule-skinners? I'm not used to having men stand at my elbow and begin fights! You two have no business quarreling, anyhow. Burk! You owe entirely too much to Mr. Gregg, for help in managing your property, to take this attitude. You should be —'

'I've been trying diligently to decide just how much I do owe the — counselor.' Burk nodded cryptically. 'As soon as I decide how the matter stands — don't worry! I'll pay him, with interest and something for *pelon!* With heaps and heaps of pleasure, too. Until that time of reckoning, the less I see of him, the better!'

Lance Gregg's face grew suddenly cold and set. His eyes were no longer angry, but very watchful. Once more, gun-hand twitched about the empty holster. From behind him came Turkey's voice:

'It's under yo' shirt, Gregg,' he drawled blandly. 'In the half-breed holster under yo' arm. Jist thought I'd mention it, me carryin' mine like that — oftentimes . . .'

While the three men stood stiffly there, from downstreet near the courthouse sounded the gabble of many voices — excited voices. They whirled toward the noise. Gregg's hand dropped away from the gunless scabbard. But Turkey's thumb stayed where it had been — hooked in the front of unbuttoned shirt.

There was a buckboard, drawing to a halt before the courthouse door. It was possible to see only the two figures on the seat, because of the thick press of men ringing it about. When it stopped, the crowd jammed in closer. They saw Judge Amblet come out and gesture authoritatively, trying to make a passage. The two men on the seat stood up. Their high-pitched voices seemed to be turned to the same effort as Amblet's.

'Now, what?' Turkey wondered, aloud. 'Burk! Reckon me an' yuh might's well hightail down the' — so's all the prominent citizens'll be represented. Yonder comes Faraday! An' the's only three things could git our noble marshal on any spot, quick's he's comin' to this'n': free whiskey; a circus; or a dead man. An' I don't reckon she's free whiskey, nor yet a circus. So it must be a dead man, an' with this sneakin' gang we got loose —— '

He and Burk cleared the porch-rail at a jump and went trotting down to the courthouse. The first man Burk touched on the arm turned grim face.

'That Cattle Raisers' detective an' his mouthy sidekick, the Fargo agent. Both deader'n Judas Iscariot. Been dead some time — a day, anyhow. The Peters boys was comin' into town an' found 'em propped up alongside the trail. They been shot into doll-rags.'

Burk pushed through the packed men to the buckboard's side. He knew neither of the dead men whom the marshal and a few bystanders were getting ready to lift out of the vehicle. But beside the bodies was a cottonwood branch, one end sharpened to a point. Sticking upon it was a large piece of paper, and at sight of the terse, sinister legend on the improvised placard, Burk felt queer along his spine.

'*Next!*' was all it said. At the bottom was the signature Yates County had come to know well: the figure '1.'

It was his first actual contact with the gang which had been chewing the Y to pieces. He stared at the notice, and men about him — seeming to become gradually aware of his presence and his identity — turned curious eyes upon the big young figure and the unconsciously set face. Obviously, some there were wondering, as they looked at him, if Burk Yates might not be that 'next' mentioned — virtually promised! — on the notice.

One of the Peters brothers, standing at the buckboard wheel with Judge Amblet, was talking excitedly:

'Y' see, we was comin' along towards town, an' when we got to Arroyo Seco an' topped out o' it, I seen them two fellers settin' alongside the trail. An' I seen this-yere sign alongside 'em. I says to Andrew it looks funny; what're they settin' down there with a sign for? I says. Then we come up to 'em . . .'

'No traces of the killers — that you could see?'

'Nary sign, Judge. Y' see, the trail's right hard along there. Whoever'd set 'em by the side o' the trail had just rid up on the road an' off the same way. They must've been plumb dead when they was rested up ag'inst a big rock. There was blood all over the

84

ground — looked like a dam' butcher-block!'

'The One-Gang!' Turkey drawled in Burk's ear. 'Uh-huh, the ol' One-Gang . . . Well, Burk, what d' yuh 'low? Me, I was plumb expectin' it, like I much as told yuh. A couple saloon-detectives that ever'body knowed, they wasn't apt to last too long.'

'Let's hightail for the ranch,' Burk shrugged. 'This is really none of our affair. We won't bother Myra any — we're not apt to be bothering her for a while, I'd guess! I can hire a horse at the corral. We've lots of work to do, Turkey. Lots! And I'm anxious to be about it. We —— Come on! I don't want to do any more talking here. No telling who's listening.'

Chapter VII

'They call it "Violent Village . . ."'

Burk and Turkey sat their horses in the home pasture. Here it was that the One-Gang had struck its last blow at the Y. From this pasture had vanished a hundred head of cows.

Burk was in waist-overalls and jumper; in new gray Boss Stetson and worn, comfortable boots. As he sat the big curly black five-year-old, he looked very much the puncher. The triggerless white-handled Colt, seven and a half inches barrel-length, sagged on his thigh in its old holster as in other days it had hung from his father's belt. It added to the picture. Turkey, looking thoughtfully at Burk, nodded slightly.

'That's shore a hawse yuh picked out,' he drawled. 'To spill plumb-gawspel truth, I never 'lowed yuh'd stick Funeral *too* much o' yesterday. He's been th'owin' all the cowboys that had all the luck. He ain't a born bad actor, neither. Jist spoiled, since Ol' Burk died. He was aimin', yo' pa was, to ride Funeral hisself. Then, after he died, Funeral shore earned his name by pilin' all comers. Happy Jack named him — from the ground.'

'Best horse I ever saw on the Y,' Burk nodded. 'I'm thinking, Turkey, that a good horse, a good Winchester, and a *right* good Colt hogleg, are going to be our regular uniforms, for a good while to come. . . .'

'Can happen! It's always like this, Burk: Ever' time stuff's been missin' yuh'd think 'twas took up in a balloon. Nary track — an' some neighbors a man'd be a fool to trust: Lance Gregg an' his Wallop–8 — that's too dam' much like a Y to suit me. Then ol' Booboo Emerick an' his Axe

86

brand, right nawth o' us. An' that ol' side-winder, Cactus Gunnell, with his Goblet outfit nawthwest o' the Wallop–8 — right up ag'in' the Tortugas. Then, the's a tol'able gatherin' o' hard cases usin' Prester, these days.'

'Prester?' Burk frowned. 'How-come? What's there to attract anybody? Used to be nothing at all but a side-and-a-half of the road through to Crazy Horse Pass.'

'Do'no' what brung 'em, but the's plenty hard cases ridin' in an' out o' the', allatime. They call Prester "Violent Village" these days. The's a dep'ty sheriff the' name o' Bill Grimm. Some call him "Greasy" Grimm — but not hardly to his face. Grimm, he runs ever'thing to suit hisself. I have thought a time or twelve that if we knowed exactly what suited Grimm, we'd figger it never suited us a li'l' bit! That's how Bill Grimm strikes me.'

'You reckon our stolen stuff moves through Prester?' Burk frowned. 'On to Crazy Horse Pass?'

'Do'no'. I was doin' some wonderin' about it, though, when I was fo'man. But Myra, she cut my laigs off from under me about that time. Before I got around to ex-plorin' the in'ards o' Prester an' Greasy Grimm.'

'Suppose we ramble over and have a look-see!' Burk grunted, on impulse. 'You know, Turkey,' he grinned, 'it just won't do to have an officer of the law lying down on the job. Much less can we endure his openly siding with questionable characters. We'll have to look into this business and, if we find grounds for reasonable suspicion, we'll have to take steps — toward those fellows . . .'

'Can happen!' Turkey nodded, grinning. 'Yes, sir!'

They turned southeast, toward the hamlet of Prester, which sprawled beside the road that crossed the Crazy Horse Range through the Pass. Burk studied the rolling country about them. Slowly, his mouth twitched and he shook his head slightly.

'I'm glad I came back to it — and stayed,' he thought.

All this live-oak country, with the vast blue reaches of the Texas sky above and behind it; with the cattle grazing over short green grass; with brown-faced, wide-hatted, leg-ginsed riders moving up and down — it was all his country.

Sitting Funeral, with the like of Turkey Adkins at his stirrup — grizzled, faithful, salty little old Turkey — with the little wind in his face and the warm sun upon him ——

'Yeh, it does beat playing soldier in a

flashy uniform, riding at the head of a troop . . . Beats the bright lights and the liquor and the party-ladies — yes, Elinor! that includes you! Kid-stuff, all that. This is the real thing . . . Boss of the Y . . .' He said that under breath and liking very much the sound of it and all its implications, repeated it, lips moving soundlessly.

Boss of the big Y . . . It was a little empire, the old ranch that Burk Yates and Duke Yarborough had hacked from a virgin Texas; it was larger by far than many a county back in the Eastern States; than many a petty kingdom of Middle Europe. And he was king of it. But, like all kings, he had to be ready, willing, to fight for it. And — there was Myra, of course. He frowned a little as he remembered her stubborn red mouth. He hoped that she would not carry out her threats.

'Lance Gregg'll probably keep hounding her to assert herself, just to annoy me,' he thought grimly. 'Well ——'

'I wisht yuh'd hit the Y couple months back,' Turkey broke in upon his musings. 'If yuh'd jerked up the ol' picket-pin an' come hightailin' down before Myra an' Lance Gregg got so thick, we'd have a salty outfit behind us, Burk.'

'She fired the old bunch, did she?'

'Yuh might've figgered the' was prickly pear leaves in their beds,' Turkey nodded viciously. 'That was after I'd been chopped off. The bunch'd have quit when I did, but I wouldn't encourage it. They stuck for a while, with Shorty Willets, after she made Shorty range boss.

'Ain't a chancet to loop that bunch ag'in, neither. They up an' scattered like a covey o' quail. Sandrock Tom an' Happy Jack an' Three Rivers, they headed for Utah. Henry Hill, he hightailed back to Menardsville where his folks has got a ranch. Blue Jay, he 'lowed he would try the Davis Mountains or the Big Bend. He'd punched cows down the' years ago.'

'And we've six alleged bowlegs in the bunkhouse, doing about half as much as that old five used to do and taking twice the time to get it done.' Burk shrugged irritably. 'Not a warrior in the bunch, either — to judge by passing examination. If ever it comes to an open fight with this bunch of thugs — well ——'

'Me an' yuh'll be in a nice li'l' boat with a Y brand on her left hip, 'way up Salt Crick, with a hole in the bottom an' both oars leakin'!' Turkey endorsed the unfinished prophecy.

Thereafter, they rode in silence toward

the thinly wooded ramparts of the Crazy Horse Range.

'Prester!' Turkey Adkins grunted at last, with jerk of the head toward the dingy huddle of frame buildings, littering a small flat at the mountains' very feet.

Ostentatiously, then, he readjusted the six-shooter in its holster on his right thigh. Burk grinned at this. For Turkey's gray eyes were glinting like silver *conchas* against the weathered brown of his lined face. Evidently, thought Burk, the Y's foreman anticipated action here.

They jogged on up the road between the warped and paintless buildings. Turkey drew rein at a hitch-rack which was already holding a half-dozen cow-horses. He grinned tightly at Burk as he swung down. When Burk would have tied Funeral with ordinary hitchknot, Turkey shook his head and retied the knot.

'Make it a slip-knot,' he counseled. 'Yuh never can tell. Mebbe we won't need to leave in a hurry. But in a place like this, yuh don't want to take no chancet . . .'

They went with click of boot-heels and clink of spur-chains across the sagging, warped floor of the porch and so into a long, cheerless bar-room.

There was a middle-sized man, very dark

of hair and eyes and skin, lounging at that end of the bar nearest the front door. He was carelessly dressed, in overalls and rusty boots and battered hat. But lest anyone take him for ordinary rider of the range, he wore upon faded denim jumper-front a nickeled shield that pronounced him a deputy sheriff. Burk observed with appreciation the way Turkey Adkins greeted this man. He put into his nod the precise shade of recognition courtesy demanded, without the least of friendliness.

' 'Lo, Turkey,' the dark deputy sheriff remarked tonelessly. Then his black eyes came roving to Burk, to wander up and down the big, almost-slim, figure; and to linger for an instant on Ol' Burk Yates's white-handled, long-barreled .45 Colt, that bore no notches, but could properly have borne a dozen.

'Howdy, Yates,' said Grimm to Burk.

'Howdy, Grimm,' Burk replied colorlessly. To himself, he said that the name "Greasy" which Turkey had said was sometimes applied to this two-gunned deputy was aptly chosen. For in his appearance he was very much the 'breed.'

'How's tricks at the Y, Turkey?' Grimm asked idly.

'Ask the boss,' Turkey suggested in an

even, indifferent sort of drawl.

Burk understood that right here began Turkey's declaration to the world that the old Y had an owner-manager once more; one capable of answering plainly for the outfit. He was very grateful to the loyal little man. Unconsciously, almost, he set his teeth on the resolve that if Turkey's faith in him were not justified it would not be for lack of effort on his part.

'I've hardly been back long enough to look things over,' he said slowly. 'But plenty long enough to have seen a lot I don't like and won't put up with! I've made up my mind to have a plain talk with the authorities. Turkey tells me that old Charley Doane's dead, leaving Ed Freeman acting sheriff.'

'Well . . . Ed was Charley's chief dep'ty,' Grimm shrugged, with vaguely sullen shrug and unpleasant twisting of loose mouth. 'Reckon the commissioners figgered they couldn't do much else but let him step up.'

Burk stared at him. Obviously, Freeman's promotion — 'Irish' as it might be — had not pleased Greasy Grimm.

'I do'no's yuh could go so far's to call Ed Freeman a detective — anyhow, not like them I read about in the books yuh buy on the train,' Turkey drawled judicially. 'Nor he ain't no ex-high-bition o' chain lightnin' on the draw with the ol' sixes. *But* he's be'n a dep'ty under Charley Doane it's nine-ten year, now. He's had that experience. An' he's got plenty hawse-sense. An' he's somethin' else, too, Grimm . . . He's straight as a die! So, *I* figger the commissioners, they jist done the plumb best thing. Anyhow, *I* do'no' how they'd have done better . . .'

Throughout his statement of opinion, he had looked Grimm straight in the face. Not in the eyes, for the Grimm eyes were roving, wandering from point to point, rarely focusing for long on any single object.

'Nobody's kickin' about Ed steppin' up,' he growled, somewhat belligerently. 'An' I reckon he'll do the best he can.'

'At heeling the thieves and killers? Roping the One-Gang?' Burk inquired abruptly, catching for an instant the deputy's shuttling eyes. 'It does seem to me that after a year of this gang's operations in a limited territory, the sheriff's office might reasonably be expected to have done something — at least to have some ideas on the subject. But I haven't heard of anything done! Not even any ideas of what to do!'

'Listen, sonny ——' Grimm began, with contemptuous grin.

'Save the "sonny" part for somebody else, Grimm!' Burk interrupted him instantly, in a tone that jerked Turkey's head toward him; that for some reason caused Turkey's normally hard-shut mouth to sag slightly, as if he saw Ol' Burk Yates standing once more before him. 'That's a poor way to begin an alibi! An alibi made to the man whose property has suffered through the plain damned inefficiency of the office you're working for!'

He leaned a little forward, thumbs hooked in shell-belt.

'Nobody's asking the impossible of a peace officer,' he went on, more slowly, but with the same grimness in his voice. 'But when we big taxpayers who are supporting you fellows don't get what we're paying for, we're due an explanation. If the explanation's not satisfactory, then the sooner we chop your names off the county payroll, the sooner we'll get somewhere!'

'Is *that* so!' Grimm snarled. He thrust out his head truculently at Burk. 'I reckon you learnt that preachin' up at that dam' school you been goin' to! Well! I just want to see a swellhead' kid, comin' down yere an' tryin' to run things! You try some o' that on me an' you'll be backin up ――'

'Shut up!' Burk Yates told him explosively. Again, it was Ol' Burk Yates's voice, coldly deadly. 'When I back up as much as a long inch, it'll be from somebody a dam' sight woolier than you'll ever be. You're just hunting a hole, Grimm! You haven't an alibi and you're just trying to wriggle out of responsibility by a lot of yammering!

'I'm telling you — right here and now! Things are certainly going to change in this county, in so far as the Y and the One-Gang are concerned. I'm tired of having Y stuff stolen. And, as one of the three biggest taxpayers in Yates County, I'm telling you that I'm tired of a lot of other things — of having this county get to be a nest of bushwhackers and miscellaneous criminals, without any action out of the sheriff's office. Don't you think for a minute that you can yell me down! Your play is to start wondering whether or not you want to keep on wearing that badge. Some very peculiar tales are floating around, about Prester!'

CHAPTER VIII

'We're help them to git sick — ha?'

There were eight or nine men besides Grimm, Burk, and Turkey Adkins in that bar-room. One or two seemed ordinary cowboys, men free for the time being from their work, stopping at Prester for a drink or a card-game.

But there were others, hard-faced, alert-eyed, silent men, who did *not* seem to be ordinary range riders. The argument between Grimm and Burk had drawn everybody pretty close. Burk saw, but worried about them not at all. Turkey, with thumbs hooked in his shell-belt, was fronting all of the men.

Burk realized that he and Turkey might be facing deadly danger here. What Turkey had said of his suspicions of this place and of the deputy sheriff Grimm had been enough to let Burk realize that his foreman considered Grimm either an active member of the One-Gang or, at least, a paid associate.

If Turkey's surmises were as correct as most of Turkey's surmises had a way of being, then, if the two of them should be abruptly and conveniently killed here, some sufficiently plausible excuse could be easily manufactured to account for it. There might be suspicious minds in the county, but it would be hard to prove suspicions correct.

But there was another angle to the situation, besides that natural urge to caution. It was an angle that overrode all consideration of danger, for Burk: Old Burk Yates had settled in this country and served grim notice on raiding Indians and Mexicans and whites that it was a place highly unsafe for their kind. Then Duke Yarborough — a Texas man out of the same hard rock as Burk Yates — had joined him. The two grim-faced frontiersmen had hit back and held their own against all who had elected to war with them.

Burk Yates's name, in particular, had become known over all that great scope of country for utter disregard of odds; for entire ignorance of the most elementary meaning of the word Fear. He had pounded his enemies with heavy fist and hot, straight lead, wherever and whenever he had come upon them. Not for expedience had *he* ever held his hand or his tongue!

'If I'm going to do anything to make the Y brand read precisely the same as "Hands Off!" ' — thus Burk phrased it flashingly in his mind, as he watched Grimm with inscrutable eyes — 'it'll have to be by using the old man's methods. *He* weighed a lot more than I ever will; no doubt of that. But I've got to stand in his boots and *try* to walk in 'em as if they fit me!'

Interruption came, strange, rather interesting to everyone, before Grimm gathered together his wits, and — it might be — his nerve, for the answering of Burk's amazing ultimatum.

It was a tall man, very much the cowboy-dandy. A lean and graceful and sinewy six-footer of clean-carved mahogany-brown face in which shone happily arresting eyes of a sea-blue color.

Out of a box he might have come — to judge by the absence of dust and saddle-sweat upon his fine blue flannel shirt, his trousers of hand-woven woolen cloth, his fifty-dollar boots and fifty-dollar black Stetson. There was a pearl-handled Colt hanging in hand-stamped holster, sagging low from a wide shell-belt of many loops, of the same exquisite, hand-tooled workmanship.

Momentarily, the stranger stopped in the doorway, with a strong, brown hand absently at the spike-point of small black mustache. Then, at sight apparently of bottles and glasses upon the pine bar, the blue eyes twinkled in high-nosed, daredevil face. He came with clink-clump of spur-chains and boot-heels inside, angling toward the bar-front.

'Ha!' he grunted explosively. 'She's the w'iskey, ha! *Sangre de Cristo!* Me, I'm have w'at you don't lie a bit, to call them terrible thirst. *Señores todos!* Will you be giving me the pleasure to grab them glass, w'ile I'm set 'em up down the line, ha? Me, I'm hurt to drink alone. With good company ——'

99

Grimm had turned with the others to watch this man. Perhaps he regarded the interruption with something of relief — it seemed to Burk that he did. For, whatever he might think of Burk Yates, Turkey Adkins was a gentleman whom he knew very well indeed. And there was no doubting that, whatever Burk Yates might start, Turkey would certainly help to finish.

'Who the hell you think *you* are?' he snarled, now, moving toward the stranger. 'Might think you owned the State o' Texas, way you come hellin' in here, a-orderin' everything around!'

'Your pardon!' the tall, blue-eyed man cried in tones most aggrieved. 'Me, *I* am not w'at you're call claim this fine Texas! *Nunca! Jamás!* Not any! I'm the stranger, *señor.* Me, I am be just w'at you're call polite, back in them country of mine — them Territory, *señor.* I'm come in — you're *see* me come in . . . There are them gentlemens by the bar. Me, I'm ask' them to take one drink with me. In these fine Texas, *Señor de la Estrella,* Mister the Deputy Sheriff, she's not w'at you're say *permit?*'

Very sad was the daredevil brown face. But neither meek expression nor meeker tone could overbalance the twinkle of the bold blue eyes. Grimm saw the latter;

100

ignored the other.

'Say! Don't you try none o' that funny business on me!' he snarled furiously, with another angry half-step toward the tall stranger. 'You ain't in the dam' Territory now! You're in *my* bailiwick, an' I wouldn't give a whoop if you was Frenchy Leonard! You'll walk soft an' talk soft, around me! I don't like your looks an that's plenty! No dam' Greaser dude ———'

'*Señor!*' purred the tall stranger — he had taken a long, tiger-smooth step toward Grimm. Now he stooped a little, so that when his face was close to Grimm's face their eyes were level — 'You're look at me — hard! Oh, so close! W'en you're look, you're see that you're make the sad mistake, w'en you're say them name "Greaser"! An', w'en you're see them mistake, you're tell these gentlemens you're mistake ———'

For answer, Grimm snarled furiously and his fist whipped up. It came looping toward the other's chin. But the tall man turned a little, stooped and caught Grimm neck and crotch. Off the floor he lifted him flashingly, then turned in a twinkling movement. He hurled Grimm bodily through the air, to crash into the wall nearly ten feet away, crumple and lie still.

'Dam yo' eyes!' roared a hard-faced

lounger, gaping from Grimm to the man who had handled him so deftly, easily. 'Why — Why ——'

His hand jerked, where it was thumb-hooked in his belt. But he was unfortunately within six feet of the man he addressed — a distance that the tall man covered in a smooth racing stride, reminding Burk Yates of nothing so much as a coachwhip snake. The pearl-handled Colt had somehow got from holster to hand, without any there observing the draw. It lifted, now.

The long barrel struck the hard-faced gunman twice — across the wrist with a force that brought the snap of breaking bone; again upon the temple. The gunman crumpled to the floor. The stranger looked up, lifting dark brows inquiringly.

'An' now,' remarked this most efficient one, 'if we're all them good friend, I'm ask again about them drink . . .'

He spun the Colt upon its trigger-guard and looked from face to face of the gaping men with that sardonic twinkle he had never lost. It seemed obvious that he cared not at all which they elected — a drink or a fight, it was all the same to him.

'If yuh-all want my ad-vice — an' I'll tell yuh beforehand it's good advice,' Turkey drawled humorously to the watchers, 'yuh'll let them two bold warriors on the floor fight their own war an' yuh won't buy into it a nickel's worth. 'Twas all Bill Grimm's fault, anyhow. An' he's got a hell of a crust, callin' anybody a "Greaser" — *he* has! When ever'body in this country knows him as "Greasy Grimm"! Yuh can tell him that, barkeep, when he wakes up. Tell him 'twas signed "Turkey Adkins" too. I see yuh wrinklin' up yo' forrud, makin' shore yuh'd remember it. Stranger . . . my boss an' me, I reckon we'd be glad to have that drink with yuh. Oh! Some o' the rest would, too!"

For all the others lined up, too. The bartender pushed bottles and tin cups along the row of drinkers. Bill Grimm's groan cut through the clatter. He was sitting up, blinking stupidly and touching hand to head. He scowled uncertainly around, and Burk Yates, after a thoughtful glance at their host, set down his cup and went across to Grimm.

'That was exactly what you had coming to you, Grimm,' he said evenly. 'My advice to you is to forget it. So long as they let you wear a star, you'd better try to act the officer, not the hard-case bully. You don't seem to have much luck in that part, anyway! But you'd best cut out the hell-raising. I have some talking to do, you know, to Ed Freeman *and* to the county commissioners. You chew on that awhile, Bill Grimm!'

Grimm scrambled to his feet. He said nothing. But in his face, as he looked from Burk Yates to the tall, sardonic-faced stranger standing so negligently at the bar, there was a promise of remembrance — and a reckoning. But if the stranger understood the meaning of that long stare, as Burk understood it perfectly, and Turkey Adkins understood it, it seemed to worry him as little as it worried them. He — like Turkey and Burk — merely let his eyes stray after Grimm as the deputy went out of the door; watched for a moment to see that he did not stop there.

Back at the bar, Burk picked up his tin cup, lifting it to face height. He and the tall man looked each other very steadily in the eye for an instant. At the end of the brief, analytical process, each was impelled suddenly to smile.

'How!' said Burk. The tall man nodded in return:

'Saludo!' he said smilingly. 'Me, I'm glad like everything to find some *hombres de bien* here, where I'm think to find nothing but them fight. Not,' he hastened to add, 'that I'm mind them fight, either!'

'Like to talk with you — about a little job,' Burk said in an undertone. 'We're riding out, now.'

'With me, she's *'sta bueno!*' shrugged the stranger, with another flash of very white teeth under the spike-pointed mustache. 'For me, I'm ride nowhere, in the particular. There will be no hurry to get there. You're ready, now, ha?'

Burk nodded. The stranger turned back to the bar and spilled silver from his hand upon it. Burk and Turkey, after waiting at the door for him, went on to the hitch-rack. Beside their horses was a magnificent pinto, with silver-trimmed saddle and bridle — and with a sleek, brown .44 carbine in the saddle-scabbard. The tall man came out and loosed the paint horse. He swung into the saddle without touching the *tapidero'd* stirrups. The three of them turned away from the saloon and rode down the street.

As they rode out of Prester, from the steady-eyed, hard-faced men at store or saloon doors or loafing on the galleries came no token of active hostility. But there was an atmosphere of unfriendliness that was quite apparent.

Like that long, steady glare of Bill Grimm's, directed at Burk and this tall, competent daredevil, the lingering stares of these men of the 'violent village' held a promise of reckoning to come. Burk and

Turkey, seeming to feel this at the same time, looked one at the other, then grinned a thought grimly.

'Seems to me,' Burk gave voice to his thought, 'we'll be in pretty bad shape if we start worrying about 'em before they go for their hardware. It'll probably take up enough of our time — worrying after they've pulled and gone to shooting!'

'Can happen!' Turkey nodded, mouth smiling, but eyes hard and narrow. 'Can happen — an' likely, it will happen!'

'I don't want to get inquisitive,' Burk said to their companion, when they had covered a mile of the road back toward the Y. 'But, watching you perform in the saloon there at Prester, it seemed to me that you might very well be the answer to a question Turkey Adkins, here, and I were asking ourselves this very morning . . .

'I'm Burk Yates. Half-owner, full-manager, of the Y outfit. We run to cattle, with a fair amount of good horses. The reason the question came up was — some of these folks around here seem to want to see us in the peanut business; anything but the cow business . . . We're standing a fair chance to lose everything four-legged on the place. Somehow, the idea hasn't appealed to us. So ——— How'd you like a job on the Y? Fifty a

106

month. *And* cartridges! Cartridges, of course. Oh! Very specially cartridges . . .'

The twinkling, sea-blue eyes went flashing from Turkey's seamed and weathered face to Burk's, then back again. Then for a moment they seemed to study the rolling country ahead.

'W'y, me, I'm not *hunt* the job,' the tall man drawled very thoughtfully. 'I'm ride because my foot, she's itch an' — w'at the hell! How will a man scratch that foot, except against a trail? A new trail! So, fifty a month, she don't sound so good to me ——'

'Forty's about top, around here,' Burk explained. 'I said fifty because — we'd really like to have you and there's more than a little chance that there'll be war ——'

'*Momentito!* Me, I'm say that fifty a month don't sound so good, or so much. For them money part, good enough! But me, I'm not so much for them money . . . But w'en you're say *"an' cartridges!"* Ha! Then she's sound much better! She's sound like them job I'm have back on the trail, in them Territory, w'en me, I'm wear one deputy sheriff star. She's sound like good time again!'

'You've been an officer? Fine!'

'Oh, me, I'm wear them star two-three time. W'at the hell! Me, I'm Carlos José de Guerra y Morales — w'at them fella in them

dam' Territory she's call "Chihuahua Joe."
My father, she's them Spaniard. *Sí!* From
Madrid. My mother, she's them Navajo
chief daughter. Now, w'at's it we're have on
our Y? Rustler, ha? They steal them little
cow an' them ni-i-ice horse an' so — *Por
dios! We're* help them to get sick, ha? W'at
the hell!'

CHAPTER IX

'It's war or go broke!'

Burk told him briefly the conditions in the
country, and the blue eyes of Chihuahua
Joe grew brighter with each mention of the
One-Gang's activities. He smacked his hand
enthusiastically upon his knee at the end.

'They're say, all time, "W'en you're want
the fighting, come to Texas!" Me, I'm glad I
listen. I'm like this place — Yates County,
w'at? — an' I'm like the job on the Y. You're
not so old, Burk, like Turkey an' me, but —
w'at the hell! Me, I'm think that very soon
you're look for them white hair in the head!'
These One-Gang, they have the salty sound!'

They came up to the big two-storied
house in which Burk and Myra both had
been born; came up from the rear to the
corrals that were set well back from the neat

108

grassy house-lot. Unsaddling, Burk stood thoughtfully for a moment. He felt that their visit to Prester had been profitable. With two such as Turkey and this Chihuahua Joe at his elbows, bucking the One-Gang, even, did not seem so hopeless!

'I'll take Chihuahua over to the bunkhouse,' Turkey drawled. 'The's plenty bunks. Allred an' Skinny Egbert, they're combin' the country up at Star Creek. Won't be back for two-three days.'

'We'll augur a while after supper,' Burk nodded. "See you some more.'

He went slowly up to the big house and around it, heading for the front veranda where one might expect to find both Myra and 'Aunty' Ferguson at this hour. But when he came to the corner of the long veranda — that extended along the sides as well as the front of the house — he heard Myra's voice and then another, in answer, that was assuredly not Aunty's.

Burk stopped with mouth tightening grimly. Lance Gregg was certainly becoming a fixture at the Y, he thought. He started to go back and enter the house by a rear door, then whirled again, with fists doubling.

'He's just a kid,' Lance Gregg was saying in tolerant, contemptuous tone. 'I don't hold it against him. But the trouble is, Myra, that he's all swelled up over having a whole ranch to run and he'll be ordering everybody and everything around to prove that he's boss. And your interest in the property will suffer. Now, my advice is for you to stand on your legal rights and don't agree to his doing anything without your approval. You can count on me for judgment of the wisdom or unwisdom of whatever he proposes.'

'He absolutely squelched that deal with Jennison — for the mares and colts,' Myra said doubtfully. 'He said we needed that stock ourselves and needed it badly. And he said the price offered wasn't more than a third of low market values.'

'You see!' cried Lance Gregg. 'Just what I was saying! He has to boss everything and so he wants to kill a deal and lose you money. He ——'

Burk came quietly along the veranda, laid a hand on the rail and vaulted over. They whirled at the thud of his heels on the floor and Myra, at least, looked taken aback. Lance Gregg had better command of his face. He sat moveless in the big porch chair and regarded Burk without expression.

'Listen, Gregg — listen once and for all,' Burk said grimly. 'I'm running the Y. Maybe

I'm not an old grizzled cowman, but I was born on this ranch and I worked with the two best cowmen Texas ever saw — my father and Myra's. I have the best foreman between this and over where the winds come from, too. Putting it all together, I think we'll manage to rock along without any help from you.'

'I — don't think you are authorized to speak for the person to whom I've been talking . . .' Gregg drawled. 'Myra has a half-interest in this ranch, you know. She is naturally interested in seeing the place properly managed. When she asked me to advise her about the management, I was glad to help in every way I could. I am glad to help, now. I don't see how you figure to stop my talking to Myra.'

'Mr. Gregg has been most kind, Burk,' Myra said quickly. 'I wish you wouldn't take this attitude. I ——'

'Just where,' Burk drawled, ignoring the girl, 'did you acquire all this terrific amount of cowology? And how is your possession of it proved? You have the Wallop–8 — or, rather, the old Double-Bar Z which you renamed for — well, for some reason or other . . . It never was any good. The range is poor. Old Jim Zelman was a good cow-man and he went broke on it after throwing

111

in all his wife's money to try to save it. A steer to a square mile is about the right stocking — and you can't do much with the place no matter what you know! No-o, can't credit you with much on the Wallop–8.

'Then there's the matter of your advice to Myra, during my absence . . . Where has it proved a profit to the Y? You were advising, all the time I was back East. And I come down to find that we've lost fully half our cattle through the operations of the One-Gang or through sales that just lifted our scalps; lost more than half of our horse-herds in the same way. And now, I find that the pick of our brood-mares have been tentatively offered, at a third of lowest value, to that thief Jennison.

'Jennison! So big a thief that he doesn't even get excited when someone calls him that! Jennison, whom neither my father nor yours, Myra, would let inside the big gate! Did I set my foot down on that robbery that you were advising? Don't be silly! It may pay you to remember, Gregg, that I was born and raised in this country. I know all the oldtimers and I know conditions, too. And certainly it doesn't take much time to check stock-prices.'

'But, Burk!' Myra protested uneasily, with quick side-glance at Gregg. 'Mr. Gregg only said that Jennison wouldn't give any more. If we want to sell at all ——'

'We don't!' snapped Burk. 'We're going to have to rock along as best we can until we build up again. Thanks to the One-Gang! I can't see that we'll have one aged cow to sell this year. We really ought to be buying to restock; not selling. Now, Myra! There's one way you can stop my running things. You can go into town and get our legal papers. But that will mean splitting the property in two. I'm not going to listen for one minute to this Confidential Adviser here. And you'll have to admit that, until I have lost the rest of what we own, I won't have done what has been done in my absence, since Dad died.'

He whirled back to Gregg and caught upon that gentleman's face an expression which reminded him, flashingly, of Bill Grimm. For in the way that Gregg regarded him was the promise of a reckoning to come. Burk's mouth twisted unpleasantly as he faced the Wallop–8 owner:

'So far as I'm concerned, your status is just this: as a visitor to the Y, you are welcome — to Myra. But as the power behind the throne, Gregg — you'll oblige me by keeping your nose out of my affairs. Unless Myra mistakenly brings about a division of our stock, I'll continue to manage the ranch. I'll be glad to tell Myra what I'm doing — and why. But your approval of what I do is not going to be tolerated, for one — single — instant!'

Gregg turned with a sneer; turned to Myra. His shrug and his expression were plain signals that this was precisely what he had expected. Myra sat staring down at the toe of her shoe, with scarlet under lip caught between her teeth. Burk watched them both for a moment, then went into the house. And he heard the murmur of their voices as he went upstairs to his room. But he had small curiosity concerning their talk. For it was — it had to be — precisely as he had said.

When he came downstairs, to the table, Lance Gregg was not in view. Myra sat down and Aunty Ferguson came bustling in. She was a distant relative of Myra's, some sort of fifteenth cousin. She had been a fixture in the house since Myra's babyhood and, in that thinly settled region, she was known by her charitable works as 'Aunty' for some two hundred miles in any direction.

'Well, well, well!' she cried cheerfully. 'If this ain't like old times! But here's you, Burk, all growed up into a man might' near's big as your pa. An' here's Myra a young lady — an' I do declare it don't seem like no more'n late yesterday that the two o' you was gallopin' through the house — Myra a-howlin' bloody murder an' you a-comin' after with a horny frog to put down her back, Burk.'

'The same *camaleon* she'd put in one of my boots,' nodded Burk. 'I remember very clearly. Mother always saved Myra and you took my part, Aunty.'

It was unnecessary to talk, with Aunty Ferguson present. Toward the end of the meal, Burk heard the sound of singing, with a guitar's twanging, down at the bunkhouse. He turned his head; it was a splendid tenor voice:

'Una mujer por amor;
Una botella de vino;
Un cancion que cantar
Y mucho dinero en mi camino.
Un buen cuchillo en mi mano;
Un buen juego que jugar;
Ni por friele o rey ufano
Desear yo cambiar!'

' "A woman to love; a bottle of wine; a song to sing and much money in my path. A good knife in my hand; a good game to

115

play; and not with friar or haughty king do I desire to change lots!" ' Burk translated swiftly. 'I reckon that's the new hand, Myra. He is — quite an individual . . . A big, blue-eyed, very handsome fellow who is known as "Chihuahua Joe." I — fancy he has a record, somewhere over in the Territory. I hired him in Prester this morning. He is half-Spanish, half-Navajo.'

'A record? You mean ——'

'As a gunman. He seemed to me to fit very neatly into the scheme of things in Yates County — as the One-Gang has made them.'

'You think it's necessary for the Y to begin hiring killers?' the girl frowned.

'I think just this,' Burk said slowly, and Myra's eyes were held fascinatedly by the grim hardening of his face that was beginning to be so like his father's, as she remembered Old Burk in his moments of anger. 'We've come back to a state of affairs that I had believed past and done. We have the choice of fighting in the old way — just as our fathers fought — or giving up the ranch. So — every man who counts on this place is going to be a man who can and will shoot — kill — if necessary.

'Now, now! Wait a minute! I'm not figuring to load up with a bunch of swaggering gladiators who'll go out and kill everybody in sight. I mean that every one of us who runs upon any evidence of rustling is going to be ready to protect Y property. Turkey Adkins; Chihuahua Joe; myself. For this rustling — and the other crimes that seem to go with it — is going to be smashed, or I'm going to be smashed. This is a war to the finish. It has to be! It's war or go broke!

'Did it ever occur to you, Myra, in connection with this wholesale running off of Y stuff, that there are two outfits right up against us using irons that fit *very* neatly over a Y brand? The Goblet and — the Wallop–8 . . .'

'You're not implying that Mr. Gregg ——'

'I'm not implying anything. I'm merely beginning to collect facts. When I have enough of 'em, I'm going to put 'em together and do some checking. And then, there will be no insinuations made. I'll get up and talk out loud! It has merely occurred to me that these two brands are on our skirts. I'm going to see if that is a mere coincidence, or if it means something. For I'm going to get these rustlers, no matter who they are. And — since we can't seem to learn the identity of the members of this precious One-Gang — it may very well be that when we hang the hides on the fence and go out to look over their brands, we'll find — some we hadn't expected . . .'

She stared at him narrowly, under lip caught between her teeth in a way that he remembered. Suddenly, something seemed to dawn upon her; something she hadn't expected; a phase of this business of the One-Gang which had never occurred to her before tonight, as she sat studying Burk.

'I believe you're enjoying this!' she charged abruptly.

'Why' — Burk looked at her; suddenly grinned — 'I believe I am, too! It is a lot more fun than playing the cavalry leader. This is a real war — and it's apt to be a pretty ferocious one, too.'

He recalled something that Turkey Adkins had said to Chihuahua Joe that afternoon as they rode homeward — about this coming fight with the masked forces of the gang.

'It'll mebbe be a long war,' said Burk.

CHAPTER X

'Fights lost — none!'

Burk rode off alone the next morning. Turkey had directions to give the four cowboys; Chihuahua Joe went with him. Burk turned the big curly black horse north and west, and Funeral moved effortlessly, in a mile-eating foxtrot, over toward Dead Horse Creek, where it formed a part of the line between the Y and Wallop–8. As he rode, Burk thought of that point he had made the night before, in talking to Myra — of the renaming of the old Double-Bar Z (=Z); of Lance Gregg's choice of the Wallop–8 (⋈8), an iron that could fit so neatly over the Y of his neighbor.

From what Turkey had told him of Y losses, Burk knew that the thieves had worked on a wholesale scale not often found nowadays. The price of steers being what it was, a rustler could work very profitably indeed and never handle more than four or five animals at a crack. There was money for a rancher, too, whose cowboys confined their efforts entirely to mavericking calves, letting the mothers go without bothering the original brand. But this One-Gang had run off anywhere from twenty to a hundred head at a time. Nothing small about those fellows! Yet this pretentious scale on which they operated left less sign than would have been the case with petty thieves. An organization which would attempt to run off and to market a hundred animals was big enough to formulate a system that took care of details; wiped out tracks.

He studied the One-Gang's history, mentally. His father had been dead nearly two years now. And this outfit of thieves had started something like six months after Old Burk's death. It had begun with stock-stealing on a rather elaborate scale; then graduated to the more aristocratic field of stage, bank, and train robbery.

Burk wondered if its beginning had waited for his father's death. If the leaders of the gang had been in the country during Old Burk's lifetime, they had deemed it wise not to lock horns with a man who had Old Burk's record of *'Fights lost — none!'* This was a perfectly plausible theory, but still, it might be purest accident that their operation had commenced only after the passing of the formidable old pioneer.

He felt that he had to do some theorizing. He had nothing like hard fact to go on in trying to drag the membership of the One-Gang out into the light. The only thing he could do was to start by studying those men in the country at whom suspicion might logically point. For instance, here was Lance Gregg, three years in Yates County, owner of a ranch adjoining the Y — and a ranch that never had and never would pay anyone a profit. Not on stock, anyway.

Lance had bought the old Double-Bar Z

from the bank for little or nothing. He had changed the brand. But, Burk recalled, Gregg had *not* changed the brand immediately. A man might think, Burk told himself with eyes grimly, thoughtfully, narrowed, that Gregg had come into this country and sat back to look things over. Well, suppose he had decided that the Y offered a good field for cattle-stealing? Naturally, he would choose for himself a brand that would most easily serve to cover the Y iron. The Wallop–8 served that purpose to a fare-you-well.

The Goblet (Y) was not in the same class. Old Cactus Gunnell had been in Yates County for twenty years. Originally, he might have been thought to have the same scheme as this Burk was crediting to Lance Gregg — of choosing an iron that would work sweetly on the Y brand. But Old Burk had been a hard man to fool. He had seen the possibilities of the Goblet instantly, and the result of his conference with Cactus Gunnell had made an honest man of the snarling old Arizonan up by the Tortugas. Honest in actions, anyway.

But now, Burk thought, if he were required to suspect somebody on nothing more than the evidence he had in hand, he must name Lance Gregg and Cactus Gunnell. And, on

121

general principles, he would add Booboo Emerick as being the sort to join enthusiastically in anything dishonest — provided it were not too dangerous.

'So I've three suspects!' he told himself, grinning. 'Simple! All I have to do is hang the old deadwood on them and — there we are! Better not forget, though, that Lance Gregg packs a pair of derringers in addition to a six-shooter. Have to thank Rufe Redden — that dam' old surly, honest bear! — for telling me that. I suspect that about twenty minutes a day devoted to practicing the draw will not be wasted time; figured as insurance . . . I can shoot well enough, but that military style target-practice doesn't fit a man to buck a quick-draw artist — he'd likely be dead before he got his heels properly together and his elbow in just the right position . . .'

He pulled in Funeral on the bank of Dead Horse Creek. It was quite a stream for that country, an unfailing source of water for the west range in the dryest season. Normally, it was from two to five feet deep and had several kinds of bottom; gravel, sand, solid rock, and mud. Burk turned Funeral downstream, heading toward Emerick's Axe (⌐) outfit and, beyond that, the junction of Dead Horse with Star Creek twelve miles past the Axe.

As he rode slowly, he watched for a sign of cattle crossing over the Wallop–8 range. Allred and Skinny Egbert were supposed to be working the north range now and coming down this way. But Burk had little confidence in either the flat-faced, shifty-eyed Allred, or the gaunt and shambling Egbert. In Turkey's judicial phrase, neither had half enough brains to wad a .22 shell. They would hardly notice tracks. He came after a while to where the creek ran between banks of rock. Here the bed was tricky footing, for there were potholes five and six feet deep, Burk knew, that were masked except in times of very low and very clear water. But if no man would normally choose this section for a crossing, still — somebody *had* chosen it . . .

He sat and frowned at the shallow gully that ran down into the creek-bed on the other side — a sort of trough that drained the land over there in wet weather. Here it was a rude 'chute' up which it would be possible to drive cattle out of the creek — and leave mightly little sign, either. But if those were not the prints of cloven hoofs over there in the thin carpet of earth on the little gully's floor ——

He found a place on the Y side near by

which might have been used to throw the cattle down into the bed, preparatory to hustling them up via the gully. He pushed Funeral down this break in the bank and they came to the water with a clatter and splashing of loose stones. Then up the creek forty yards or so; with the big black twice stepping off into hidden holes and once swimming a stroke or two. And up the gully. It was possible to get out here and those *were* cow-tracks, with horse-tracks pointing inland and toward the Wallop–8.

This was rolling country, becoming increasingly rough as it neared the foothills of the Tortugas over the Goblet fence. The trail of the driven cattle vanished within fifty yards of the creek-bank in a jumble of gravel and big stones. Burk hesitated a moment, wishing for Turkey or Chihuahua Joe. Then he shrugged and rode forward, loosening the Winchester in its scabbard as he went. He wanted to know where those tracks went and, if it were possible to find soft ground along their path, approximately how many had been pushed along here.

He had to circle to pick up the trail, but when he found it, he whistled amazedly. Fifty, sixty — a hundred, perhaps, of cattle . . . He sat there with hands clenching on the saddle-horn and face like stone.

There was no doubt in his mind, now, concerning Mr. Lance Gregg's connection with the gentry of the long rope who had been working on the Y herds. Independent thieves would hardly take stolen stock straight across the Wallop–8 range. They could more satisfactorily drive them southwest toward a market. This caution in crossing the creek, to Burk's mind, pointed to a plan to hold the stolen herd close by — where swift pursuit would discover them. Now, where would that secret holding-ground be? Somewhere on the Wallop–8 range, probably; though, if old Cactus Gunnell were in on this business, it might be in some canyon of the Tortugas on his range.

A moving object caught Burk's eye; the merest flash of something yellow-brown moving across his front far ahead of him. He shook his head irritably. The one tiny glimpse he had, as the object disappeared behind a swell, was not enough to let him say if it were a horse or a cow. But as he sat scowling alternately in the direction of its disappearance and down at the pounded ground, it came to him presently that Lance Gregg or his men would not particularly fancy this investigation of their range. And he was alone, far into the Wallop–8 bailiwick.

He turned Funeral and rode back toward the creek, aiming at a point where the banks were low, upstream from where he had crossed and nearer the Y house, but requiring a longer ride over Wallop–8 ground. And suddenly there was the flat *whang!* of a rifle. A puff of smoke blossomed with the sound, beside a low swell ahead. Automatically, Burk drove in the rowels and Funeral leaped into a racing stride in midair. Behind a head-high swell, Burk jerked him to a stop and jumped off with his Winchester out.

CHAPTER XI

'You're a cow-thief!'

He ran to where he could see that other swell, estimated its distance, then set his sights. He aimed at the spot from which the shot had come, and waited. But no other shot came. Burk studied the lay of the land, then suddenly came to his feet and ran back to Funeral. He flung the reins over the black's head and went into the saddle without troubling to touch stirrups. That silence doubtless meant an attempt to flank him. It was merely a question of the direction the bushwhacker would take — whether he would circle to right or to left.

126

Burk decided to head on his original course — toward the creek. If he ran into the gentleman who had burned his ears, he would run into him. Better take that chance than get cut off from the line and holed up, while more Wallop–8 men came up to scientifically and easily shoot him to pieces. He sent Funeral at a break-neck pace on the home-trail. But, alert as he was, he was utterly taken by surprise when a tall figure suddenly showed, afoot, beside a boulder, with a rifle in his hands. Burk jerked up his own Winchester, almost before this man saw him. It was all over in a twinkling — he got in three shots and saw the tall man drop his rifle. Burk surged forward triumphantly, but stopped himself in time.

For the other had only dropped his Winchester for an instant. Immediately, its barrel reappeared over the boulder-top and a bullet hummed waspishly past Burk's head. He was at a disadvantage, there in the open. He hauled Funeral around and spurred him furiously off to the left toward the cover of a tiny hill. He had almost made the shelter, though bullets pelted the ground around Funeral's flying hoofs and whined viciously past Burk as he lay almost flat, when he had the sensation of a rough finger — red-hot — jerked across his face. The next minute he was behind the hill.

He made no stop here. All that firing would bring up any Wallop–8 men within hearing and there might well be more than enough that near. He continued on to the creek and not until Funeral surged up the bank and came out on Y land did Burk so much as lift his hand to his face. The numbness was gone now. In its place was a stinging. His fingers came away dabbled with blood. He looked at reddened finger-tips and grinned tight-lipped.

'First blood to you, Gregg!' he acknowledged, aloud. 'But first blood isn't last blood, by a long shot!'

He rode back to the house, and before the bunkhouse yelled for Turkey and Chihuahua. The latter appeared, and at sight of Burk's face his black brows went climbing and into the blue eyes came a glint like polished metal.

'Ha!' he grunted. 'She's them war, ha? An' me, I'm not there. W'at the hell!'

'Where's Turkey?'

'He's ride for them south pasture to see w'at them mares will do. You're — find somethin'?'

'Rather! Found where between sixty and a hundred head of our stuff went across the creek to the Wallop–8. And I found a gentleman on that side who made me very welcome. Very. He wanted me to stay there permanently . . .'

'An' now,' purred Chihuahua, 'we're ride over an' we're salivate 'em, ha? Me, I'm like these Yates County, Burk, I ——'

'What did you do to your face?' gasped Myra, from behind them.

Burk turned slowly in the saddle to face her. Chihuahua swept off his hat, but Myra's eyes were fixed fascinatedly on Burk's bloody cheek and neck. One hand had come up to her breast; all trace of color was vanished as if washed from her cheeks. Burk regarded her somberly — but with a shade of curiosity, too. He wondered vaguely at her show of emotion, for he recalled that, in her pigtail days, she had normally been hardly more moved by the sight of blood than he had. But he dismissed the thought swiftly; after all, it mattered nothing.

'This is a brand donated this morning by your friend, Mr. Gregg,' he drawled. 'Oh, not personally, perhaps. I never got a good look at my opponent. But it was on the Wallop–8 range that I was jumped, while I explored a little to find where some Y stuff had gone, after it crossed the creek from our side with some of Mr. Gregg's merry men chaperoning.'

'I don't believe it!' she flashed. 'He's not that sort, at all! You're just prejudiced against him, Burk. Anybody might have shot at you.'

'You don't believe it? Why, what has that to do with it?' Burk scoffed, unpleasantly. 'Chihuahua' — he turned away from her abruptly — 'when Turkey comes in, we'll augur a little. I have an idea in my head and I want to see how it strikes you two.'

He rode over to the corral and unsaddled. Myra had gone back to the house, and he followed. He washed the scratch on his cheek and went down to lunch. It was past the regular meal-hour, so he ate alone. But Myra came in as he was getting up from the table. Her face was set and pale.

'Burk, you have to stop accusing Mr. Gregg of stealing Y stock. I know him better than you do. I know that he's absolutely incapable of dishonesty. Why, don't you see that when you accuse him of rustling, you're also accusing him of being a member of the One-Gang? A gang of stage-robbers, bank-robbers, train-robbers, cowardly murderers!'

'Yes, they're all those things . . . And now that I think of it, Lance Gregg looks perfectly capable of any or all of them. Which is all the more reason for jerking off his mask and replacing it with a black cap.'

He brushed past her, going through the great hall toward the front veranda. But she followed quickly and caught him at the door. She was furious. Almost, he grinned. It was so like other days. Myra was a born partisan. She never did things by halves and, if she liked a person, she would listen to nothing in the world against him. But this business of Lance Gregg had to be settled.

'You — You ——' she began, then caught her breath. 'Mr. Gregg is a friend of mine! No matter what you say about him, he has been the one person to help while you were gone. And it's perfectly ridiculous ——'

'— For you to sit up here at the house,' Burk broke in upon her, 'and try to tell me that our stuff went across the creek to his range and never came back and that *he* knows nothing of it. He's a rustler and he's going to have his neck stretched. You might just as well save your breath, Myra! This is man's business and it's going on to the end.'

He turned and looked through the door. Lance Gregg was standing on the lowest step below the veranda. Burk looked at him with narrowed eyes. How much had Gregg heard? And had he interpreted it as applying to him? Then, at Myra, Burk looked flashingly. With sight of her expression he made a decision. There was no use postponing the flinging down of his gauntlet. Myra was going to tell Gregg. There was no doubting that, after seeing her face. So ——

He stepped out upon the veranda and moved aside from the door, then regarded the big swaggering Wallop–8 owner steadily.

'I was talking about you, Gregg!' he said coldly. 'When I told Myra that I had found, this morning, where our stuff went over to your range. You're a cow-thief and mixed up with the One-Gang. And you're going to get yours by lead or a rope!'

It had occurred to Burk, standing there, expecting swift reaction to this charge, that what Rufe Redden had said of Lance Gregg's scant skill with a gun applied only when Gregg faced a skilled gunman; one of those wizards on the draw like little Turkey Adkins or Old Burk Yates. It would not apply when Gregg faced him — who was not particularly fast on the draw. So he watched Gregg keenly. There was nothing slow about Burk's brain, whatever lagging might be noted in his gun-hand.

He saw Gregg's eyes narrow; grow murky. He had the idea that the Wallop–8 man was calculating the desirability of two or more courses of action as he stood there looking up. And saw, too, the tightening of his mouth that denoted a decision made. So it surprised him not at all that Gregg suddenly slapped hand on the smooth white butt of his .45. He had rather expected the Wallop–8 owner to take this opportunity to kill him.

For himself, he had decided flashingly in the beginning not to accompany his charges by drawing a gun. That was the sensible thing to do, for a man not sure of his speed. But it would weaken the effect of this encounter. Gregg would shrug and sneer and Myra would be surer than ever that Burk was a stubborn boy, with an un-founded prejudice against the big-hearted, tolerant Lance Gregg. So he had made up his mind to give Gregg the chance to draw first.

It was a twinkling draw; a blur of hand-movement as the big pearl-handled .45 came out of the holster. Myra screamed thinly. But Burk, trained athlete, owned a coördination of mind and muscle this cow-country knew little about. He was pulling the triggerless right-hand gun of his father as Gregg's gun flipped out of its fancy holster. But he was also moving — so rapidly that Gregg, shooting from the hip, had no chance to hold his shot, to alter his instinctive aim. So, as Burk covered six feet of space in a jump, the bullet thudded into the house-wall and Burk dropped lightly, jerked back the big hammer twice and his second bullet ripped into Lance Gregg, knocking him backward.

He crashed face upward across the graveled walk. Burk slid forward and waited at the veranda-edge, mouth a white line, eyes hard as agate, instinctively falling into the killer's crouch. His left hand was a stiff claw; the Colt in his right, held at hip-level, menaced the still figure on the ground below. He heard, but gave no heed to, Myra's scream. And, as these three were rigid, so, around the corner of the house, like a racing snake, came Chihuahua Joe with a Winchester carbine across his arm, the light of battle in his sea-blue eyes.

'Ha!' he said. The .44 muzzle jerked down to cover Lance Gregg.

Lance Gregg moved a little, and groaned. Before his eyes could open, Chihuahua Joe spat out a bitter oath of disgust. He slid forward and jammed the muzzle of the carbine into Gregg's belly, then stretched a long arm to take the .45 out of Gregg's hand.

Burk recalled suddenly the derringers that Rufe Redden had said were Gregg's secondary battery. He went down the steps and stooped over Gregg. There they were; two wicked, stubby-barreled .41 Remingtons, in the watch-pockets of Lance Gregg's pants.

'Let him up, Chihuahua,' he ordered. 'Let's see how badly he's hurt. Reckon he was just faking that knockout.'

'Faking?' Gregg snarled. 'Damned lucky thing for you that I hit my head on a rock! I'd have hung your hide on the fence, otherwise.'

'She's nothin' but them bullet in his gun-arm an' one knot on them *cocobolo*,' Chihuahua announced contemptuously, after swift and practiced examination. 'Nobody but them *pilgrim* would be bothered in them fight by so little. But w'en one fella, she's want to *crawl* from them fight — anything's do for them excuse. W'at the hell!'

He spat eloquently and twisted a spike-point of his black mustache in manner supremely insulting.

Lance Gregg propped himself up with a hand on the ground and staggered to his feet. He stood for an instant, lowering at Burk, then Myra came quickly forward.

'Come into the house, Mr. Gregg,' she said shakily. 'I'll bandage your arm.'

Burk stood back and let him pass. When the two had gone inside, he looked at Chihuahua. That gentleman shrugged sympathetically:

135

'She's hell!' he said sadly. 'For them fella, she will kill you from the back or w'at way she can. *Sí!* She's them kind. She will shoot from the front w'en that's all right. But she's them *buscadero* w'at will dry-gulch you w'en that's better! I'm wish you're kill him then.'

CHAPTER XII

'Of course, I'm going to smash you ——'

Burk nodded; shrugged. He stared blankly at the door. Then: 'You see him ride in?'

'*Sí!* But I'm not see them brand on his horse. So I'm think nothin'; till them shots.'

'Where's his horse?' Burk grunted suddenly. Chihuahua, who seemed to be busy with certain thoughts of his own, looked up with a grunt of inquiry, then replied that the horse, a sorrel, was in the corral.

Burk turned that way with Chihuahua trailing. The sorrel had been unsaddled. Evidently, Lance Gregg had intended to remain at the Y for a time. The saddle was hanging to a peg in the shed. Burk saw a Winchester in a saddle-scabbard. With an odd, small smile, he went over and drew the weapon from the sheath. Along the stock was a long, lead-burned groove.

'Ha!' grunted Chihuahua interestedly. 'These fella she's have the bullet hit them Weenchestair, ha?'

'Very recently,' Burk drawled. 'This morning, in fact. Dam' near collected him, too. See? He had his face against the stock and the bullet came over his right arm, glanced along the stock, and passed within an inch of his face and off.'

'I — see,' nodded Chihuahua. 'Twice she's have them devil's luck —— Well! She's only them third time w'at is the charm, ha? An' third time, she's next time.'

Burk went back to the house, having left both Gregg's .45 and a pair of derringers in the saddle-pockets. He watched through a window, from the veranda, Myra's ministrations to the sullen-faced Gregg. When she went out, carrying her rolls of bandage, he went swiftly through the hall to where Gregg sat in the great living-room. He moved up to Gregg's chair and stood looking down at him. Gregg stared at him, in turn, like a trapped wolf.

'I'm in a sort of complicated situation,' Burk drawled ruefully. 'Of course, I'm going to smash you and your outfit. That's not only a duty to the country at large, you understand; it's going to be a real pleasure. But my problem is this: You're such a Smart

Aleck of a thief, Gregg, that just stretching your neck or seeing you go down with a .45 through you wouldn't be complete satisfaction.

'That's why I just shot you in the arm a while ago . . . I want to stand you up in the Congress barroom in town; then, before an audience, show them what a four-flusher you really are; show them with my fists. I suppose that the only way to settle the problem of treating you as a rustler and all-around crook, *and* as a four-flusher, will be to first knock your block off, then jail you. Well, that will work itself out, of course.'

Lance Gregg's twisted face was maniacal. He had been shown up once that day by this boy whom he had been treating so condescendingly. Now, Burk's lazy, contemptuous drawl was the most maddening irritant possible. He could not speak. He struggled with the fury that choked him. Burk watched with a small grin.

'Won't come out?' he inquired sympathetically. 'Now, that's just too bad, it is. But it really doesn't matter. Nothing you can say, hereafter, is going to alter anything. We've already made our plans for you, Gregg.'

'I'm going to kill you on sight!' Gregg burst out suddenly. 'On sight! You — you got away today, but you won't get away again! You ——'

'Of course,' nodded Burk, sympathetically as before, observing how this treatment most infuriated Gregg. 'You'd have to say that. It's expected. All the best dime novels recommend it. I'd have been disappointed if you hadn't said that. But I reckon that, for all practical purposes, it won't really signify. Oh! I was just looking over your outfit. That's quite a fancy saddle you sport. Good horse you've got, too. Where'd you steal him? Doesn't matter, of course. That Winchester of yours — sorry to have skinned up the stock the way I did, this morning. I didn't mean to do it. I was aiming at something else. But I'll try not to hit the rifle next time. Not just the rifle . . .'

He went out to the bunkhouse. It seemed to him that right here and now it was time to be talking to county commissioners and to Ed Freeman, the acting sheriff. He found Turkey Adkins and Chihuahua Joe alone in the bunkhouse and Turkey looked up at him speculatively.

'Chihuahua was jist a-tellin' me how yuh locked horns twicet with the Wallop–8 today,' he grunted. 'Burk! I'm downright sorry yuh never drilled that skunk plumb center. Like Chihuahua says, he's the breed that don't give a dam' how he gits his man, so long's he gits him. I sized him up that-away quite a spell back.'

'*Seguramente!*' nodded Chihuahua energetically. 'Me, I'm try to think where I'm see them fella before. But I'm ramble here, somewheres else, very much. I'm see plenty fella. Now, I'm still wonder . . . But, I'm bet some money I'm remember — an' she will not please them Lance Gregg w'en I'm remember.'

'Myra still stickin' with him?' grunted Turkey.

'I reckon,' shrugged Burk. 'She told me that when I accused Gregg of rustling our stuff, I was also accusing him of membership all paid up in the One-Gang.'

'Ex-act-ly!' snapped Turkey. 'An' I was jist a-figgerin' along that line, Burk. Yuh got to watch out, now! He's a rattler, that fella. An' he's out to collect yo' scalp. An' yuh ain't forgittin' Shorty Willets an' Pedro Garcia? Nor the Association detective an' the Fargo man? I tell yuh, Burk; this country's seen some trouble an' seen it through the smoke. But the' never was a outfit that could do jist the things this One-Gang's done. We're goin' to hub hell, boy!'

'Maybe we had better plan to sell out and move into Dallas or Fort Worth,' Burk said sadly. 'You and Chihuahua are too old to stand this strain and everybody tells me I'm too young . . .'

'I reckon,' grinned Turkey. 'But le's try 'em a tussle first. Well — what's to do?'

'Who's working for Gregg?'

'High-pocketed hairpin name' Powers — looks right salty; quiet an' mean, I'd call him. Bob Tetter from the Uvalde country; don't jist figger him another King Fisher, though, even if he does come from the same neck o' the woods. He packs two sixes an' lets his hair grow kind o' long an' shoots off his mouth right smart. Then the's The Animal — looks like one o' these-yere circus apes. I'd figger him a knife artist ruther than a deesciple o' Ol' Jedge Colt. That's all the riders he's got that I know about. But ——'

'But there's the gang over at the Violent Village, you were about to say,' Burk nodded. 'Turkey, I reckon as how it's time for one of Yates County's leading taxpayers to hightail for town and engage in earnest conversation with those leading lights of the community known commonly and profanely — very profanely, right now — as the county commissioners and the acting sheriff.'

'Hell of a lot o' language an' fancy, at that, to keep from sayin': "that dam' courthouse gang," ' grinned Turkey.

'Oh, you don't know the half of it,' Burk grunted. 'I can drop a loop over some real hyperpolysyllabicses quipedalianisms when the spirit moves me. But I'm beginning to believe that the education I got back there was important chiefly in another phase than the literary.'

'Such as?' suggested Turkey. 'Be'n more to the point, I'd figger, if they'd learned yuh somethin' about fannin' a couple hawglaigs.'

'*That's* what I'm referring to,' nodded Burk, taking out his father's old triggerless .45. 'Now, you see that fly up there on the front wall over Happy Jack's old bunk? Well ____'

He lifted the Colt and sighted. Turkey Adkins winked solemnly at Chihuahua, who grinned shadowily. The .45 roared and Turkey's chin sagged, for that bluebottle fly had vanished. There was a bullet hole in its place.

'Turkey,' grunted Burk, as he shoved a fresh shell into the chamber, 'I want you to ride herd on things here until Chihuahua and I get back from town. Now, now! We aren't going off to war and leaving you for home-guard. I'm going into town to have a nice, peaceful auguring with the gentlemen we mentioned. When we get back, I've an idea that there will be much rushing up and down through the smoke. For I'm going to have a look-see at the land's lay between Dead Horse Creek and the Tortugas. There's a holding-ground *somewhere* over there to the northwest. And if that little expedition doesn't furnish an old, feeble, peace-loving *hombre* like you all the excitement he can digest — then I'm a Chinaman, the which I'm not.'

He rose and stretched himself, grinning. Turkey looked at him curiously from under lowered lids. Chihuahua's wide mouth was stretched in pleasant grin.

'Yuh're boss!' Turkey exploded suddenly. 'But tell me one thing, Burk, was that dam' fly business jist a happen-chance?'

'If you'll promise not to tell on me,' Burk grinned, 'I'll confess: when I was in school, I held the State Pistol Championship two years. I'll be ready to high-tail in a few minutes, Chihuahua. I want to see if Little Poison Oak's still infecting the house.'

He went whistling out, and Turkey shook his head and regarded Chihuahua thoughtfully.

'Chihuahua!' he remarked, 'I knowed his pa for a good many years. I figgered the' was a streak o' fat — a wide streak — in that kid's bacon. But *dam'* if I ain't beginnin' to believe that he'll turn out as good a

143

man as Ol' Burk hisself! He's got a trick o' usin' his head an' a gift o' tongues, too — that his pa never had. I reckon he gits that from his ma; she was a town-lady an' high educated. Yes, sir! I have sort o' cottoned to him since I see him fight Lance Gregg up in town. I plumb liked the way he *lost* that fight. An' more 'n' more I'm figgerin' that the Boss o' the Y is turnin' out to be a *Hand!*'

'Me, I'm go very slow to say she's not so,' Chihuahua nodded, as he got up to follow Burk. 'I'm figger we're make these One-Gang find it very easy to git sick!'

Burk glanced into the living-room and found it empty. Turning, he faced Myra, who had come into the hall and stood watching him steadily.

'The One-Gang cleared out?' grinned Burk. 'Just wondered.'

'Mr. Gregg rode away a few minutes ago,' she answered evenly. 'I — listened at the door when you were talking to him in the living-room. Do you realize that you made it practically inevitable that he will kill you?'

'I do not!' he told her promptly — and flatly. 'If you listened, you should understand that. Didn't you hear me tell him what I intend to do?'

'Oh, you're intolerable!' she flashed. 'You're just a schoolboy and, as he said,

you're all swelled up over being the manager
of a ranch! In the few days you've been
home, you've narrowly escaped being killed
at least twice. And you can't realize that it
was not because of any wonderful capabili-
ties of yours that you weren't killed. It was
because men tolerate boys' actions.'

Burk regarded her thoughtfully.

'You certainly have a case on that cow-
thief, haven't you?' he drawled. 'I wonder if
you realize how foolish you seem — how
gullible you must seem — to him? You
refuse to admit plain proof when it's put
before you. Well, that's not particularly
important. Gregg's future doesn't depend
on your judgment. And perhaps I am nothing but a schoolboy — *quíen sabe?* But, all
the same, when Mr. One-Gang pulled his
gun on the veranda awhile ago, it wasn't to
prove his tolerance of me. Not in my opinion! Whatever you may think about it. If
you'll look at the bullet mark, remembering
just where I was standing before he fired, I
think you'll admit that it was well inten-
tioned. It was meant for my anatomy, my
dear Myra!'

'You said — to him — that you had just
shot him in the arm!' she said abruptly, not
answering his charge. 'I don't believe that!'

'Quite right. You shouldn't believe that. I

was merely aggravating him. For I certainly tried my best to kill him where he stood. He had it coming to him. He is responsible for a return, in this country, to the old ways; the smoking six-gun ways. Until he and his friends of the One-Gang started operations, Yates County was pretty peaceful; there was regular law and order. So when a bullet knocks Lance Gregg from here to Boot Hill, it will be precisely fitting. For he started bullets to singing again, when our people had stopped that.'

'But he's going to kill you, now!' she cried — and now her voice broke. 'Burk, he's going to kill you! He will be forced to.'

'Not if I can help it, he's not! For, it's going to be shoot on sight, my darlin', my dear!'

Chapter XIII

'We're on the One-Gang's list'

'— Ni por fraile o rey ufano
Deseo yo cambio!'

Chihuahua broke off his humming with the last two lines of his favorite song, and Burk eyed him whimsically sidelong.

'How-come all the joyful spirit?' he in-

146

quired. 'Why wouldn't you change lots with a fat friar or some nice, well-fixed king?'

'I'm tell you — *verdad!*' Chihuahua grinned, eyeing with satisfaction the pleasant, rolling country ahead, as they rode toward Yatesville. 'Me, I'm born for to be them *viajero* — one wanderer. Me, I'm never settle down for long time, anywheres. An' so I'm hunt them good time, all time. You're hear them song of the Long Rider? No? Well, me, I'm hear it one time, by them campfire in Chihuahua, w'en me an' some boys w'at ride from them Blue Mountains in Utah, we was steal the Mex' cow:

'Long ridin', she's them easy life;
   Them life w'at's full of fun.
Them prairie, she's our lodging-house;
   Them moon, she is our sun!
Dancing, drinking, gambling, fighting,
   Are them pastimes of our gang.
Enjoy yourself! Them password she's:
   Tomorrow you may hang!

'That's me! W'at the hell! Tomorrow, I'm maybe stop them bullet. *Bien!* Today I'm have them good time. An' me, I'm like this country. She's suit me fine, Burk. Ni-ice country; ni-ice One-Gang peoples; ni-ice job . . . Back in them dam' Territory, I'm

147

dep'ty sheriff like I'm tell you — one, two, three time. I'm fight by them Texas man — Lit Taylor w'at's own them Los Alamos outfit; Curt Thompson w'at's one time sheriff in Gurney. Texas men, both them fella. All time I'm fight, she's by one Texas man. Well! Now I'm by them Texas man an' — will I not fight now? Ha!'

'I reckon you will!' Burk drawled. 'Well, yonder village upon the horizon is our destination, Yatesville. I don't look for any excitement there. Turkey says that the county commissioners get down and knock their heads against the floor in pious supplication, every time the One-Gang's mentioned. All I aim to do, this trip, is start 'em on their obeisances. Yes, sir! I'm going to speak my li'l' piece and ask how-come they stand for the One-Gang, and what they allow to do about it . . .'

They rode up the street of the town, past the First Chance Saloon; on by the Congress; past Judge Amblet's general store, where Faraday the lank city marshal snapped a suspender upon his gaunt shoulder and stared hard at them; up to Rufe Redden's. Burk grunted and Chihuahua turned his bay in to the hitch-rack beside Funeral. They swung down and looped the reins over the cross-bar, then went clicking across the plank veranda, two salty-looking cowboys.

'Howdy, Rufe,' nodded Burk to the grim-faced redhead. 'Get used to the Y's latest acquisition, *Señor* Carlos José de la Guerra y Morales — Chihuahua Joe, for practical purposes. Chihuahua, this is my old and dear friend, Mr. Rufus Redden. Rufe' — abruptly his tone altered from whimsy to a hard evenness that brought a narrowing to Rufe Redden's eyes — 'I'm in to do some auguring.'

'Yeh?' drawled Rufe; 'Got ary scalp to show you got a *right* to augur?'

'Well, one — with me . . .' Burk lifted his hand and touched the inch-long weal upon his face, left by Lance Gregg's rifle-bullet. 'One more you can see any time Lance Gregg brings his .44 carbine to town — you'll find it on the stock where my bullet glanced off! And if he rides in soon enough and you feel like asking him what's wrong with his gun-arm *and* he sees fit to elucidate, with or without gestures ——'

'You been tanglin' ropes with Gregg?' There was an unconscious skepticism in Rufe Redden's voice. *'You?'*

Elaborately, Burk looked behind him, took off his hat and examined the sweatband.

'I reckon I'll have to say "Guilty!" your

honor. Unless I'm twins, and nobody ever mentioned that fact to me. Yep! I've seemed to do nothing *but* lock horns with Gregg, ever since I stepped out of the buckboard here in town. You know that he knocked me kicking in the Congress. Well, I told him to keep his nose out of Y business, out at the ranch. Then I hightailed off the Wallop–8 range with Lance doing his best to dissuade me from that emigration. And left him with that scar on his carbine-stock. Today, that was — early.

'This afternoon I told him something that he didn't fancy, on my own doorstep. As a result of my poor shooting, he got off with a snag in his gunarm.'

'You beat Lance Gregg to the draw!'

'No-o — not exactly. He beat me to it, but I figured he was going to pull and shoot and I jumped a minute ahead of him. So *he* missed me and *I* whanged away at him twice from where I lit; casualties as reported before.'

'What'd you tell Lance, that got him hostyle?' Rufe Redden was staring at Burk very much as Turkey had stared at that young man, in the bunkhouse; as if finding himself under the necessity of revising all past opinions.

'I told him' — Burk glanced swiftly over-shoulder and found the store safely empty — 'that he was a cow-rustler and a horse-thief and tied up with the One-Gang; and that I intended to bust him wide open in the middle and kick the pieces out of Yates County!'

'Sufferin' Moses!' breathed Rufe Redden. 'Damme if it don't look like the ol' Y's goin' to step front an' center an' do somethin' toward runnin' the county ag'in! Gi' me your paw, Burk — we're passengers in the same boat, now! Me 'n' you both, we're on the One-Gang's list, an' we might's well figger to stick her or git piled, together.'

'What do you know — actually know — about Lance Gregg? And the One-Gang?' Burk demanded.

'Nothin'. But I been suspicionin' Gregg for a right smart while. He shows too much money for a fella runnin' the ol' Double-Bar Z. Changin' the brand ain't goin' to make things grow better — not honest! It did look to me like he figgered that the change'd make his calf-crop a lot better; make it one o' them oldtime crops where ever' cow calved ten at a throw . . .

'Then the' was the robbin' o' the bank yere, nine months ago. I swear I see that long-coupled hairpin a-hightailin' for home when I come within a mile o' town, that night. I come on in, *wonderin'* why he cut off the trail the way he done, before I got up to him. An' when I found the bank'd jist be'n stuck up, I thought a lot about Lance Gregg. But ever'body says he left town three hours before the robbery an' he come in with that fella Powers an' that windy Bob Tetter, an' they says he got home before ten o'clock. An' it was close to ten when I see the gunie I figgered was him on the trail.'

'Nothing else?' grunted Burk, watching Rufe grimly. 'That's a good deal, from our angle, and very little, too. I mean that it points the way, but it isn't anything a man could take into court, as you found.'

'Yeh, I found that out next mornin' when I asked Gregg if it wasn't him that skipped off the trail ahead o' me, between me an' town. No-o, it ain't all; not quite . . . I be'n gatherin' samples o' Mr. Gregg's fist; he writes a mighty, mighty purty hand, Lance does. When I got my ideas about him an' the One-Gang, I began collectin' his writin's as I could. An' I got a couple labels the One-Gang left, an' the hell o' the thing is, Burk, I do'no. I jist do'no'. Writin's different from print an' it ain't easy to pick out likenesses. But I do find some resemblances between his writin' an' the printin' on them signs the gang's been so free with . . .'

'We have to pile up a big vote to elect him,' Burk said doubtfully. 'Turkey says he's got friends — some of the solid old ranchers. He can make himself agreeable.'

'*You* got proof o' that, right out at the Y,' Rufe nodded dryly. 'What you aimin' to do, Burk?'

'I thought I'd worry the county commissioners a bit, then ride Ed Freeman some. Turkey is suspicious of that gang that's making Prester its hangout. And that fellow Bill Grimm over there is a poor excuse for a deputy.'

'Ed Freeman don't think so. He ain't crazy about Grimm, exactly. But he figgers he's a hard man for a hard spot. You can talk to Ed, o' course. But I wouldn't say nothin' much to him about what you think o' Gregg. He likes Gregg, Ed does. An' as for augurin' with the commissioners — hell! You might's well save your breath. They won't do a thing. Don't I know? I'm one of 'em!'

'Well, I'll ramble down and see Ed. I never figured him as much of a heavyweight on the head end of him, but I do believe he's a square-shooter and anxious to do a good job of law-enforcement — when he can.'

'Le' me know what happens before you ride back,' nodded Rufe. 'An', say! You fellas

153

better le' me take care o' your plow-handles while you're in town. That nitwit, Faraday, is enforcin' the gun-totin' ee-dict high, wide, an' handsome — it bein' one law he ain't skeered to enforce.'

'I don't just like that,' Burk shrugged, scowling. 'I saw two Wallop–8 horses at the Congress hitch-rack as we came by. I feel sort of naked and helpless without Dad's old cutter sagging on me.'

'Oh, I wouldn't *never* su'gest you-all stickin' in town plumb nekkid!' Rufe cried painedly. 'You'll jist want a couple der-ringers apiece, that's all. Keep you from rockin' when you walk, .41s does. I can fit you-all up like tailor-made!'

'Me, I'm have them fit already,' Chihua-hua grinned. He slipped hands into trousers-pockets and they flashed out again with a pair of pearl-handled, silver-and-gold-plated Remingtons.

Burk took the pair of vicious little weapons from Rufe's hands and slipped them into overalls-pockets.

'See you some more, Rufe. And — I hope I'll return these with the same loads in 'em . . .'

'Can happen,' Rufe said philosophically. 'An' — can happen the other way, too. Don't be too hard on Ed Freeman . . .'

Chapter XIV

'I'll learn yuh-all somethin'!'

Ed Freeman they found in the sheriff's office. He was perspiring over some sort of statistical report of scouts made, arrests and prisoners convicted. He lifted pale blue eyes almost relievedly. But his nod to Burk was colorless. He was stocky, weathered the dull red of an old saddle, tow-haired. Looking back upon the years that he had known Freeman, Burk thought that the acting sheriff was a year or two over the forty tally. Recalling those years of acquaintance with Freeman, Burk realized that here was a man who would listen to nothing — because he could understand nothing — save the hardest, most obvious, of facts. That was Ed Freeman's constitution ——

'And there's never been an amendment to it,' Burk thought.

'Glad to see you back, Burk,' said Freeman.

'Thanks. I — hope you'll stay in that state of mind.' Burk grinned dryly. 'Let me make you used to the new Y-man — Mr. Morales. He won't scalp you if you call him "Chihuahua Joe." '

Freeman got half-erect and shook hands

with the taller man. Then he slumped and looked vaguely at Burk, who was frowning.

'Ed . . . Who's that hawk-eyed bunch using Prester these days? I was over there yesterday. Place seems to have changed plenty. Looks precious tough to me. And — the way things are going ——'

'Oh, they ain't so bad, I reckon.' Freeman shrugged easily. 'Likely, some hard cases do drift in, come-day, go-day. Same as other places — not all of 'em in Yates County, either. You come home through Chicawgo? I was in Chicawgo, once . . . You remember I went up with a solid train-load o' Y steers, ten — no, it's eleven — year back. You bellered that time, because yo' pa never let you go. I never will forgit that Hinky Dink's place . . .'

'Yeh. I came back that way. It's a great town. But, Ed . . . About Prester . . . They call it "Violent Village," I hear. How-come? Unless there's been a change — and for the worse?'

'Aw . . . That's just a joke. If some hard eggs hit Prester, Bill Grimm'll comb 'em down soft. You see Grimm yeste'day?'

'See him?' Burk cried. 'See him? I not only saw him, I heard him! And he saw me! And heard me! See him — hell! I saved his life!'

Briefly, he described Chihuahua's entry to

156

the saloon in the 'Violent Village.' It lost nothing by his telling.

'I don't reckon Bill meant as much as you figgered he did,' was Ed Freeman's apparently sincere verdict. 'He's sort o' overbearin' like, but I don't believe he means the half o' it. Still, I got to tell him to soften down some.'

'He's doing a good deal of hiding behind that star.' Burk frowned. 'He has the ordinary man at a disadvantage. He starts a row and if he gets hurt, the other fellow has assaulted or killed an officer.'

'Oh, I don't reckon it'll go so fur's that.' Freeman shrugged easily. 'How's tricks out at the Y?'

'They've been pretty bad, as you know. What in the devil do you figure to do about this One-Gang? Pass the word along that all of us are to move out and let 'em have the country? If the authorities have done one single thing, in eighteen months, toward putting the twine on that outfit, I haven't heard of it.'

'It's been a hard thing to run down,' Freeman said in the same emotionless voice. 'We've done a lot o' scoutin' around an' runnin' down what looked like leads. But the's been nothin' to work on. A stage is stuck up; a bank's robbed; a bunch o'

157

stock's run off; an' there's the place where it all happened an' nothin' else. Nary sign. Nary smidgin o' sign. I don't know a thing to do but just keep waitin' an' watchin' till somethin' does show up that'll let us cut the trail.'

'You think any of my stuff has gone out through Prester?' Burk shot at him suddenly.

'Don't think so. Can happen, o' course. Might've gone just anywhere. But Bill Grimm'd likely stop that hole.'

'If he's standing in with the rustlers?' Burk demanded grimly.

'Now, don't say that, Burk!' For the first time, iron showed in Freeman's slow voice. 'Not unless you got some proof to gi'me. I got none, an' until I see a reason for changin', I'm backin' Bill Grimm — to the limit.'

'No, I haven't proof,' Burk admitted. 'But I've got some tolerably tall suspicions of that deputy of yours. I'm going to do my best to find out whether they're justified or not. I'll be quick to tell you, either way!'

'I'll listen, but don't go callin' Grimm crooked till you plumb know he is, Burk. An' don't go lockin' horns with him just because you don't like him.'

'Well, I've locked horns with him once.

And, deputy or no deputy, Ed, if I find proof that he's standing in with the One-Gang, I'm going the whole hog to the last bristle. The Y has lost the last cow it's going to lose — quietly. I reckon I have found out what I came to town to ask; what you people intend to do about this gang. The answer I see is that the Y is going to smash the One-Gang — if it's smashed.'

'Gi' me somethin' to go on an' you dam' well won't have a kick comin' about how fast I tie into 'em!' Freeman said grimly. 'I ain't one o' them dam' story-book detectives, though. I can't look at a busted safe door an' tell you how many's in the gang that busted it an' where they come from an' where they went.'

'I reckon you can't.' Burk grinned, in spite of himself. 'Well, I won't ask too much of you, Ed.'

He went whistling tunelessly, eyes on the ground, with Chihuahua at his elbow, toward the Congress Saloon. Coming abreast the hitch-rack, he stopped short to look at those two Wallop–8 horses, a white-faced bay and a stubby iron-gray. As he stood there wondering to which of the three riders Turkey had described these belonged, Chihuahua tapped his arm.

'Listen!' said Chihuahua, with a metallic

159

ring in his voice. 'In them saloon.'

It was a drunken man singing. The song was that which Chihauhua had sung on the trail; the trail-song of the Long Riders. They listened to the end, then Burk lifted his brows.

'Me, I'm think somebody's come "from over where them winds come from," ' grunted Chihuahua, using the ancient rustler term. 'Ha! She's come to show us!'

In the doorway of the Congress stood a lean, dark man, with Indian-like black eyes set close together against the bridge of a high, thin nose. His hair was somewhat longer than was usual among cowboys. About his lean hips sagged crossed cartridge belts, on which hung empty, tied-down holsters.

With sight of all this, into Burk's mind flashed Turkey's remark about Bob Tetter, 'from over in the Uvalde country.'

Tetter — if this were he — was beginning again on the Long Riders' song. Then, turning in the doorway, swaying a little on his high heels, he saw Burk standing beside the Wallop–8 horses. The little black eyes narrowed swiftly, speculatively, it seemed to Burk. As he noted this, Burk noted also the twin bulges beneath the black-and-red checked shirt; bulges just under the arm-

160

pits . . . He saw Tetter's eyes flash to the empty holster at his hip, then to Chihuahua's.

'Whut the hell yuh doin' with them hawses?' yelled Tetter. It was a tone artificially belligerent, to Burk's ear. 'I'll learn yuh-all somethin'!'

Up to the open front of his shirt his hands flashed; disappeared like snakes racing into a hole; reappeared flashingly, each with a Colt from a shoulder holster. Suddenly, Burk understood: this was no accidental business, this running foul of Tetter over so small a matter as having stood beside the Wallop–8 horses. It was one phase of a put-up job. Tetter had his orders to deal with him, Burk, at the first opportunity.

There was nothing else which would explain Tetter's show of fury over so flimsy a cause. No, Lance Gregg had passed the word to his riders, probably before today, to 'get the kid from the Y.'

Tetter was lurching forward. Upon the thin face was that exultation of the killer ready to strike; sure of his prey. A sort of sinister ecstasy. But abruptly it faded; he stopped dead-still. For Burk's hands had slid into his pants-pockets only faster than Chihuahua's had moved. They were out, now, cocking the pair of derringers of Rufe

Redden's lending. He stepped forward —
Burk.

Up jumped Tetter's Colts with desperate
hurrying of the motion. But Burk was walking in on him and, as he walked to shorten
the range of the stubby little pistols, he
began firing. Right-hand, left-hand, at that
point-blank range, he blazed away. Tetter
staggered, spun in a quarter-circle with
blood spurting from his neck, from a hole
in his breast, from a gash on right hand.
The Colts dropped from sagging fingers.
Suddenly, his knees bent. He crashed face-
down with arms outflung.

As Burk stood with one shell unfired in
the left-hand derringer, men came running
from up and down the street; came pushing
out through the swing-doors of the Congress.

Chapter XV

'An' yonder he lays!'

Through the crowd pushed the lank city
marshal. His .45 was out. It wavered from
point to point as he glared ferociously —
albeit a trifle uncertainly, too — at the fallen
gunman, then looked up at Burk and Chihuahua, who stood each with derringers still

mechanically held at waist-level.

'Here! Y'-all put up them durringers!' Faraday cried shrilly. 'An' whut'd y'-all shoot Tetter about? Put up them ——'

'Presently! Presently!' Burk said frostily. He met Faraday's wavering eyes grimly. 'First, take a look at that cheap thug. See if I killed him. I certainly intended to, but — hell! I intended to kill his dry-gulching boss today, too, and only snagged him in the arm. I don't seem to have much luck, this week. Well! Look at him, will you? What the hell are you paid for?'

Automatically, it seemed, Faraday was moved by that compelling snarl. He stooped toward Tetter. But at that instant the sprawling Wallop–8 man moved and groaned. Back went Faraday with a gasp, as if he had burned his hand. He moved his Colt hand and the thumb slipped on drawn hammer. The .45 roared. A slug rapped within a foot of Tetter's head. Men gave back hurriedly.

Chihuahua slid in. Deftly, he kicked Tetter's Colts out of reach of the clawing hands. Then he stepped back. He bowed with exaggeration of courtesy to the panting marshal.

'Now' — it was the tone one might use to a timorous child — 'she's all ni-ice an' safe. You're look at him without having the fear.

An' you're not need to shoot him again.'

Faraday's lean face went violently red. For around the ring of watching men ran the hoarse sound of amusement. He swallowed audibly, then stepped forward, squatted beside Tetter and put hand on the fallen one's breast. When he straightened, importance had returned to him. He waggled a wise head at Burk.

'Y' never killed him. 'Cause he ain't dead. But y' admitted y' wanted to; that y' tried to. No use tryin' to deny it, neither. All these men hear y'. What was y' tryin' to down him about, Burk Yates? Come on, now! Talk up! Y' cain't bring yo' feuds into Yatesville where I'm marshal. How-come y' tried to kill Tetter?'

Briefly, Burk related the circumstances. Faraday stood with unpleasant expression upon his face, as if taking pains to disbelieve the account. And through the crowd came shouldering a squat, apish figure; a cowboy in middle twenties with a beetling forehead and tiny, yellow-tinged black eyes and great loose-lipped mouth.

'That's a dam' lie!' he snarled. 'I seen it all, an' this feller, he jerked out them derringers an' told Tetter he was killin' off all the Wallop–8 hands he could find. Pore ol' Bob, he went for his hawglaigs, but he couldn't quite git there.'

'Ah-ha!' cried Faraday triumphantly. 'Ah-ha! So y' brung yo' feud to town, did y', Yates? Well, y' cain't work nothin' like that around me!'

'Just a minute!' drawled a man from within the crowd. Burk, turning slightly that way, saw the familiar thin, distinguished face and mop of incorrigible gray hair of his father's old friend and attorney, Robert E. Lee Carewe.

'I happened to be looking out of my office window,' drawled Carewe. 'It was pre-cise-ly as Burk told you. If there were a feud being brought to town, Faraday, it was working in the other way — Wallop–8 against the Y . . . As for this *thing;* it was not in sight, any-where, until the crowd gathered. Let's get the bartender out of the Congress. I fancy that he can tell us where *this* was standing when the shots were fired . . .'

The Animal — Burk had placed him quickly — looked defiant. A man slid inside the Congress's door and quickly came out again, with a pasty-faced, be-curled and be-perfumed man in tow. The bar-tender wiped his pinky hands nervously on his apron and faced Carewe.

'Well ——' he began, then his eyes fell upon The Animal's brutal face. He gasped audibly, swallowed something and tried again. 'I don't reckon I could jist say, gents. You see, I wasn't ——'

He gulped again. For in Chihuahua's hands, the derringer-muzzles lifted like curious bulldogs. They were trained squarely upon the large glass stud in the bar-tender's bosom.

'Oh, The Animal!' he cried. 'Oh, shore, gents! Yeh, he was standin' down the bar, *he* was, when we hear the shots. He looked around to where Tetter'd been in the door, gents, an' then he run out.'

'Could he have possibly seen what Tetter was doing?' This was Burk, moving so that he could stare icily at the luckless man of drinks. 'Could he?'

'N-no, sir! Least, I don't see how he could've done it. I was closter'n he was by six-seven foot, an' *I* couldn't see.'

'Sort of rolls up that ball of twine, doesn't it, Faraday?' inquired Carewe pleasantly.

'Well ——' the marshal growled uncertainly. Then he had a brilliant thought: 'He was packin' them derringers, he was, anyhow. An' that's ag'inst the law!'

'Le' me in on this a minute!' called Ed Freeman, shouldering into the inner circle. 'It's plumb plain Burk shot Tetter to keep from bein' killed, Faraday. I reckon no-

body's going to doubt Mr. Carewe's word
——'

'I hope not,' sighed Robert E. Lee Carewe
sadly. 'Oh, I *hope* not!'

'— So what you better do is let this slide
till Judge Amblet comes back to town,
tonight or tomorrow. Then you can put
what charges you want to against Burk —
an' against Tetter, too. It's assault with
intent to murder, in *his* case, on Mr. Carewe's testimony. Meanwhile' — his quiet
eyes found Burk, where he stood watching
The Animal with a sort of patient air of waiting — 'Burk, you'll have to pass yo' word
you won't start no row with The Animal.'

Burk scowled at this reading of his
thoughts. Chihuahua trod lightly on his toe;
significantly. Burk nodded unwillingly. Chihuahua fixed his eyes upon a point above
the Congress's bar-room door and hummed
pleasantly to himself.

'You'll have to hand over them .41s, too,
Burk.'

At this, the small black eyes of The Animal
lit smolderingly, but the light faded at Ed
Freeman's next words:

'An', Faraday, The Animal is packing two
hawglaigs under his shirt right now, in violation o' the law you was talkin' about . . .'

'Hand 'em over!' Faraday demanded of

167

The Animal and sullenly the apish Wallop–8 man fished out of their shoulder-holsters a pair of .45s.

Burk held out the derringers, and, as men picked up Tetter to carry him to Doc' Stevens's office down-street, he moved over to Carewe.

'Thanks, Uncle Bob,' he said earnestly. 'I reckon you haven't forgotten that you're the Y attorney. Why haven't you been out to see us?'

'Well,' smiled Carewe, laying palms together and regarding them judicially, 'I haven't been the Y attorney of late. And I haven't been out since you came home because — well, I have an unfortunate tendency to offer advice to my friends and, while it's usually accepted as honest, if not wholly wise, that rule doesn't always govern.'

'I see!' nodded Burk. 'D' you know, Uncle Bob, I'm beginning to believe that — *he* must be a thoroughly wonderful character . . . For, apparently, he compensates for everything and everybody else, to her. At least, everywhere I turn I find where she's slapped some other old friend in the face, for — or because of — him.'

'Myra is a thorough partisan,' the old lawyer nodded in his turn. 'I understand

168

that you're moving to abolish the One-Gang and Lance Gregg . . . I hope you manage to stay within the law.'

'I'm trying to,' Burk said frowningly. 'But I noticed that you differentiated, then, between the two objects of abolishment. I don't. I think that when the One-Gang is settled, so will be — everything.'

'She'll hate you forever if you kill him!' Carewe said suddenly, his blue eyes sharp on Burk's face, probing.

'Can happen!' shrugged Burk. 'But all the same, it's apt to happen if he isn't luckier. I'll just have to put up with whatever she feels.'

The blue eyes searched his face for a long half-minute, then Carewe frowned a little, as if puzzled at failing to discover what he had expected.

'When I said I hoped you'd keep within the law,' he drawled, jumping back to the other topic, 'I perhaps didn't make myself quite clear. There's the law of the books, Burk — too damned much of it. Cluttered with ambiguous terms and Latin phrases; even to lawyers very frequently anything but clear-cut. But there's a fundamental law, too; the simple, primitive code out of which the other has grown like a mushroom. That law gives a man, for instance, the right to protect with his own hand the property that is his. Does that simplify your problem? Good! Come to see me, soon.'

'Now, we're have them drink, ha?' Chihuahua grunted. 'In here, at these Congress. I'm seem them sheriff an' them marshal go down yonder. Me, I'm rather drink in here.'

Burk shrugged indifferently. *He* had not observed The Animal returning to the Congress's bar.

Inside, Chihuahua glanced keenly about. The Animal was glowering at that bartender who had testified. Very evidently, the bar-tender was aware of this attention. For the hands with which he dispensed drinks were shaking. He looked at Burk and Chihuahua with a relief that was almost prayerful.

Chihuahua moved down until he stood on the right of The Animal. He was perhaps two feet away. He ordered whiskey for Burk and himself. When the bar-tender set bottle and glasses before them, he poured their glasses brimming and picked up one. Then, turning as if accidentally, he faced the glowering Wallop–8 puncher and recoiled with furious oath.

'Sangre de Cristo!' snarled Chihuahua. 'Bar-tender! Bar-tender! W'at the hell! W'at for do you let them dog in, for to stand at

them bar with gentlemen, ha? W'at the hell! Me, I'm never mind so much for to drink with them pigs, but these yellow *chucho* that live from them alley-scraps ——'

He spat eloquently. The Animal snarled furiously at this sudden assault. His hands jerked up instinctively, then he remembered that he wore no guns. Chihuahua laughed in his face. The murky little eyes were reddened. He growled like a vicious, but helpless animal, far down in his throat. And his hand went up to the back of his neck. Chihuahua, watching, lifted both his hands. With one he twitched the silken neckerchief from his brown throat; the other went back, as the Wallop–8 man's was going, to produce from a sheath beneath the shirt a glittering long-bladed knife.

'You're think you're them knife-fighter, ha?' grinned Chihuahua. 'Me, I'm think you're nothin'! But if you're want them fight — w'at the hell! Me, I'm never stop you. Take this in your filthy mouth! Me, I'm take them other end. Ha! *I'm* make you let go!'

The Animal snapped at the corner of the silken neckerchief. Chihuahua put the opposite corner between white teeth and struck flashingly at his opponent. Burk, who had an odd crinkling of the spine at the sight of this shining steel, saw nothing; he

171

heard the click of metal; saw The Animal's lip jerk. Then Chihuahua had moved slidingly away from the bar and struck twice more. The Animal, it seemed, was no novice at this deadly play. He seemed to guard the strokes and in his turn struck. But Chihuahua gave the impression of something fluid; his long, sinewy body giving to right or left and letting the wicked blade of the other go past him.

Men ringed the fighters about. Burk frowned as he watched. He understood how his friend (certainly this tall, ever-smiling hand of his was friend, more than mere employee) had slid in deftly to take from his hands a fight that was sure to come and in which he would have been helpless.

Suddenly The Animal sprang in, snatching for Chihuahua's wrist with his left hand, striking with his right. Chihuahua did not give ground this time. Instead, he stepped in flashingly and met The Animal. There was the veriest twinkling of movement. Then Burk saw blood leap out on Chihuahua's knife-hand. The Animal threw back his head. His face was horribly contorted.

'*Aggghhhh!*' he snarled, and, as the neckerchief fell from unclenched teeth, his whole front showed blood-covered.

Quietly, Chihuahua wiped his blade on

172

the neckerchief. He balled the silken square and flung it into the nearest spittoon. His blue eyes were like polished turquoise, for brightness and for hardness, as he stared calmly down upon the dead man.

Pounding foosteps sounded on the gallery outside of the street-door. Ed Freeman flung back the swing-doors. He was alone this time. He shouldered through the press of gaping men. Normally stolid, expressionless, his face was angry. From one to the other of the principals he glared. Chihuahua lifted dark brows.

'Ah, she's them sheriff . . . Me, now, I'm wonder if these town she's so dam' full of them law that always them fella w'at's *win* a fight is arrested? Them Animal — she's pull one knife. *Pues,* me, I'm like always for to have them politeness, them — manners, an' so — w'at the hell! I'm give him one corner of my neckerchief an' me, I'm take one corner. So . . . we're try, then, for to cut each them other one's heart out, ni-ice an' polite. She's against them law? Me, I should be kill? Them Animal, she's should be not?'

'Aw — hell!' Ed Freeman cried helplessly. 'If she's like you say, *I* don't want you none. But — *amor de dios!* I shore do wish the Y an' the Wallop–8 could manage to settle their rows outside town, once or twice. It'd certainly be doin' somethin' different, for a change. You men! All o' you see this? 'Twas like this fella says?'

'Just like he says!' the watchers assured him in chorus. 'The Animal, he pulls his toothpick an' — yonder he lays!'

Chapter XVI

'There's your trouble!'

They had a drink, at the far end of the bar, away from that spot where The Animal had fallen. But Burk's eyes came wandering back to the reddened sawdust. Then roved up to the sardonic, thoroughly competent, friend who had put the killer there. As soon as he could, he drew Chihuahua away; outside.

He led him downstreet toward the Municipal Hotel of Yatesville. Presently, he shook off the effects of what he had seen. He even grinned, as he looked ahead to the shabby front of the hotel.

Fat, sharp-tongued, belligerent, softhearted — 'Ma' Whittington of the 'Munysippul' was all of these. 'Pa' Whittington was her shadow in appearance as he was in fact — a jockey-sized, white-headed, scragglymustached man whose faded, meek blue

174

eyes were trained generally upon his feet and whose tongue — Yatesville swore it! — stopped automatically the moment that Pa came within a measured hundred yards of Ma's shadow.

Burk had known the Whittingtons all his life. Tonight, he much preferred eating within the friendly dining-room of the Municipal to going farther along to the larger and better Star.

'Well, well, well!' cried Ma Whittington at sight of Burk and Chihuahua. 'I was jist a-sayin' to Pa yeste'day I wondered if that long-laigged boy o' Ol' Burk's was clean for gittin' ol' friends, like somebody else right close't to him. Come on inside, Burk, an' set down. Friend o' yo's with you? Come in, stranger! Any friend o' Burk Yates is mighty welcome in the Muny-sippul Hotel.'

'Couldn't stay away from your cooking, Ma,' grinned Burk. 'Where's Pa? How's ever' thing? Well, if there isn't Old Satan himself, as sour and opinionated as ever. *Como 'sta, El Diablo?*'

'Go to hell!' replied the green parrot amiably. 'Go-to-hell — go-to-hell — go-to-hell —'

'He remembers you a' right, Burk,' nodded Ma. ' 'Member the time yo' pa held you up to his cage an' Satan got his beak in

175

on yo' finger?'

'Got the scar, yet!' nodded Burk. 'What's new in town?'

The dining-room was empty, except for themselves. A Negro girl brought in steak and fried potatoes and feathery biscuits and coffee. Chihuahua, after one bite of steak, turned squarely in his chair and grinned at Ma Whittington.

'*Señora,*' he said courteously, 'me, I'm ride them thousand an' thousand mile in my time an' never find them steak, before, w'at will not need them axe!'

'It's all in how you handle 'em,' smiled Ma; then turned to Burk: 'Nothin' much new, Burk, except what you an' yo' friend've pulled off today. This must be the fella what carved up The Animal! Blame' good job, too! 'Minded me o' some big, ugly ape, that fella. An' et like a pig, he did! I ain't noways fancy, Burk, but the's some things that'll jist turn my stummick, an' seein' The Animal eat was one. You crawled that no-'count Bob Tetter, they say. Too bad you never settled him. He'll be all to plug over ag'in soon's his holes mend up.'

She rattled on, passing a scorching opinion of the Wallop–8, its hands, its owner, and its works. If there were anything on the face of earth that could halt Ma Whittington's tongue when she wished to express herself, Yatesville had never discovered what that might be.

'Myra don't never eat with me, no more,' she said suddenly. 'Likes the style up at the Star, I reckon. They started in to puttin' tablecloths on an' havin' a bunch o' li'l' tables instead o' one long'n an' Myra goes up the', nowadays. How you two gittin' along? Good, I hope! Even if Myra has kind o' froze up toward ol' friends, it would be a downright shame for you two to augur. It'd jist leave things like that onery Lance Gregg wants 'em.'

'We're not fighting,' grinned Burk. 'If that's what you mean . . .'

' 'Tain't what I mean, an' you know it blame' well!' Ma Whittington informed him flatly. 'For oncet, I'm goin' to horn in on somebody else's business, Burk. I'm goin' to say right out that it'd be a crime to let that girl go on an' marry Lance Gregg. First place, he ain't no good; I'll bet this here hotel on that. He'd jist make her plumb miserable. Second place, it'd mean bustin' up the Y an' you know it. You an' Lance Gregg'd fight.'

'My goodness, Ma!' cried Burk. 'This is a free country, you know. If Myra wants to marry Lance Gregg, that's her privilege.'

177

'Her fortune, too,' Ma Whittington said grimly, ominously, 'unless somebody I know mighty well steps in an' stops it. Now, wait a minute! I'm talkin'! I know you think you been tryin' to stop her thinkin' about Lance Gregg. But you been tryin' man-style, by tellin' her what you think Lance is; an' threatenin' to down Lance. I know that's well as if I'd listened to you. An' that way's all wrong! The thing to do is *crowd* him out, not try to *shove* him out. With a girl, Burk, you got to fill the place where you haul out a man.'

'You're beyond me!' confessed Burk, shaking his head bewilderedly. 'How am I to crowd him out? What're *you* laughing about, Chihuahua?'

'*Pues,* me, I'm have them tickle,' Chihuahua grinned. 'I'm see, fine, w'at the *señora,* she's mean . . . Ha! Somebody's w'at you're call very innocent, eh, *señora?*'

'Dumb-headed or mule-stubborn!' snapped the lady. She fairly glared at Burk, who watched her with puzzled face. 'How'll you crowd him out? says you. Why, by comin' in between an' shovin' him to one side, o' course!'

With fat hands upon her hips, she glared at the suddenly reddened Burk.

'You mean that I should make love to

178

Myra?' he gasped. 'Why — why ——'

'Why not?' she demanded belligerently. 'Ain't that the sensible thing to do? Here's the purtiest girl I see in I do'no' when, to begin with; an' the two o' you ownin' the biggest an' best cow-outfit in this part o' the country. Why, what better could you want?'

'Well, if that doesn't beat three of a kind! Who told you I was even thinking of — of marrying anybody?'

'Well, if you ain't, it's certainly time you started thinkin' about it! The's nothin' so good for a young fella, Burk, as gettin' married to a good girl. Now, I know young folks has a lot o' idees about marryin' — mostly foolish. It's ol' folks like me, Burk, that knows what's what. Let two young calves try to settle things to suit their story-book idees an' they git into all kinds o' trouble that they could easy have missed. So I'm talkin' jist like you was my boy an' I'm tellin' you that you ought to step in an' make Myra see you're three times the man Lance Gregg is!'

'Who was the girl I saw on the street awhile ago — a slim, gray-eyed girl with brown hair?' Burk asked desperately, trying to stem this tidal wave of talk. Chihuahua was sputtering over his food.

'With a red hat on? My stars! You ain't been makin' eyes at *her,* I hope! That's the girl they call Frisco Fanny; Tom Mason brought her in from Dallas to be boss dance-hall girl at the Blue Mouse.'

'She? A dance-hall girl?' frowned Burk. 'Never would have taken her for that. She's not only a looker; she's — she's nice-looking. There's a difference.'

'Well, she —— See that fella goin' by? Reckon you don't know him; he's come in since yo' time. Name's Barney Settels. He's the white-haired boy with Fanny, they say. He drifts back an' forth, buyin' an' sellin' stock an' mixed up in all sorts o' things. He fell for Fanny so's you could hear the crash halfway to Fort Worth, an' she seems to fancy him, too.'

'Looks like a gambler,' Burk decided, coming back from the door, at which he had stood studying Mr. Barney Settels.

For the favored of Frisco Fanny was a black-haired man of thirty-five or so, somberly and immaculately dressed, with his creased trousers legs pulled over gleaming boots. And he had the pallid, still face of the professional gambler.

'Well,' said Burk swiftly, to anticipate any further lectures on the Benefits of Marriage, 'I reckon we'd better drift, Chihuahua. See

180

you at breakfast-time, Ma.'

'Don't you be forgettin' all the good advice I give you, now. The's nothin' you could do, better. An' don't you git interested in Frisco Fanny, neither! That Barney Settels they say's a curly wolf with the hawglaigs, Burk!'

'Oh, I'll remember everything, don't worry!' Burk said hastily.

'The *señora,* she's one — w'at will you say? — wise woman!' grinned Chihuahua, as they moved along the sidewalk in the darkness. His grin widened at the inarticulate sound Burk made in answer. '*Si!* I'm think she's know . . .'

At the door of the Blue Mouse, light shone out in an elongated rectangle that lay across sidewalk and street-dust. Early as it was, relatively, there was already the sound of music and of voices from within. Burk turned in. It was the first time he had ever observed the interior of Mr. Tom Mason's dance-hall-saloon. Just inside the door he stopped and looked around with interest.

There was a big dance-floor, ringed about with tables. A balcony ran around three sides of the room, which had a small stage at one end. For Tom Mason sometimes staged a variety show, when he could arrange a list of entertainments. A small bar was against the right-hand wall and at its end a doorless opening gave upon the main bar in the adjoining room.

There were a good many men in the place tonight. Glancing at them, Burk thought that the Blue Mouse must draw patronage from ranches thirty and forty miles away. Yatesville being a stop-over for freighters, there were a good many knights of the mule-whip here also. The girls — two of whom swooped down upon them instantly — were unusually good-looking, for that place.

Burk shook off his fair accoster with a smile and Chihuahua followed suit. They found a table and sat looking around, with drinks before them. Chihuahua suddenly touched Burk's foot with his own:

'Look at them table two away. She's them fella we're see go by the hotel, an' them girl you're talk about.'

Turning slowly, Burk saw Frisco Fanny sitting with face toward him. Directly opposite her at the table, so that the back of his head was presented to Burk's view, was Barney Settels. There was that about the set of his shoulders which spelled displeasure. Fanny seemed bored. Then she looked squarely at Burk; seemed to study him impersonally, feature by feature, detail by detail. Settels said something and her steady gray eyes came back to him.

'You're such a liar, though, Barney!' she said lazily, indifferently.

He got up quickly and stood looking down at her. Then he whirled and went over to the small bar. She sat there, apparently oblivious to his going. And Chihuahua stood up and smiled at Burk:

'*La señora,* she's not tell *me* to stay away . . .'

He crossed to the table and bowed low to Fanny. She tilted her small head, that was crowned by a tall Spanish comb, and regarded him levelly.

'If you won't think me impolite,' she drawled, 'I'll decline with thanks the request. But, will you ask your friend to come here? I want to talk with him.'

Chihuahua's black brows climbed, but he shrugged and returned to where Burk was scowling over what he had heard in an intermission of the music. Scowling hesitantly. Should he heed her invitation? Why was she inviting him to this *tête-à-tête?* Because of his handsomeness? He grinned slightly at this thought. More likely he was recognized as the boss of the Y and she took him for Ready Money.

'*La señorita,* she's want —— Ah! You're

hear, ha? Well, me, I will grab them yaller-haired girl an' dance. But, you will remember the words of *la señora?*'

Chihuahua grinned at Burk over his shoulder and went swaggering toward the blonde down the hall.

'Good evening,' Burk said evenly, taking the chair Settels had deserted so waspishly. 'I was just wondering why I should be so honored . . .'

'And you're the man who nearly rubbed out Bob Tetter's mark today . . .' she said thoughtfully, as if but thinking aloud. 'It hardly seems possible, as I recall how Tetter sat across from me last night and expatiated upon his skill with the Colts.'

'It was purely accidental,' Burk grinned easily. 'He was looking for an unarmed man, you see. The derringers rather disconcerted him.'

'Let's dance!' she proposed abruptly, standing up. Then, as Burk sat motionless, watching the slender grace of her in that Spanish shawl and short, beaded skirt, she said: 'Oh, don't be frightened! You won't have to buy *me* a drink . . .'

'It isn't the dollar that scares me,' Burk assured her smilingly. 'It's you! Of course, there's Barney Settels to be considered, too. It's warm weather, but hardly warm enough

184

to sleep comfortably without one's scalp. And Barney's over there talking with that old wolf, Cactus Gunnell, from the Goblet. Do you blame me for being scared?'

'I want to dance with you. Perhaps I can pay you for your trouble,' she said, with odd gravity in her face, but, most of all, in the level gray eyes. 'Come on!'

He stood up. There was something moving here, he felt. It had hardly been the mechanical, professional invitation of the dance-hall girl which had brought him over to Frisco Fanny. His mind flashed to Settels. Why had she said to him, 'You're such a liar —'? He slipped an arm about her waist and turned her deftly. It was a waltz and Burk's waltzing was on a par with his boxing.

'You do this — divinely . . .' he told her presently. She made no answer for a time, then looked up at him sidelong. Only her mouth was smiling.

'And *you* dance too well to let be murdered without warning!' was her unexpected reply. 'Don't look at me so, please! It might attract attention in the wrong quarter . . . Had you guessed that you were marked for removal — very quickly?'

'Ummm — yes, I reckon so,' he said. It was the truth, but hearing it from her had an odd power to affect him. He considered it and found the thought highly unpleasant. 'But I *had* figured to dance with you hereafter.'

'That's possible,' she nodded, but her tone was not overly optimistic, Burk thought. 'Yes, possible. But you're bucking skilled performers. Be careful. Oh, be very careful; in every step you take; large or small! I would hate to see *you* dangling to that corral gate like those two poor devils who greeted me one morning as I took my walk.'

The dance ended and he took her back to the table. He glanced absently toward the door, and Ed Freeman, standing there, made a small beckoning motion with his head. He repeated it when Burk frowned and did not heed it otherwise. So Burk excused himself and went across to Ed.

'Listen, Burk,' the acting sheriff drawled. 'You have shore crowded yo' luck today. Now you better listen to me: Shake that Fanny woman an' hightail for a bed at the hotel. You are just beggin' for grief when you make up to Barney Settels's gal that way. Now, go on up to the hotel like I tell you.'

'Listen to me!' Burk snapped, for this dry-nursing pleased him not at all. 'If you've any particular reason for worrying about my health, I'd like to hear it.'

'I ain't got a single reason,' Freeman snapped in his turn. 'I don't give a damn what happens to you, so long's it comes off accordin' to rule. If you don't want to take good advice, go on up an' *ram* yo' fool nose through the Gates Ajar!'

With which he whirled and went out. Burk went back toward the table, but in passing the small bar, he found Barney Settels easing out into his path. Old Cactus Gunnell's lips writhed back from yellow fangs in a grin of pleasant anticipation. Burk watched Settels. The man wore no visible weapons, but that was no proof that he lacked a pair of Colts under his coat, or a brace of derringers in convenient pockets.

'You're a long-tail pup,' remarked Barney Settels, without any preface whatever. 'You been a-yappin' around town all day an' I reckon it's just about time you traded your bark for a howl!'

Silence came into all that great barnlike room, like a ripple spreading upon the surface of water. Those around the two principals fell quiet and from them the hush was conveyed until the musicians stopped playing in the middle of a dance. Burk saw from the corner of an eye that Chihuahua had left the blonde standing in the middle of the dance-floor and was now less than ten feet away. But there was nothing Chihuahua might do. The etiquette of this sort of thing was very strict. Let any of Burk's friends, well-wishers, interfere, and Burk might as well leave the country.

He considered flashingly. The pair of reloaded derringers was in his jumper pockets. It would be an awkward draw and, against this fast gunman, would likely be far too slow. It was not probable that Settels had picked this quarrel without being entirely ready to follow it to a quick and smoky climax. Gunplay was Settels's meat — therefore the play to be avoided.

'I have *heard* you're quite a trader, in certain mysterious ways,' he drawled — and was rewarded by the sudden narrowing of Settels's eyes. 'But I think you're taking in a lot of territory if you're figuring on making the trade you mention. For ——'

He struck like a rattler, with open hand. The edge of his palm came down like a knife-blade upon Settels's gun-wrist as the trader reached for the weapon in hip-pocket holster.

He struck again, with the same numbing *jiu-jitsu* blow. But this time palm-edge was across Settels's neck. Delivered with terrific force, the blows were paralyzing. Settels's gun-hand dropped limply; his still, pale face twisted agonizedly. In that instant, he was completely offguard. Burk stepped to one side. Over Settels's shoulder he could see the dance-floor, with its moveless couples. Suddenly, he saw Frisco Fanny's pallid face. Something about her expression seemed odd to him.

But he ticketed that for later investigation. Now, he put head a little on one side, shifted feet the barest trifle. Over came whipping a long, perfectly timed right. Straight to the unguarded chin it snapped; landed crashingly. Settels dropped like a poll-axed bull; fell sprawling like a jumping-jack dropped, all limp arms and legs.

Burk looked down at the unconscious gunman for long enough to be sure of the effect of the blow. Then he stooped swiftly. From Settels's hips he took twin 'stingy guns' — bulldogged .45 caliber Colts, self-cockers. He went through Settels's clothing — with an eye-corner devoted to Mr. Cactus Gunnell. In side-pockets of Settels's coat he found matched .41 derringers. These he placed sadly upon the senseless one's chest, before he stood up to grin at Ed Freeman, now running in the door.

'*There's* your trouble, Ed,' he drawled. 'In a sack!'

Chapter XVII

'I knew you hadn't a gun, so ——'

Ed Freeman made an ugly sound deep in his throat. Half-snarl, half-growl, it seemed to contain irritation, disgust, something like resignation, all in one. He moved heavy shoulders and stared down at Barney Settels with under lip pursed.

Burk waited, watching them both. His eyes were narrowed and his face was hardened to stony fixity. When Ed Freeman said nothing, Burk leaned a little toward the acting sheriff, to speak without being overheard by the watchers.

'Ed . . .' he drawled, voice very low. 'Ed . . . there certainly seem to be two sides in the county these days. If a man isn't on one side, seems he must be on the other. You have heard it before, maybe? *Bien!* Then I'll add a small observation of my own: it does seem to me that the officials are paying just a — a hell of a lot of attention to the way cowboys hitch their horses and pitch their voices. So much attention that — maybe it explains why just about no attention at all is paid to some other things — murder and stock-stealing and lynching and

— Oh! several things! For instance — here's this!'

'You dam' fool!' Ed Freeman snarled. 'You drunk, maybe? You think I was raised in Boston, maybe? You think *I* am botherin' about fool cowboys gettin' drunk an' fightin' among thei'selves? Or worryin' about you knockin' Settels for a loop? I got lots more on my mind than that, I can tell you! I got the whole dam' county to bother about. An' it ain't you layin' Settels out — it's what Settels is goin' to do when he gits up!'

'I'll take that last off your mind!' Burk said stiffly. 'I will be glad to. Whatever Barney Settels wants to do, when he wakes up, will be per-fect-ly all right with me. And I'll handle it as a private affair. Meanwhile — about this gun-toting — who started that congenital imbecile Faraday on his crusade? And — since he's started — how is it that the only ones who pay any attention to it are the law-abiding citizens? You've got sense enough, anyway, to see that all you're managing is a chance for a man obeying the ordinance to get himself killed. Here's Settels, for instance: packing two stingy guns and a pair of derringers; jumping me for no reason at all that anybody could see, simply because the ordinance made him sure I'd be unarmed and, being unarmed, would be

191

helpless ——'

'For no reason at all!' Ed Freeman exploded. 'An' me a-tellin' you to keep away from Frisco Fanny because he had his iron on her an' wasn't a man to monkey with ——'

'Ed! Ed! I'm afraid that you're as crazy as a country-bedbug on a folding bed. Or do you really believe that, yourself? That he chose me as a candidate to down, simply because I sat at table and danced once with her? I'd hate to think that you believed that! It makes you seem so — so ——'

He broke off short, shaking dark head sadly. Then he grinned down at Settels, who had moved and groaned. Settels rolled over on his side and gaped up at them.

'You can get up!' Burk told Settels. 'I'm not going to hit you again — right now. But I'm going to tell you something: you overplayed your hand. Or, rather, Lance Gregg overrated you! If he had to use someone out of your family, he ought to have picked the twins. Funny! I just had a thought! I'm wondering who that *One* may be — the one who amounts to something; when he has to work in the open, you know, and from the front!'

Settels scrambled to his feet with an oath. The derringers slid from his breast, apparently unnoted, to make a hollow double rap upon the floor. Settels's pallid face was flushed. Nor was it expressionless now. For that reference to 'One' had been too pointed to pass over. Too many had heard and understood. He glared venomously at Burk.

'You — you think so!' he said thickly. 'You're due to find out — a lot o' things! An' a lot o' good it'll do you. You ——'

'Maybe I should poke you again!' Burk drawled thoughtfully.

'Cut it out! Both o' you!' Freeman cried angrily. 'I had about all I want, tonight! Go on about yo' business, Burk. Settels! same for you! But the first thing you do, go by the recorder's office an' lay down twenty-five bucks — bond. Come to recorder's court in the mawnin'. For packin' guns in violation o' the ordinance. I never knowed you make trouble before. I hope you don't make no more. Go on, now.'

Settels lurched toward the door. Freeman gathered up the guns and rammed them into waistband and jumper pockets. He looked irritably at Burk, then shrugged and followed Settels. Burk grinned mockingly after him, met Chihuahua's seraphic face and grinned the wider. He was still grinning when he turned slowly back toward the table at which Fanny sat. Abruptly, he so-bered.

He zigzagged through the couples who had stood watching the fight and its ending and who looked curiously at him now. He sat down across from the girl as the music began with squeal of fiddles. He did not look at her. He brought Duke's Mixture and brown papers from a pocket and rolled a cigarette. She reached over and took the tobacco and papers. He watched while she shook the yellow flakes into the paper and twirled it one-handed.

He leaned over with a match and set it to the end of her cigarette, continued to look into the gray eyes while he lit his own. Her hand was on the table. He put his own over it.

'Was I right?' he said quietly. 'In believing that Lance Gregg sicked him onto me? Or was Ed Freeman right? Did he jump me because he was jealous of you?'

She looked at him steadily without answer-ing. Slowly, she lifted one shoulder — and he noticed that she had lovely shoulders. The semi-*décolleté* effect of the waist left no doubt of it.

'Which would you rather believe?' she countered indifferently. 'He is a very good friend of Lance Gregg. And — jealous.'

He lifted a hand in the direction of the bar. A bar-tender came over. Burk looked inquiringly at her.

'My usual, Tony,' she said, without looking at him.

'Old Crow,' Burk told him, turning in the chair. 'Bring the quart. And give that tall gentleman with the blonde some drinks, with my compliments.'

He faced her quietly, then.

'I couldn't fence with you. I know that. I'll not try. I happened to be looking at you after I'd worked that *jiu-jitsu* on Settels. You had a mechanical sort of smile — but your eyes weren't smiling. They were — calculating. I wondered why. If you don't choose to tell me, forget it. But I wondered why you showed no nervousness, no alarm.'

'Perhaps I was sure of the outcome.'

'You shouldn't have been. Not just then. A moment before, you might have been.'

'Not sure that you'd handle him! When you'd been sitting here so — sure of yourself? You surprise me!'

'My — stars! Was I swelled up so much? I didn't know it. Certainly, it was unconscious! And — even so — it wouldn't have fooled you, any more than Bob Tetter's bragging. No . . . When I sat down here the first time, I was merely the Y's spoiled kid. I know what the town, the county, would have called me. That was what you thought, if you'd heard anything at all. So, when I walked out there against Barney Settels, you had reason to believe that I was a one-to-ten shot. No better.'

'And yet — I didn't believe any such thing,' she said calmly. 'Let's dance. Tony won't have your drink here for minutes. And mine's nothing but cherry-and-water. I won't miss it.'

She stood up, quick, graceful. He was frowning a little as he got to his feet. Who was she? What was she? He was hardly the untraveled cowpuncher, to be fooled by 'airs' such as most dance-hall girls assumed. She had none of the mannerisms of the tribe. She was as natural, as real, as any woman he had ever met. Put her in street-clothes and the last thing in the world anyone would suspect of her would be her profession.

She slipped close to him. It was a waltz, again. He looked down at the smooth brown head frowningly and danced mechanically — so much so that she lifted her head suddenly and looked.

'I was wondering — about you,' he told her. 'Why you're here; how much Barney Settels means to you; why you've troubled to be interested in me; and — why you're here . . .'

'I'm here because I'm Frisco Fanny, boss dance-hall girl. Barney Settels is a good customer. I mustn't offend any good customer. Perhaps that explains my interest in you, too. Of course, you are rather handsome, in a way. But a dance-hall girl can't go by that. It makes no drink-checks . . .'

Burk scowled. The waltz ended, he took her back to the table. He poured himself a drink while she moved the taller glass aimlessly before her. He gulped down the whiskey, lifted the side of his mouth in a sort of grin to Chihuahua and the blonde, then filled his glass again. The devil of it was — regardless of its effect upon his vanity or his sense of the romantic — what she had said might very well be the truth and the whole truth! The half-owner of the great Y was Ready Money.

He emptied the glass and made a cigarette. She shook her head as he pushed the tobacco toward her. She was looking around the dance-floor absently, without expression. She got up, excusing herself briefly, and went toward the little bar. She spoke to man after a man as Burk watched her. That manner — it was perhaps plainest in her walk. He remembered something his mother had said, about carriage and walk showing breeding, in humans as in horses. He had another drink and watched her go behind the bar. She leaned on it, talking to a fat, red-faced bar-tender on the inside, and to a group of cowboys outside. Burk shrugged.

'What the hell!' he said surlily. 'If she says she's nothing but a dance-hall gal, why should I deny it! Singed angel, she may be. You might say, must be. Barney Settels's brand on her with a *Hands Off!* sign. Maybe I was wrong about Gregg sicking him onto me. Maybe he *was* going to show the world that he alone could look closely at her. Ah — hell! I'm going to bed!'

But she was coming back, now. It was the same as when crossing the room before. She smiled and spoke; stopped sometimes at a table. But she was coming back here. He poured his fourth drink. She was facing him. She came a little faster, leaned on the table before she sat down, and put her hand on his wrist. Carelessly affectionate, the gesture seemed. But her fingers were like ice — and they held his glass-hand to the table.

'Please!' she breathed. 'Ah, please! Don't take it!'

She sat down. He was slightly fuzzy of brain. But he looked past her; his eyes shuttled to right and left. He saw nothing, nothing to explain her tenseness.

She was close to the table-edge. Suddenly, he felt her hand upon his knee. Something hard rapped his leg. Her face was blank:

'Take this! Take it and slip it into your waist-band — and I hope to God you won't need it! But "Pocomalo" Charley is sitting over to the right, behind you. There's a tough with him whom I know only by sight. But they're watching you. This is the bar-gun. It's loaded all around. I knew you hadn't a gun, so ——'

He stared at her. His hand was taking the short self-cocker. He worked it into his waistband. But that was mechanical. She was amazing. There was no other word he could apply to her. How deftly she had got behind the bar and abstracted that gun; got back to him with it!

'I owe you — more than I ever owed any woman. More than I ever owed more than one or two men,' he said quietly. 'I'll try to pay you. Now, I wish you'd go. I'm going. Whatever it is they have decided on, the chances are it's to be staged here. If I beat 'em to the jump by leaving, it's bound to throw 'em off-balance. And — thanks to you — I know what to expect.'

He stood up, smiling flashingly at her.

Then he turned toward the front door. He lurched as he walked and upon his dark face was a set grin. Passing Chihuahua — who frowned slightly — he said thickly that he was going to bed. He went on, shaking his head when Chihuahua answered. He heard Chihuahua talking to the blonde; heard her answer in reassuring, if slightly lifted voice. *He* would be all right, she said. Sure he would!

He made the door and went with realistic lurch through it. The street just there was empty. He flattened himself against the wall by the door and looked into the room. Chihuahua still sat with the blonde girl. But coming toward the door, also unsteady of feet, were two cowboys, one dark, the other very dark, of hair and eyes and complexion. He nodded shadowily and slid along the wall of the dance-hall. He went fast. He got to the watering-trough, beyond the light of the oil lamp, before the two made the doorway. They looked both ways. Burk began to sing — then he sat down upon the watering-trough.

'That's him. Drunk!' one said sharply.

They made no pretense, now. They came walking with no unsteadiness toward him. He had the gun out of his waistband, now. It was on his lap. So was the derringer out

200

of his left jumper pocket. He swayed a little on the trough.

They came up abreast of him. They stopped. They looked all about. He seemed to ignore them. He was on the outer side of the big trough. They stood almost against it.

'Yates?' one said with a trace of accent. 'Yates!'

'Yeh — Yates!' he answered. 'Pocomalo? Who's your friend?'

'Give it to him!' the accented voice snapped. *'Pronto!'*

Their hands jerked. Burk went flashingly to the ground as their guns roared. They ran to the trough's end. He was lying with hands, shoulders, and head projecting there. The self-cocker hammer was back. He pulled trigger; pulled it again and again; while from behind them there sounded the heavy roar of .41s.

'Burk! Burk!' Chihuahua yelled. 'You're not hurt?'

Burk had scrambled to his feet. The dance-hall door was spewing men. But as yet nobody came their way. Pocomalo Charley and his helper were swaying, empty-handed, between Chihuahua and Burk. One fell across the trough, into the water. Chihuahua caught the other by the shoulder, swung him about and sent him crashing into the wall of the store across the sidewalk. The man slipped down the wall and sprawled upon the planks.

'Whut's all this?' Faraday yelled — from somewhere in the darkness out of sight. 'Y' men! Put down them cutters! This is the marshal talkin' ——'

'I could tell it was you the minute I heard you yelling so valiantly from your hideout!' Burk answered him. 'Come on out into the light! Nobody's going to hurt you — now!'

'Burk Yates? That y', Burk? What y' been doin' now? Y' shot somebody else? By Gemini! Y' goin' to git into trouble ——'

'Come on out!' Burk interrupted him impatiently. 'I want you to identify these bushwhackers.'

Faraday appeared like a skittish horse, from the shadows at the corner of the store. He leaned to peer at the body of the man by its wall, then came laggingly across to see that one whom Burk and Chihuahua were pulling out of the trough.

'Pocomalo Charley . . .' the marshal muttered. 'An' *was* he a plumb hard case! This feller in the water — I seen him around town a few times, last few days. But *I* do' no' who he was.'

'What's this? More Wallop–8 an' Y

trouble?' Ed Freeman demanded. He shouldered through the slowly advancing group from the dance-hall's door.

'You'll have to inquire of Barney Settels, I reckon,' Burk said slowly. 'I can answer for the Y end, of course. These two trailed me out of the dance-hall and when I sat down here for a minute, they walked up, called me by name, and, when I answered, opened up. It happened that I hadn't exactly obeyed your fool gun ordinance. I had a pair of .41s on me. I smelled something. I dove off the trough and met 'em coming around the end. Then Chihuahua Joe, who'd got suspicious when he saw them trail me out, arrived and helped mop up.'

Faraday stooped and picked up two Colts. He held the short self-cocker up to catch the light from the oil lamp before the dance-hall. He cried out triumphantly:

'Why — why — this is Tony's gun! From behind the bar at the Blue Mouse! I know it by that 'ere mended grip! Which o' them was shootin' it, Burk?'

'I wasn't asking 'em questions,' Burk said dryly. 'I was trying my damnedest to keep from being killed. Well, Ed?'

'We'll move 'em up to the office,' Ed Freeman said resignedly. 'Inquest tomorrow — along o' the one over The Animal. But —

my Lord! We ain't had this much trouble since I been actin' sheriff! You certainly do fall into more ——'

'Trouble!' Burk exploded. 'You talk as if I picked this! And I suppose Shorty Willets's lynching wasn't trouble? Or the murder of those two detectives? Ed! I swear I don't know what to make of you!'

'He's be'n associatin' with Amblet an' the dam' county commissioners so much he's gittin' bad as them!' Rufe Redden said grimly, from the crowd. 'An' I ought to know how triflin' the commissioners is. I'm one of 'em!'

Chapter XVIII

'You're next!'

'Me, I'm think them Turkey, she's scalp us!' Chihuahua grinned, as they came out of the courthouse at noon. '*Segur' Miguel!* Plumb scalp us! W'at the hell! You're tell Turkey, we will ride so-o-o nice an' peaceful into town. Now — w'y, almost we're git locked up, *no es verdad?* Turkey, she's raise hell!'

'But now we're pure as the lily, sweet as the rose,' Burk said grimly. 'Thanks to Uncle Robert E. Lee Carewe . . . And — to give him his due — thanks to Ed Freeman.

204

If Uncle Bob's testimony and his — call it manner! — cleared up the Tetter affair and sort of set a tempo for the little knife-business you had with The Animal, it was Ed Freeman's testimony in the case of Pocomalo Charley and his little side-kicker that set Amblet back on his heels. Ed's no lightning calculater, but he is honest. And with the authorities of the Amblet, Henderson, and Faraday caliber, an honest sheriff is something to thank God for.'

They moved to one side of the door at the rap of heels behind them in the courthouse. It was Barney Settels and the fat, red-faced bar-tender from the Blue Mouse. The man of drinks was denying earnestly that he had given Pocomalo or the other killer the bar-gun. He had no idea how it got away from the bar.

'You dam' fool!' Settels snarled. 'What I'm tryin' to do is settle for certain that Pocomalo or Wilbur used it! Because if they never — an' each had his own — then Yates used it. And if he used it, how'd he happen to have it? If I knowed that ——'

'You'd know a lot you don't know now,' Burk grinned at him, as Settels broke off short with sight of him. 'I'd like to keep you in suspense — that means, not sure, Settels — by telling you maybe I did have the gun from behind the bar. But, really, it was Pocomalo's heavy-footed tip toeing to the bar to get it that roused my suspicions. You see, I was suspicious of everything and everybody in the joint about that time. Well, run on, Settels. I'll be seeing you — likely through the smoke!'

Settels glared furiously. The bar-tender looked relieved, somehow. They went on, without speaking. Chihuahua looked questioningly at Burk. Burk seemed not to see. He turned his head sideways to watch Amblet come out. Amblet went on without noticing them. Then Burk turned and lifted his hat. Frisco Fanny nodded and was going on when Burk fell into step with her.

'Thanks!' he said slowly. 'I wanted to come back, last night, to thank you. But it seemed better not to. I want you to know how much I appreciate what you did — and the way you did it. I may have opportunity to pay the debt — or pay on it ——'

'Your lying to Barney, just then, paid it in full,' she told him, without inflection. She looked blankly straight before her. 'Naturally, I didn't want to see you murdered. Naturally, I don't want to be in trouble about it, if I can help it. You settled that, I think. They'll believe Pocomalo got the gun out from behind the bar.'

'I hope so! Now, I'd like to talk to you . . . You don't have a thing to do until evening, do you?'

'But you have!' she said flatly. 'You have plenty to do besides spreeing in town. You have a war on your hands. You've done a little too much winning of late. You'll face something serious, now, very quickly. You — traded a garter for cartridges, once, so I understand. Don't even think of trying to trade the cartridges for a garter, again . . . Your place, Burk Yates, is on the Y! Not hanging around Yatesville, drinking and talking to dance-hall girls! "Women are mockers and strong drink is raging . . ." '

' "Wine is a mocker ——" ' he began, then stopped short, reddening, to look at her. She was smiling with a sardonic little twist of the corner of smooth, unpainted red mouth.

' "Women are mockers ——" It's my quotation and I'll stick to it. You started to lick Lance Gregg and the One-Gang and whatever else in Yates County you didn't fancy. Don't hesitate, Burk, or — nobody will have any faith in you.'

'Do you think we can lick 'em?' he asked slowly.

'My money's on you!' she breathed tensely, looking straight up at him, very earnestly. 'You'll smash that murdering crew! Now, this is as far as you can go with me. I have things to do. But I'll be expecting news from the war — not from you, directly. But a dance-hall girl hears everything, sooner or later. Luck, boy!'

Burk stared after the quick, trim figure. Chihuahua came up to him and, after one flashing glance in the same direction, put out his hand to Burk's arm. Burk nodded silently; crossed the street. They headed for the Municipal Hotel, in which they had spent the night. But, passing the Last Chance Saloon, Burk stopped suddenly and lifted hand to Chihuahua, who halted beside him. Burk edged closer to the swing-doors, listening. Voices rose dolorously within the saloon; voices betraying the effect of liberal moistening, but none the more musical for the dampness:

'Drunk last night,
Drunk the night before.
If ever I git sober,
I'll NEVER git drunk no more!'

Even as Burk stared incredulously, out of the doorway reeled two men arm-in-arm, one a lean and hawk-faced four-inches-and-six-footer, the other no more than up to his shoulder, but twice as wide, with a face made unforgettable by twisted nose and ever-twinkling bright blue eyes. Behind these two came disgustedly a fat cowboy in skin-tight clothes; a round man with the saddest face and the reddest hair in all the world.

The first two out stopped mechanically before Burk and Chihuahua. Then the tall man peered down, the shorter man peered up; then both turned to gape at each other. Finding no information in this way, they turned again to stare at Burk.

'Ish my eyes a-deshevin' me, Three Rivers?' demanded the tall man in a bass that fairly shook the wooden awning above his head. 'Ish they? Tha's all I'm a-askin' yuh, Three Rivers.'

'Looksh like Burk an' ' — Three Rivers put out a huge paw and touched Burk — 'feelsh like Burk!' he added triumphantly and confirmed the testimony with a wolf-howl.

'You dam' nitwits,' snarled the disgusted red-haired fat man, 'it *is* Burk!'

Then the first two seized Burk and waltzed him unsteadily about the wooden gallery, until men came to the door of the saloon and looked out curiously.

'Well!' cried Burk, when the dance of

welcome was over. 'I thought you Three Mesquiteers had headed for Utah to gather unto yourselves harems and quit chousing little cows around.'

'Harems!' cried Sandrock Tom in his most violent bass. 'Me, I had a wife oncet, Burk, an' if yuh figger I'd ever multiply *that* by nine or ten — Nah! We 'lowed to try Utah a whirl, but we decided to come back this way — 'twas all Happy Jack's fault.'

'Like hell it was!' snarled the red-headed fat man. ' 'Twasn't no such ——'

'Dry up!' commanded Three Rivers, grinning. 'I can't recollect jist how-come we got broke an' started back, Burk, so it must've been Happy Jack's fault. Which that dam' joy-killer's be'n responsible for more trouble, since he was born, than all the eggs Old Crow ever laid.'

'What do you 'low?' said Burk abruptly. 'About working?'

The question seemed to sober them somewhat. They looked awkwardly, one at another, then all at the ground, at the sky over the buildings across the street, anywhere except at Burk. For with Henry Hill and 'Blue Jay,' they had been on the Y for upward of ten years, Old Burk Yates's handpicked riders, of whom he was wont to remark with grim pride that they could outride, outwork, outfight, outdrink, out-*anything,* any seven others in the State of Texas.

'Thought mebbe we'd gi' the Wagonwheel or the U-up-an'-Down a chancet to see some real punchers,' Three Rivers said presently, in a far-away voice.

'You will like hell!' Burk said with vicious sincerity. 'You'll unroll your beds in the Y bunkhouse and the next time you ride off we'll all ride together — for there won't be any Y to stay on!'

Furtively, they eyed him from under their brows. Then Sandrock Tom studied the roof of the Municipal Hotel with unwavering black eyes:

'Uh — about the Wallop–8, Burk,' he said slowly. 'That Lance Gregg, he's shore a ringtailed whizzer for a cowman, now, ain't he? An' *friendly!* Why, me, I figger he'd jist let the Wallop–8 go plumb to blazes while he he'ped out the Y.'

'Turkey's back as foreman,' grinned Burk, understanding perfectly. 'Why, I reckon you must know about Gregg. First time you see him, you might ask who skinned up his carbine-stock, and who put a .45 through his gun-arm. And, if you're really curious, you can ask him who threatened to smash him and the One-Gang and shove the pieces over the county-line . . .'

They gaped at him; then at each other. The hawk-face of Sandrock Tom took on an expression of seraphic joy. Three Rivers was grinning from ear to ear, with the broken nose making it a sinister leer. Happy Jack's deep-seated gloom seemed more intense, sure proof of his pleasure.

'Uh — we'll be out!' nodded Three Rivers. The others jerked their heads.

'We'll be out!' they chorused.

'Happy Jack's got fo' dollars left,' Sandrock Tom explained. 'We got to he'p him to git over startin' out to be a miser. But we'll be out, Burk; we'll be the' with our hair in a braid!'

They shook hands with Chihuahua, eyeing him keenly and placing him very accurately. Then Burk and Chihuahua went on to the hotel corral and got their horses, while the three cowboys went on up-street, as far as the next saloon. Burk grinned at Chihuahua as they took the homeward trail.

'Now, I can fire three or four of those grub-destroyers! We've got somebody to back our play, Chihuahua! They're no lightning gunmen, but *how* they can handle their guns! That fat red-head, Happy Jack, is fat for just about one quarter-inch of his

212

outside. Under that, he's rolled steel and whang-leather. I saw him fight the Lazy-D rep' one time, over a rope the rep' had borrowed without leave. The rep' had fifty pounds on Happy Jack and about six inches of reach. They fought for a solid hour and the rep' rode the wagon for a week!

'Sandrock Tom is the best pistol-shot I ever saw in my life. For accuracy, not speed on the draw, though he's pretty fast. But his Colts certainly do shoot where he holds 'em!'

'An' them Three Rivers fella?' grinned Chihuahua. 'Me, I'm like 'em all fine.'

'Three Rivers? He's a sort of barbed-wire-and-streaky-lightning cross between the two others. Oh, but I have a feeling that events are about to cloud up and rain all over you, Mr. Lance Gregg! You've bought yourself a party.'

They rode up to the bunkhouse and Burk sat thoughtfully, staring across to the neat three-roomed bungalow that Old Burk had built long before for a married foreman. It stood empty, now, and sight of it gave Burk an idea.

'I'm going to move my traps in there,' he told Chihuahua. 'I've an idea that the way things are going to happen in the immediate future will necessitate a more elegant

213

central location than upstairs in the Big House.'

He put Funeral in the corral and hung up his saddle. In the house he stopped in the hallway. Myra had come out of the living-room and stood facing him with the oddest expression he had ever seen upon her face. Uncertainty; speculation; a sort of fear and — relief? He wondered. Then recalling suddenly Ma Whittington's advice, he flushed cherry-red up to the roots of his dark hair. At sight of this, her eyes widened. Then, as he continued dumbly to stare at the slender beauty of her, with an appreciation utterly new to him, her own clear cheeks went swiftly scarlet.

'I — I ——' he began. 'Happen to know where Turkey went? I —— That is, I — wanted to see him. Anything happen while I was gone?'

'Why, I think he went up to the Star Creek range. He had told Allred and Skinny Egbert to come in this morning, at the latest, and when they didn't, he rode up to see why. He said he was going to fire them if they hadn't a good excuse. I —— You had trouble in town? Max McGregor stopped for supper yesterday and he said you'd shot that man Tetter. You — you weren't hurt? He said you weren't, but ——'

'Nary scratch. Tetter'll be out soon, too soon. Think I'll ride up to Star Creek after Turkey. I haven't seen that bunch of mares yet and I want to. I'm going to put my stuff in the foreman's house, Myra. I think we'll be in and out at all hours for a while and that'll be handier for all.'

He jerked his head awkwardly and ran up the wide stairs. She was too much for him, he confessed. Why this abrupt change of manner? This strange air of friendliness? He had almost thawed to her, then the tall figure of Lance Gregg had sprung up within Burk's inner eye and, with visualization of the Wallop–8 owner, Burk had hardened again — automatically, as in obedience to some control against which he was helpless. Now, as he opened the door of his room, still with the picture of Myra as she stood in the hall with face hotly scarlet, there came to him abruptly — and for no reason at all that he could discover — another picture. This one was of that 'boss dance-hall girl' who styled herself 'Frisco Fanny' . . .

He stood stock-still for an instant before that visualization. As clearly as when she had looked up at him from the circle of his arms, he could see her — slender, lovely, calm of face and grave of wide, gray eyes.

He repeated Ma Whittington's phrase to himself — 'a boss dance-hall girl.' And what difference did it make if she were chief of the tribe! A girl could hardly be a 'boss' dance-hall girl without being — a dance-hall girl!

Burk knew far too much of that class to be other than very cynical concerning them. Why — he put it to himself — should he be twisted, by certain kindnesses, human-nesses, of Fanny's, to impulse to believe her more than the others? No matter what she had of manner, she was still within the class the frontier knew very well indeed — the Ancient Order of the Painted Women; of the Loose Women. Payday companions of hard-drinking cowboy and miner and freighter; consorts usually of bar-tenders, saloon-keepers or gamblers. He recalled Ed Freeman's grim yet matter-of-fact remark — 'Barney Settels's gal . . .'

Ed's tone had shown that he was merely stating something which the country knew — or believed, if it did not know. Then, Burk asked himself for the severalth time, why had she turned so on Barney Settels? Why had she so favored him? He shook his head at last. He couldn't answer the question. But there was no denying his debt to her. Whatever her motive might have been

— anger toward Barney, or sheer kindliness, decency of character, she had warned him; saved him from Pocomalo's bullet.

He moved into the room and, glancing carelessly past the bed, stiffened, glaring at the neat counterpane. Everything about the room was comfortably tidy. For Burk's own carelessness of habit had life-long counter-balance in the iron régime of Aunty Ferguson, who ruled her Mexican servants with heavy if kindly hand. But — on the bed a ragged bit of paper offered a jarring note in the order of the place.

Burk moved closer, staring hard. With identification of the paper, instinctively his hand snapped to the smooth white butt of Old Burk's right hand Colt; instinctively, too, he glared about him and stepped back to look under the bed.

For this was such a note as that which had been found beside the luckless detectives of the Cattle Raisers' and Wells-Fargo, when discovered beside the trail in pools of blood. But with an additional word on this exemplar. That other notice had read simply *'next!'* This one said *'You're Next!'* The signature was that which Yates County knew so well — *'1.'*

He came back to the bed and picked it up. With hand on gun-butt he studied it.

He found himself wondering if that were the writing — printing — of Lance Gregg.

He thought that he would certainly make opportunity to compare this with the collection of samples in Rufe Redden's possession. But right now he wanted to see Turkey Adkins . . .

'But how'd that get there?' he asked himself suddenly. 'Who put that there? It wasn't here when I left yesterday, so ——'

Swiftly, he checked over the list of their servants; all Mexicans; all old in this service, with the possible exception of a new kitchenmaid or so. Not much possibility of treachery there. Who among the white employees could be suspected? There were only two of the new punchers Myra had hired who could be even vaguely connected with this. Maguire and Sweet were the only ones at the bunkhouse the day before. And neither had access to the Big House. Rule them out and there remained only the men's cook, and he had no more access to the house than had the punchers, for his kitchen was behind the mess-hall that formed one side of the bunkhouse.

Yet Burk found himself recalling the cook's surly face and roving, close-set eyes. Perhaps it was unjust to pick on him merely because of his looks, but he had disliked this fellow at sight. Jones, he called himself, when he called himself anything. The cowboys addressed him as 'D. D.' from the initials he signed on the payroll.

'Well, I can't bother with sleuthing right now,' Burk shrugged. 'But I think I'll tear the other leaf from Dad's book, this minute!'

He went over to the mounted sheephead, from which dangled odds and ends. There was another belt and holster and another Colt. Old Burk's left-hand six-shooter. Its taking down and the buckling around Old Burk's waist of the second cartridge-belt, had always been a virtual declaration of war. And as Burk buckled it around him now, he recalled this and the saying he had heard Turkey Adkins quote; he grinned tightly:

' "I reckon this is going to be a Number Two Gun war." '

Down at the corral he looked over the horses. Funeral he didn't want to ride again so soon. There was a snaky yellow horse with the lines of a goer. But 'The Eel,' as the *amarillo* had been named for his lankiness and height, was a vicious brute, by Turkey's word.

Burk shook out a small loop and moved toward the Eel. As the *amarillo* moved off, Burk tossed up the loop expertly and it settled over the long yellow head. Chihuahua, drifting up, looked keenly at the Eel. Burk led him over to the gate and bridled him. Chihuahua roped a stocky black and saddled quickly. He sat the black and watched the ominous quiet which the Eel maintained as Burk cinched him.

Burk swung up, mindful of the left-hand gun in open-topped holster. He had just found the right stirrup when the Eel unwound. He went into a paroxysm of bucking.

'*Yaaaiiiaaah!*' Chihuahua yelled enthusiastically. 'She's them show-horse, Burk. She's leave you sittin' on nothin'!'

Stiff-legged, grunting, bawling, scooping up hollows each time the jerking forefeet struck ground, the Eel bucked across the open space before the bunkhouse; bucked toward the Big House. One of Burk's guns flew out of the holster. His hat came down over his eyes. He slapped it back even as he scratched the yellow shoulders, the snaky flanks. Chihuahua followed, bright blue eyes appreciative of the ride Burk made.

'She's say: "I *want* you! I *want* you!" She's one fi-ine bucker,' his voice came dimly to Burk amid the dust and the jolting.

The Eel was emulating the immortal bronc' of the ballad, with sunfish, fence-rail, and do-se-do. Finding these useless against the long burden that shifted center of gravity fluidly with each jump, the Eel began to run around in dizzy circles like a puppy chasing its tail — but with spasms of bucking inserted in the performance. Then he rose on his hind legs and, to Burk, the ground fell away. Burk swung the heavy quirt to land between the flattened little ears. The Eel came back to earth, rose again, dropped under a second blow and, this time, trotted meekly forward like the veriest old buggy-horse — as if nothing were farther from his evil mind than tantrums such as those just ended. Burk expelled breath in a great gasp.

He looked about for his Colt. Chihuahua had picked it up. His hat was well behind him. He rowled the Eel and the lank *amarillo* plunged over to the Stetson. Burk leaned from the saddle and snatched it up. He was settling it again upon his head when he saw Chihuahua sitting the black under the rail of the side veranda — with Myra leaning upon the rail. She straightened as he looked at her, with a long breath.

'Nice ride!' she called. Then she whirled and went quickly toward the front of the house.

Chihuahua rode over with his pistol. Burk reholstered it absently. What, he wondered,

221

could have got into Myra! She acted as if —
as if they had never exchanged any bitter
words. Well! Add that to the strangeness of
Fanny — and the sum-total was: You never
knew what to expect from any woman!

Chihuahua was grinning — as he had
grinned at Ma Whittington's table, during
the lecture on the Benefits of Marriage.

CHAPTER XIX

'Name a .45 for me, Boss!'

Up Star Creek way the range seemed deserted. No sign of the fifty-odd mares, nor
of the punchers Allred and Egbert — nor of
Turkey Adkins. Burk began to frown as they
rode on and could see ahead of them the
green line of cottonwoods and willows along
Star Creek itself. They turned and came
back along Dead Horse Creek, and suddenly in an arroyo saw a man lying with
saddle under his head. Burk jerked out a
gun with a grunted oath; Chihuahua was
moved by the same impulse.

Before they came up to this still figure,
Burk had recognized him. It was Skinny Egbert. He swung down, noting the blood-
soaked shirt. Weakly, Skinny opened his
eyes. Burk bent over him.

'One-Gang!' whispered Skinny. 'Run off — them mares. Allred — hightailed — dam' coyote! Turkey's — a-trailin' 'em.'

He was shot through the chest and, whether or not he knew it, as good as dead. Chihuahua brought a flask from a saddle-pocket and Skinny was lifted by the liquor sufficiently to tell how he had seen the mares moving and had ridden that way, with Allred following, as they started for the house that morning. A rifle bullet had knocked him off his horse and Allred had whirled and cut stick.

An hour or so later, Turkey, riding up, had found Skinny and made him comfortable in this degree. Burk, looking down at his dying employee with brooding eyes and hard-set mouth, understood that Turkey had realized Skinny's condition and had gone on the trail of the *mañada* because staying here would be of no use. He was a grim little rooster, Turkey.

'I'm — cuttin' stick — myself,' grinned Skinny weakly, as they looked down at him. 'Don't matter — much. Lone wolf — no folks. Yuh-all been — good people to work for. So, watch Barney Settels! He's — One-Gang — ask' me last week — throw in with 'em. Kind o' figgered — I figgered — I might. Then I was — ashamed to. Glad —

now . . .'

He lapsed into silence and was deaf to Burk's swift questions. They thought him dead, but abruptly his eyes opened and his lips moved. Burk bent quickly.

'Name one o' yo' .45s for me, Boss!' he grinned, and died.

'She's one man!' Chihuahua said admiringly. 'Now we're find them trail, w'at? An' them Turkey.'

They swung into the saddle and rode, one to the right, the other to the left. Chihuahua jerked up a hand from a quarter-mile away and Burk spurred over. There was the trampled trail of the *mañada,* and Chihuahua, bending from the saddle, estimated that from six to eight men had been in the thieves' company. He found Turkey's tracks after a little. Burk scowled.

'Now, I wonder if he's going straight after them? The little bulldog! If he catches 'em, we'll have him to bury, too — I'd rather lose every head of stock on the place than have Turkey shot up!'

They rode on, alert, watching for sign of Turkey. Then suddenly there came the far-away rattle of shooting. They set in the rowels. The Eel would have bucked, but Burk was in no mood for delay. He slipped the loop of his quirt from his wrist and banged the vicious yellow head with the loaded butt, then raced on to overtake Chihuahua.

The firing came from among a nest of low swells, and in five minutes they could see the smoke-puffs blossoming. It was pretty certain that the man closest to them would be Turkey. They rode on, therefore, intent on joining him. The firing lulled as they came close up to this point, where the last puff of smoke had shown rising in the still morning air. The *thuddah-thud-thuddah-thud* of their horses' hoofs sounded loud in the moment's quiet.

Suddenly over a mass of rocks ahead, where lay Turkey, three rifle-barrels darted. The rattle of the volley was like the flying buttons of a rattlesnake. They dropped flat over the horns and jerked their mounts aside. Burk felt the Eel shudder; then the yellow horse stopped in his stride and collapsed. Burk flew out of the saddle, tried desperately to turn himself in air and come down upon his feet, but could not make it. He struck upon his back and felt terriffic pain for an instant. Then numbness came in his back, to spread over his whole body. He could not move. He was dimly conscious that from over to the left came the rattle of firing.

He tried again to move, conscious that out here in the open was a deadly place to lie. But that alarm — which was not a keen alarm, but rather logical thought moving dimly — died away. It was growing oddly dark. His eyes were wide-open, but the swelling darkness blanketed them. Sounds faded, too . . .

He became aware of voices, after a while. The ground moved before his eyes. Then he was looking upward and it was no longer dark. He could see Chihuahua's face and Turkey's close to his own. They were very grim, very anxious, of expression. Then Chihuahua's teeth flashed under small mustache:

'Ha! That's better! Me, I'm think you're gone traveling with them Skinny feller. But we're look; we're turn you over like them flapjack. We're find no bullet's hole. You're not hurt, my friend, ha? You're knocked stiff by them fall?'

Burk tried to answer, but his lips were stiff as if frozen. He found his tongue heavy. He made only a buzzing noise. But he fought desperately to speak. At last he managed a whisper:

'I — can't move! Fell on something. It's — like paralysis. Get me back — to the house. Send for Doc' Stevens. Probably —

he can fix me — easily. Can't be — anything much.'

'Shore!' Turkey agreed heartily. 'Don't yuh worry, none! *Can't* be nothin', much. Li'l' fall like that . . .'

But after he had moved beyond the range of Burk's vision, his voice came in a whisper:

'Ain't that hubbin' hell! Jist as we was goin' so good! Yuh never can tell about these paralyzin's. Mebbe Doc' can fix it quick — but mebbe he cain't! Ah, but we owe yuh plenty, Lance Gregg! An' we got ca'tridges to pay off in!'

Darkness swept over Burk again. He came to, to see the ground bobbing, bobbing . . . He understood that he was in the saddle, held by someone. But he was not interested. He slipped away again; roused; went into the stupor once more.

When he had done that several times, he opened eyes upon a lighted room and before his eyes were several people — Chihuahua, Turkey; Myra and Aunty Ferguson — both with shiny streaks upon their faces. Old Doctor Stevens rose into view.

'He's conscious — and I — I hope he'll remain that way, except for natural sleep,' the little doctor said wearily. 'I suppose you've heard of anesthesia, Burk? That's what this seems to be. You received a ter-

227

rific jolt when you landed on a projecting rock; it bruised you badly. Also, the jolt to the spine affected certain nerve-trunks — how seriously, I can't tell now.'

He shook his white head; shrugged; smiled down at Burk.

'You could have been worse off, son! You could have been wholly paralyzed. Turkey says you can talk. These cases are encountered sometimes. It happens that you can do everything but move your body. Now, I'm leaving some directions with Aunty here, for your treatment, but — frankly, boy! you may not get over this suddenly. A week from now — a month — or ten years, even . . .'

He was very white and worn, the doctor. Those who knew him knew also that he was suffering from heart trouble of some complicated sort. It was more and more of an effort, daily, to go on with his practice. When he had gone, with the women following, Turkey moved over to the door and looked out. He turned grimly.

'Yere comes Ed Freeman, with Lance Gregg . . .' he said tonelessly.

They came inside and nodded to those in the room. Freeman moved over until he could face Burk, whose head was turned on the pillow. He was apparently a little ill at

228

ease, the acting sheriff. Nor was his composure increased by the steady, somewhat scornful, stare he met from Burk.

'Uh — I hear you-all had some mares stole yeste'day,' mumbled Freeman. 'An' that the thieves killed one o' yo' men an' somebody shot yo' hawse from under you.'

'Not just somebody,' Burk denied in the low, stiff-lipped voice that he could manage. 'Lance Gregg! He and some of his thieves of the One-Gang.'

'Now, Burk,' Ed Freeman snapped irritably, 'you're all worked up an' no wonder. Things happenin' like this. But you hadn't ought to go off half-cocked thataway. Jist because you followed them mares onto Wallop–8 range an' you don't like Gregg, the's no call to turn red-eyed an' accuse him or the Wallop–8 o' doin' the stealin'. Happens, I know he never. He told me in town about him an' Powers gittin' jumped by them fellas an' dam' near gettin' rubbed out. Must've been right after you-all had yo' fracas with the rustlers, too.'

'I admit that he's sufficiently artistic, as a liar, to handle a simple mind like you without any trouble,' Burk replied to this. 'I suppose that he and Powers were chased so far he couldn't even see which way they were heading with the mares? I'm formally charging him with the murder of Skinny Egbert and with the theft of every head of stuff that has ever been stolen from the Y.

'Of course, you won't arrest him, Ed. I didn't expect you to. The only way you could ever catch a thief would be to accidentally bite down on his hand while he was lifting the fillings out of your teeth. What are you here for, anyhow? Why aren't you over on the Wallop–8 trailing the mares and the rustlers?'

Lance Gregg had nerve — of a kind. Burk conceded this. For the big Wallop–8 owner had stood from the beginning with features calm and a small, properly tolerant, smile curving his lips. But Ed Freeman flushed angrily under the lash of Burk's flaying tone. His stocky shoulders moved in a manner that suggested it was fortunate for Burk that he lay helpless.

'I wanted to see if you-all had recognized anybody that was shootin' at you!' he snapped. 'An' I'm takin' a lot off you I wouldn't take for a minute, if you was on yo' feet! I'm runnin' the sheriff's office an' I don't need none o' yo' advice. I'll git on the trail o' them mares — though Gregg says they was cuttin' nawth across Star Creek an' on that rocky ground the' ain't much hope o' followin'!'

'Gregg was nervous, I see,' Burk sneered. 'Wanted to learn if, by any chance, he or any of his thieves had been recognized . . .'

Freeman whirled angrily toward the door. Gregg, with the sheriff behind him, regarded Burk with the mask off. A slow, maliciously triumphant grin spread over his too-handsome face. Then he turned and followed the raging Ed Freeman outside.

Chihuahua rolled a cigarette mechanically. Lifting his eyes as he lit it, he regarded Burk somberly. And his black brows drew down frowningly. For Burk's teeth were hard-set in his lower lip. From the mouth-corners came thin trickles of blood.

'To think of lying like this for years!' Burk burst out furiously. 'To be able to think and see and hear, but not to move! To know that son of a dog is making his plans; laughing at us because the cards are all stacked for him, and be helpless to do anything about it ____'

'Don't yuh fret a minute about *him* laughin' a hell of a lot!' Turkey snarled venomously. 'Yuh ain't goin' to stay there in bed no year. I don't give a dam' what the doc' says. An' till yuh do git up ag'in, the's me an' Chihuahua an' them three curly wolves yuh re-hired. We're still in the saddle

231

an' able to paint for war. They been askin'
for trouble, this dam' One-Gang. A' right!
They're goin' to git 'em a cloudburst where
they was askin' just for a li'l' rain!'

Chihuahua came like a big cat to his feet.
He began to pace up and down. For all his
high-heeled boots, he moved almost soundlessly over the big Navajo rug that carpeted
the room. He was smiling softly.

'Will these fella ride home, now, ha?' he
asked Turkey purringly. 'Me, I'm better go
for them little ride, an' take my Weenchestair
— W'at is it we're do, she's better we do
him quick, ha?'

'Not that, Chihuahua!' Burk whispered in
vigorous denial. 'We have to get him with
the evidence to show why we got him. True,
Ed Freeman's no detective. But he wouldn't
have to be, to know that it was the Y who
killed Gregg. Ed would figure it his consci-
entious and official duty to hang you.'

'To hang me?' Chihuahua laughed. 'W'y,
first she will have to catch me. If she don't,
these hanging will not be legal. An' me, I'm
half-Navajo, *amigos mios.* I'm think these
sheriff like Freeman they will find me — *if*
I'm wish for that . . .'

'I feel like the both o' yuh,' Turkey
scowled. 'I'd like to shoot it out with that
buzzard, same's you, Chihuahua. But I can

232

see that it'd make folks think the Y was all wrong. Nobody'd believe nothin' we brought in, as evidence after.

'What's the scheme now, Burk? For runnin' things? Yuh reckon Myra'll want to boss the roundup ag'in? If she does — well, Sandrock Tom an' Three Rivers an' Happy Jack, they'll land yere jist in time to git bucked off ag'in . . .'

'You're Riding Manager,' Burk said grimly. 'Between us, we'll run things. Myra may want to swing into the saddle again, but she won't do it. Now that Allred's hightailed and Skinny's dead, Maguire and Sweet and Cowell and Murdock are left of the men she hired. With the Three Mesquiteers coming back, you'll need about two of the others. Which ones do you choose to keep?'

'Maguire an' Sweet — they got the makin' o' hands in 'em. I mistrust that cockeyed Murdock. An' Cowell, with his always-grin, he's too dam' thick with Jones to suit me — me not likin' that cook a li'l' bit.'

'Reminds me!' Burk said abruptly. 'Found a One-Gang warning on my bed yesterday. I think somebody on the place put it there. Maguire and Sweet and the cook were the only white men at the house and I don't think it was one of the Mexicans. And I'm

233

like you; I think Maguire and Sweet are all right . . .'

'By Godfrey!' snarled Turkey, staring hard at Burk. 'If that ugly cook is workin' for that gang, it'd shore explain how they know so nice an' neat *jist* where our stuff is rangin' an' where the boys are! I feel like wanderin' over to the bunkhouse an' separatin' his ugly mouth from his mind, *jist* on general principles!'

'No-o, I wouldn't. I think I'd keep an eye on him. Wait awhile and catch him red-handed. Then ——'

'Then take the dam' scalp!' grinned Chihuahua pleasantly.

He had been standing beside the bed, looking somewhat absently down at Burk — as if thinking about something else. Now he turned back the sheet and pulled away the pajamas-coat from Burk's back. With deft fingers he probed and rubbed and manipulated the muscles about the spine.

'Them Navajo old women,' he explained, 'they're know something about these rubbing, Burk. An' my mother, she's a chief's daughter . . .'

Turkey whirled suddenly and glared at the window in the end of the room. His hard palm smacked on the smooth handle of a Colt as he darted across to look out of that window.

'Thought I hear somebody out the',' he grunted.

He jumped across to the door and stared out, then nodded:

'Our friend, the cook — I bet anything I got he was under the winder; he's walkin' to the bunkhouse, now. If I could prove it on him ——'

Chihuahua turned away from Burk. He ran to the window and looked out, then vaulted over the sill. When he came in through the door, he was smiling catlike.

'*Sí,*' he nodded. 'She's them cook. She's have one bootsole with them hole . . .'

'Reckon I'll drift over an' augur with that hairpin a spell,' drawled Turkey.

Chihuahua returned to his massaging, with head turned sideways toward the door. At the sound of a sudden yell from the direction of the bunkhouse, he grinned. But that yell was followed by a chorus of *yip-yipping* in which several voices blended. Presently, into the door crowded Turkey with Sandrock Tom, Three Rivers, and Happy Jack. The first two were grinning; Happy Jack wore an expression of deepest sadness; Turkey was grimly pleasant of face.

'He never hear me comin' up to the cookhouse,' drawled Turkey. 'He was packin' up his stuff for a stick-cuttin'. I see that, so I *jist* give him his powders.'

'Jist!' boomed Sandrock sardonically. 'Like hell yuh did — jist. We was ridin' up an' see the whole thing: when Turkey whispered in that gunie's ear, from behind, he hit the roof o' the cookhouse. Come down like a skeered mountain lion facin' Turkey with a hawglaig fillin' his hand.

'Turkey took the cutter off'n him an' knocked him down an' picked him up an' knocked him down three times before he could hit the floor. Then he throwed him out the door an' run out under him an' kicked him before he lit. Then he bit him on the off year an' throwed him over the windmill an' yells to him that he's plumb displeased with the way he's been actin' an' he better go git his time.'

'Sandrock always was the *blame'st* liar in any scope o' country yuh could name,' Happy Jack said sourly. 'But — leavin' out the windmill, 'twas mighty like that.'

'What was it all about, Turkey?' demanded Three Rivers. 'We jist see the rude way yuh acted; we never knowed how-come.'

'Nothin' to speak about,' shrugged Turkey. 'I was jist a-firin' him.'

CHAPTER XX

'She's too sweet to think about!'

In the ten days following Burk's fall, Doc' Stevens made two calls upon the patient. The sum-total of his decision was that nothing but time would tell. Burk suspected that the treatment which the doctor ordered Aunty Ferguson to administer was of the 'bread-pill' variety. Chihuahua's massage was a daily routine, but it had no more apparent effect than Doc' Stevens's prescriptions.

Furiously, Burk would stare at the Colts hanging over the bedpost where his eyes could lift to them. One portion of the doctor's directions he followed with all his will; would have followed without admonition. He lay there by the hour mentally commanding his helpless hands and legs to move; concentrating on this until perspiration burst from his forehead.

Turkey rode the range ceaselessly. He scattered his cowboys over strategic points, with grim instructions never to be caught out in the open; never to sleep by a fire on the range; never to forget for an instant that they were doubtless watched. Chihuahua had appointed himself Burk's bodyguard and companion. He slept on his blankets at the foot of Burk's bed and during every night he prowled several times around the buildings of the ranch. But no further blow came.

Myra and Burk had one furious argument concerning the management of the Y, in this period. She had talked to Lance Gregg, and she first suggested, then demanded, that Burk relinquish the reins. She had been trying to give orders to Turkey and to the cowboys and had been met with blank stares. But when Burk refused flatly to give over the management to her, she did not fulfill her threat to take legal steps. Burk wondered about that. It was not like Myra, somehow, and yet —

It was on his mind, the evening of the eleventh day, as he lay — alone for the time — in the dark room. Chihuahua had gone to town in the afternoon and was not due back yet. Outside, it was bright moonlight, but such light as came through the windows was not enough to do more than lighten the gloom of the place.

Burk's senses were preternaturally sharpened by his time of lying abed. So he looked up mechanically at a slight sound outside that window which was on the right side of the door. But he could see nothing. Then, through the open door, a man slid noise-lessly. There was something in his right hand that twinkled in the moonlight. Something white and dim of outline showed in his left hand. As he stood poised on the balls of his feet, silhouetted against the yellow rectangle of the doorway, there was a vague familiarity, to Burk, about him.

'Who is it?' he whispered.

The man came soundlessly over and stood looking down. In the quiet his hasty breathing sounded clearly, it and the tick of the clock on the far wall the only noises.

'Where's ever'body?' the intruder whispered in his turn.

'Bunkhouse — Chihuahua's in town,' Burk answered, frowning. Who could this be?

'Whut I 'lowed,' the man nodded, then laughed softly. 'I been watchin' this place a week, waitin' to earn two hund'd . . . Ye figgered ye was hell on wheels, didn't ye? Knowed 'twas me put the spot on y'r bed, huh? Then that dam' Greaser found my tracks under the winder yonder. An' had that dam' Turkey beat me up an' fire me. Well, a lot o' good it's goin' to do ye! I got another spot yere in my hand. I'm goin' to leave it on y'r chest — when I leave, in a minute.'

The ex-cook lifted his hands, significantly. Burk saw the wicked blade of the knife he held; saw, too, the 'spot' which would tell that the One-Gang had struck another deadly, untraceable blow in Yates County. Evidently, Gregg and the others were not satisfied merely to have him lying here helpless. They wanted him completely out of the picture. So this bitter-faced assassin had been hired.

Panic jumped into his brain. It was like lying bound while a rattlesnake crept closer. 'Jones' leaned forward a little. He seemed to be straining to see, so that he could enjoy the spectacle of his tortured victim. Burk watched fascinatedly as the ex-cook's right hand came deliberately forward with the knife. As far as his range of vision permitted, he followed it as it sank lower and lower. He guessed that the point was resting on his chest. Instinctively, he was throwing all his will into the effort to move; to lift a hand and snatch the blade away.

If only Chihuahua would come — or Turkey — or one of the boys from the bunkhouse. But there was no sound anywhere, outside, to tell of such approach. Desperately, he tried to think of something to delay that knife that must be pressing down . . . He thought of those swaying bodies of which Turkey had told him:

'If you're going to murder me, tell me something, first: Why did the gang kill Pedro Garcia and Shorty Willets?'

'Jones' laughed. His arm moved a little, relaxing, in Burk's sight.

'Willets was gittin' wise. He'd stumbled onto a thing or two, on the range. Saw a couple o' the boys maverickin' some calves. They knowed he had. Well, he started for the house, but he never got yere. Ped' Garcia was in with the gang, but the Boss got the idee Ped' was figgerin' to git off to a safe distance an' sell us out by letter. So it was right good business to hang 'em up in Yatesville an' show folks 'twasn't healthy to monkey with us!

'Now, ye're done gabblin'! I ain't takin' no chancet o' that Greaser gittin' back an' findin' me yere. Ye're goin' to be found, when he comes, jist as nice an' peaceful as ary other corpse anybody ever see. An' this-yere spot'll be on ye, like I says. It'll read *"Next!"* '

His arm stiffened. Burk glared up at him. He could see the snarling teeth a-shine between the thin lips. For himself, he was frantically biting his nether lip. He could go up against another man as he had faced Lance Gregg or that other of the One-Gang

241

— Settels. Nor would it worry him particularly. But to die here at the hand of this crawling assassin — and to die so *uselessly* . . .

Suddenly, as he waited for — blackness, he could have cried out. For he *felt* the sting of that knife-point. It flashed upon him that he was free, in part at least, of the anesthesia — but only for that split-second. He would be dead before he could move a finger. No chance to see if he could lift a hand; no time to snatch at that Colt-butt a foot from his head, even if he could move. But, automatically, he *did* turn there in the bed. 'Jones' lurched a little as the knife slid down Burk's chest and went into the mattress.

Burk's hand came up weakly. But there was a flash and roar from the door. The assassin fell heavily across Burk, knocking him flat again. Then a squat shape streaked across the room and seized the ex-cook; hurled him to the floor — again a Colt roared; Burk fainted.

Light was shining through his lashes when he recovered consciousness. He was amazingly weak. So he merely opened his eyes and blinked, but made no movement. There was Chihuahua and beside him Turkey's grim face. Turkey — Burk's eyes wandered mechanically downward — had a Colt in his hand. Myra and Aunty Ferguson, the one white-faced and tense, the other red and angry, resembling most an outraged mother hen.

'I run onto a hawse with reins trailin' in that li'l' *motte* o' cottonwoods,' Turkey was saying. 'Figgered 'twas funny. Come on up, not makin' no noise. When I got close to the door yere, I hear talkin' an' this on the floor was sayin' somethin' about not takin' a chancet on Chihuahua catchin' him an' how Burk was goin' to be found a corpse. So I sneaked up an' see him bendin' over Burk with what I guessed was a knife. I took a chancet and let drive.'

'Me, I'm tell them Manuel to get Sandrock, before I'm go to town,' Chihuahua said grimly. 'Sandrock, she will stay with Burk. Me, I'm going to wear out one fine, new quirt across them Manuel's back, *por dios!*'

'Well, Burk ain't hurt — but no thanks to us he wasn't!' snapped Aunty Ferguson. 'Turkey, I reckon you jist about own the Y right now. That pore boy a-lyin' helpless there, he would've just been murdered, hadn't been for you.'

The weakness was going, in a degree. Burk lay there watching them through half-closed eyes. He was going to sit up triumphantly, in a minute, as soon as he felt a little stronger. Then suddenly he had a thought — he considered it, and the angles of it were so many and so far-reaching that he literally forgot the cook; forgot these figures crowding in the room. So when he opened wide his eyes, there was an odd smile on his lips.

'You got him, just in time, Turkey,' he drawled. 'He had just been explaining why Shorty Willets and Pedro Garcia were lynched. And, as you heard, how I was to follow them and the others the One-Gang has murdered.'

'He — he didn't hurt you?' Myra cried, moving closer to the bedside. 'We saw the place where he had set the knife-point. And a long scratch. Oh, it's awful!'

'They're that sort of folk, you know,' Burk grinned. 'Awful. The One-Gang. No, I'm not at all hurt. But he did scare me into — I mean out of a year's growth. Now, you folks can go back to bed or wherever you were. Turkey, you and Chihuahua stick here. I want to talk to you both.'

When the body of 'Jones' had been removed and the others were gone, Burk watched Turkey and Chihuahua with a slight smile. But Chihuahua, who saw everything, came over to the bed and stared frowningly at Burk's Colt — which was lifted in the holster hanging to the bedpost until it was on the verge of toppling out.

'She's pull your gun?' he asked slowly. 'I'm remember them Colt, she's not like that w'en I'm leave . . .'

'No-o, he didn't touch the gun.'

Burk raised his hand — if shakily — and pushed the Colt back into the holster. Chihuahua spat out an amazed oath. Turkey gaped, mouth sagging.

'I reckon your massaging, Chihuahua, had put me where I only needed a tremendous shock to break the anesthesia,' Burk told them. 'I can move again! I'm weaker than an aged cat, but that will pass off.'

'W'y you're not tell them women?' inquired Chihuahua. But there was a narrowing of his shrewd blue eyes that told Burk of certain private ideas Chihuahua had.

'Can't you guess?' grinned Burk. 'I — think you can. Anyway, if our friends believe me tied to the bed here, we've a chance to surprise them . . . Suppose that we wander over onto the Wallop–8 or Goblet range and find some of our stuff and salivate the gentlemen in charge —— Nobody would guess that I had a hand in it. I'd certainly enjoy dropping a few rustlers upon Lance Gregg's doorstep, with a note to match those the One-Gang is so addicted to: *"Riders of the Night,"* say, for a signature . . .'

'*Válgame dios!*' grinned Chihuahua. 'She's too sweet to think about!'

'Plumb — dam' lovely!' breathed Turkey. His narrowed eyes seemed to stare blissfully ahead over a trail of the future that pleased him tremendously. 'A li'l' private vig'lance committee . . . A Y-brand tit-fer-tat play . . . Do good them that despitefully uses yuh . . . Dam' good . . . do 'em!'

'It'd be just lovely to have a man planted in that One-Gang,' Burk drawled. 'The idea makes me plumb yearning-ful. Wouldn't it be sweet if we had someone who could notify us of the jobs they planned, so we could wander up ahead of them — accidentally — and be there as a reception committee?'

'Not much chance to arrange that,' Turkey grunted. 'Yuh see, the One-Gang is Boss o' the Roundup right now. They ain't struck a snag yet, to amount to nothin'. So the gang naturally figgers the winnin' play is stickin' to the gang. O' course, in any outfit like that, the's like to be somebody that's sore about somethin'. But stumblin' onto the one in this gang that might be sore'd be like huntin' around for a pocketbook full o' money, an' findin' it.'

'Pedro Garcia was dissatisfied about something,' Burk nodded. 'But he never made first base. "Jones" told me they suspected him of planning to sell out the gang. Perhaps they did, but I don't think they had any proof of that. They just figured that, after he got away from their circle of influence, he *might* blab, and that there was no use taking the chance when he could so easily be rubbed out — and serve the useful end of giving warning to the likes of Rufe Redden.

'If he did spill anything, to anybody, we've never run onto any trace of it. Of course, he might have gone to those two saloon-detectives of yours, Turkey. They hardly had a chance to use information, even if he did pass it out for a price.'

'Well, anyhow! We shore hit 'em a lick yere, tonight. First time, too, that anybody's hurt the One-Gang even a li'l' bit! Ever laid eyes on 'em to know it, for that matter. Well, boy! If yuh' goin' to be able to rise up an' prowl with us, that's shore-ly goin' to be great. But we-all got to go mightily careful — walk plumb hawk-eyed! — while yuh' playin' sick. So long's Lance Gregg figgers yuh' jist playin' off ——'

'Them doctor, she's the one w'at might say Burk's not crippled,' Chihuahua broke in, grinning. 'An' so she's ni-ice that, w'en I'm in town today, I'm hear that she's very sick, too, them doctor. She will not ride out to see us, very quick . . .'

Chapter XXI

'I'm going to prophesy —'

Steadily, methodically, as he had done for four days, now, Burk flexed his muscles beneath the light covering; stretched and twisted in the bed. After dark, he would get up, as he had done on the two nights before, to walk up and down, up and down, the room. He felt equal to getting into a saddle again — on a gentle horse. But there was no urgent reason for getting out. Tomorrow night, Burk thought, he would slip out for a ride with Chihuahua. That would be soon enough.

There was the slightest of sounds outside the door. The scrape of a light foot on the ground, he thought. Instantly, he 'froze' like an alarmed rabbit. His face set; he lay with body and head moveless on the pillow, watching the door. An instant passed, then there appeared — a very charming figure in that frame — Frisco Fanny.

She held a wide-rimmed white Stetson in

gauntleted hand. Smooth brown hair was twisted into a braid that hung, now, over one shoulder of a beaded buckskin vest. She wore trousers of silvery whipcord and inlaid puncher half-boots, with gold-mounted spurs. Gravely, she looked at him, and Burk, in near-panic, wondered if she could have glimpsed him moving ——

Painfully, he studied her quiet face. But, if she had seen the evidence that paralysis was gone, there was no reading it in her inscrutable expression.

'Receiving visitors?' she asked — and smiled suddenly. 'If you are, I'll come in for a minute. This is my weekly ride. It occurred to me to stop by and see how you were.'

'Come in! This is very kind of you,' Burk said in the low, stiff-lipped fashion of his days of helplessness. 'I haven't seen anyone from town lately. Nobody's been here but just those around the place. Sit down, if you will.'

She came with small clink-clump of spur-chains and boot-heels over to the bed, drew up the chair Chihuahua had lately quitted.

'It was terrible — the way Doctor Stevens described your accident,' she said slowly. 'I suppose that it seemed much worse, even, than news of a new killing. We get rather used to hearing of murders and lynchings and pistol-battles — in my business. But crippling seems worse than killing, doesn't it?'

Burk frowned slightly when she smiled at him cheerfully. It did seem that she might take the matter with more becoming face. For all she knew, he really was doomed to lie helpless for the rest of his life. For all she knew? He looked narrowly at her with renewed suspicion . . .

'The doctor and I are quite good friends — outside of business hours,' she went on easily, looking at the big, rather bare, room. 'He told me that such a stroke as yours is always a problem to the physician. I wondered, then, if you wouldn't almost have preferred to exchange with your horse — to have taken the bullet and let him have the fall. I'm a strange person.'

'You are!' he agreed grimly. 'But — though I did feel that way at first, one of the consolations of such a condition as this comes from that very uncertainty Doc' Stevens mentions: if one isn't sure that he'll ever move, walk, again, he's equally uncertain that he won't do that very thing, tomorrow. But it isn't easy to lie here and know that things aren't getting a bit better; that they may be doing worse than that. I think you prophesied this, didn't you?'

'I don't recall prophesying that the One-Gang would cripple you. But if I did, mark one in my favor as a fortune-teller. I suppose that, having seen even one small forecast work out, I should rest on that success; not risk my reputation by prophesying any more. But I'm yielding to temptation — dance-hall girls are always doing that, aren't they? I think that — yes, I'm going to prophesy — again:

'You're not going to lie long in that bed, Burk. You're going to get up and you're going to do what you've promised yourself and others to do. You're going to smash the One-Gang and accomplish in Yates County what your father and Duke Yarborough once accomplished. You're going to bring law back!

'Now,' she said, smiling at him, but with gray eyes, red mouth, both enigmatic, 'isn't that pretty good? Considering that I haven't so much as a single tea-leaf for prop?'

'I appreciate your prophecy and I hope it will work out,' he told her somberly. 'But I find it hard to concentrate on the fortune-telling when — when the fortune-teller herself so occupies my mind. I keep wondering about you ——'

'Curiosity is a very bad trait!' she said quickly — and seriously. 'You have no business considering the prophet. Ever. And

251

particularly — oh, very particularly! — in this case. A prophet, you know, is properly a voice, not a personality. Who ever *saw* the Delphian Oracle? You concentrate on the One business!'

'Ever since I first saw you,' he burst out irritably, 'I've been asking myself a question. I ask it, now, of you. Dou't quibble! What in the devil is such as you doing in the Blue Mouse? It no more fits you than — than a pulpit would fit me!'

'Why' — she regarded him mockingly — 'dancing with all and sundry; persuading them to buy me drinks on which I'm paid a commission; keeping fifty different men at precisely the proper distance to sustain interest that will bring them back and back again; to buy more drinks on which may revered employer and I make a profit. After hours ——'

'You know what I mean,' he told her irritably. 'You're — not in the least like any other girl any Texas dance-hall ever saw. Why are you in the Blue Mouse?'

'My dear boy, you musn't be deceived by surfaces. I *would* pass as a sweet young graduate of a Female Seminary, wouldn't I? I could tell you of my innocent childhood in a great mansion; and how I followed the villain to the big city and sank lower and lower, until I reached the Blue Mouse. And — I'm not going to. I'm Frisco Fanny, just at present the star dance-hall girl.'

'I beg your pardon!' a cool voice remarked in the doorway. 'I didn't know you had a visitor, Burk.'

'Come on in, Myra,' Burk said. He thought uncomfortably: Now, how the devil mix these girls, so utterly different in background and viewpoint, if not so different — *surprisingly* not so different — in surface refinement?

'Come on in,' he said again, when Myra merely stood with chin up, looking over Fanny's head. 'This is Miss — uh — Miss ___'

'Frisco Fanny, of the Blue Mouse,' Fanny said — maliciously, Burk thought. 'I presume this is Miss Yarborough . . .'

'I'll go back, Burk. No, I just meant to look in and see if there were anything I could do for you.'

When she was gone, Fanny smiled tight-lipped at the scowling Burk. He could not tell by any searching of her face what was moving in her mind.

'She's a little beauty,' was her comment. 'You're a — fortunate young man. To be able at one stroke to keep the other half of the Y in the family and acquire a beauty like that. It's unusual. According to the novels, all beautiful girls are very, very poor; the young hero has to choose between a lovely pauper and a cross-eyed heiress. Ye-es, you're an extremely fortunate young man, Mr. Burk Yates . . .'

'Piffle!' he snapped. 'Myra and I were raised together and it happens that we get along better with just anyone else than with each other. But that's beside the point. What's happening in town?'

'Nothing, in particular. Your foreman roused some excitement by killing that assassin. I wonder if there will be other attempts. Of course, you're able now to protect yourself,' she added slowly. Then, as he looked suddenly, suspiciously, at her: 'I mean — "forewarned is forearmed." You can guard against similar attacks. Have you heard of the robbery? The Citizens' Bank at Rhettsboro? Last night, it was. The One-Gang. Word was telegraphed from Rhettsboro to Cottonwood and a messenger came from there.'

'This is the first time they've gone out of Yates County, isn't it?' he frowned. 'They're bucking trouble when they cross into Rhett County. That's old Wolf Edwards's bailiwick. He's been sheriff there since Star Creek was a puddle of rainwater.'

'No, they've operated now and then out-side of the county, and the other officials haven't had any more success at checking or catching them than ours here. They killed the cashier and rode off with about eight thousand. Do you know, I've been thinking of something:

'Wouldn't it be good tactics for the One-Gang, now, without waiting for this excite-ment to die down, to — say, hold up the through train and rob it? The ideal place for the robbery would be this side of the bridge over Dead Horse Creek. The bridge is so shaky that the trains just crawl over it. And the gang could easily arrange the robbery for, say, tomorrow night . . . About six of them, say . . .'

Burk stared at her. From her tone, this was merest speculation, as she had an-nounced it to be. But he kept recalling that she was supposed to be Barney Settels's private property; and Settels, according to Skinny Egbert's testimony, was sufficiently influential in the gang to act as recruiting-agent . . . Did Fanny know, through her relations with Settels, of the One-Gang's plans and activities? And was this, then, a warning that the train *was* to be robbed by six men at the bridge?

Long after she was gone — with a promise

to come out occasionally 'to talk gossip' —
Burk mulled this over in his mind. Chihuahua came drifting in, grinning shadowily.
Burk guessed that he had not been far from
the room during Fanny's visit. Turkey came
in a few minutes later, walking stiffly and
smelling of horse. Burk regarded them
absently for a moment, then suddenly
beckoned them to the bed.

'Listen! We're going to take two chances
tomorrow night: we're going to risk sitting
beside the track at the bridge west of
Cottonwood and seeing nothing; and we
risk, also, running into an ambush. But I'm
guessing that the One-Gang is going to stick
up the through train there. Now, there's
you, Turkey; you, Chihuahua; myself and —
who else? Can we trust Sweet and Maguire?
Better not to. There'll be only six or so of
the gang. Can you get Sandrock and Happy
Jack and Three Rivers without letting anybody know?'

'They're on the south range now. No
trouble to pick 'em up at Monument Rock
line-camp when we want 'em. That train
comes by at ten, though, Burk. Yuh-all cain't
hightail out o' yere till dark. We'll have some
ridin' to do, to make it . . .'

'There are *mottes* of cottonwoods all along
there,' Burk said slowly, eyes narrowed as

he visualized the lay of the land around the bridge. 'If we could get there ahead of 'em, it would be easy. But if we ride up after they've finished, which way do you think they'll head, after the job? My guess is toward the Wallop–8. They would attract attention trying to make Yatesville or Prester and be going right in the direction where the alarm would be given. There's plenty of rocky ground to kill the trail and nobody to see 'em, heading toward Gregg's.'

'My idee,' nodded Turkey. 'Man, man! Wouldn't it be lovely to hit 'em a lick! An' take the money off'n 'em?'

Chapter XXII

'Train-robbers from Dead Horse ——'

The moon shone dimly and fitfully through drifting cloud-banks. The way was none too smooth, either; lying as it did close to the east bank of Dead Horse Creek. Burk and Turkey rode furiously in the van of the compact little band of six. They were racing against time toward the bridge, but rather expectant of being too late on the scene to see the actual hold-up.

'Missed it!' snarled Turkey suddenly, when they were yet three miles from the railroad and the bridge. For faintly came the long-drawn blast of the whistle.

'Hold up!' yelled Burk, mechanically jerking his hand aloft. 'No use wasting time getting any closer. What we've got to do is cut across to the trail they'll come by and wait for 'em! We'll cross the creek now; they'll likely use the old road of Zelman's that runs close to the water. If they don't — well, we're shot!'

They turned to the creek and the horses slid and splashed down and went grunting up the far bank. They found the dim old road, and Chihuahua, swinging down to scratch matches and stare, announced that several horses had come this way not long before — heading for the bridge. Burk thrilled at this. It seemed to prove that the train-robbers had gathered on the Wallop–8 and ridden over this old road to the railroad. It was a good bet that they would return the same way.

They rode on down a little way to a bunch of cottonwoods growing on ground so strewn with loose rocks that fast riding would be impossible. Here Burk posted his forces. He warned them to pinch their mounts' nostrils and prevent warning whinnies.

'You tell 'em to stop,' he grunted to

Turkey. 'I'll keep quiet, and I'll look for Gregg, too. If he's leading this, I don't want a better crack at him.'

A long half-hour passed. Sandrock and Happy Jack and Three Rivers, standing close together beside their horses, kept looking at Burk's big still figure and shaking their heads with wondering grins. They had been very much amazed at sight of their 'helpless' employer materializing beside Turkey and Chihuahua at Monument Rock. So, now, their state of mind was such that they hardly considered the coming of the robbers. If a helpless paralytic could get up and ride, anything was easy.

Chihuahua lay flat with ear to the ground. He grunted presently, and Burk turned to the others:

'There's not going to be a hell of a lot of etiquette about this,' he said very grimly. 'We're dealing with a bunch of killers, and I'm going to give 'em just one chance to grab the stars. But don't count much on their surrendering! Get those floursacks over your heads and hold your guns on 'em — they'll come up almost at a walk over these rocks. If they go for their guns — salivate 'em!'

Soon the thudding of hoofs was plain even to those who stood erect. The moon shone

259

palely through a rift in the piled gray clouds. A mass of horsemen showed a hundred yards away, picking their course deliberately over the rocks.

Suddenly, someone in the gang laughed harshly:

'Did yuh see that fat woman! Oh, *dios mio!* When she tried to yank herself back into the car an' stuck in the winder — I thought I'd keel over . . .'

'Whut ye reckon we got, Boss?' another voice inquired, fifty yards from the cottonwoods. The reply came in an impatient grunt, indistinguishable as to words.

They were thirty yards away when Turkey pushed his horse out of the cottonwoods:

'Stick 'em up, yuh sons o' dogs!' he yelled. 'Speedy! Or grab a harp!'

'Dry-gulched, by Jupiter!' roared someone in the gang.

A line of orange flame seemed to run around the front of that compact group. Turkey dropped flat on his horse's neck. Bullets clipped twigs and bits of bark from the trees of the little grove. But the robbers' volley was answered by one from steadily aimed Winchesters. Nobody in the *motte* had had much faith in the One-Gang surrendering. The rattle of the rifles and carbines was deafening. The mass of horsemen was shattered as by a terrific, gigantic hammer-blow. Horses went down, kicking and squealing; men cried out furiously. Only two or three remained in the saddle.

Then out of the cottonwoods swarmed Burk and the others. Turkey, set afoot, ran to one side and squatted. His Winchester played a stream of bullets into the One-Gang. Burk fired with his right-hand gun. He wanted to get to that tall man who was jerking his mount about. Funeral stumbled and recovered himself, but in the flashing interval, the tall man had got to the creek-bank and a terrific splash told of his horse landing.

Burk rode after, but already the fellow, by some stroke of devil's luck, was up the far bank and going like a coachwhip snake. He passed a clump of cottonwoods and was sheltered. So Burk turned back, with Funeral limping a little. He found his men gathered about the fallen robbers, separating them from the horses.

There were four dead men, at each of whom Turkey was looking closely; there was a fifth who seemed on the verge of dying. There were three dead horses. Chihuahua gestured toward the wounded man. He said that Turkey had tried without success to loosen this one's tongue. Burk went over and looked down. It was a dapper young cowboy, reckless, rather good-humored of expression, whom he had seen in the Blue Mouse. The others, when he came to examine them, were without exception men from Prester. Those whom he didn't remember Turkey had seen over there.

'What to do?' inquired Turkey. 'That Gregg that got away? Did look like him, didn't it . . . Amazin' like him. Well, this gunie says he'll die with a knot in his tongue an' I reckon mebbe he will. One around his neck, too . . .'

'Show me yo' coil o' manila!' the dying one mocked him. 'Yuh — can't kill a man — twicet!'

'To Yatesville with 'em!' grunted Burk suddenly. 'We'll do a little exhibiting ourselves. Show the One-Gang they can't monopolize that trick!'

So they loaded up the robbers' own horses — on one of which they found a tow sack containing currency — with the bodies. Sandrock, Three Rivers, and Happy Jack each took a limp form behind him. They crossed the creek and turned toward Yatesville.

It was past two when they came silently to the town. All was still, but they took no chances on being seen. They dismounted in the rear of an old corral behind Judge Amblet's general store. One by one the five dead robbers were carried to the big veranda and laid gently down. On top of a barrel, the tow sack of loot was set. Then swiftly Burk wrote his challenge to the One-Gang, using a sheet of cheap ruled tablet:

Train-Robbers from Dead Horse Bridge
RIDERS of the NIGHT

That last drew a sardonic grin from him as he set the curt notice under the tow sack. It more than matched the sign of the gang he had sworn to smash. It had a mysterious sort of melodrama about it. He thought that he would have given a good deal to be in town when this exhibit was discovered.

The others were waiting for him, out behind the old corral. He was stooping to pick up a handful of pebbles, with which to batter the Judge's windows upstairs and rouse him to consciousness of the surprise on the gallery, when a hard-ridden horse came pounding into the street fifty yards away. Burk ran around the corner of the store. The rider seemed to know Yatesville. He slid to a stop before the sheriff's office, dropped off, and began to pound on the door:

'Train-robbery!' he bellowed. 'Train-robbery! Train-robbery! Wake up, every-body! Train-robbery! West o' Cottonwood!'

Burk ran back and swung up on Funeral. There was no need, now, of waking Judge Amblet. That messenger would find himself looking the train-robbers in the face very promptly, now. So would the town. There would be some tall wondering about who composed the swift-striking Riders of the Night — who delivered assorted train-robbers before Yatesville even knew that there were train-robbers to deliver! He heard the clatter of windows flung up; the squeak of near-by doors jerked open.

'I *wish* we could stop and see this! It's go-ing to be one of the biggest shows the town ever saw. Circus won't be in it, with the exhibition that'll come off. But — we've got to hightail! The town'll be out in its virtu-ous and utilitarian red underwear, in about a minute, Mex' — and that's only a half-minute, English. And day will be soon. We've got to get peacefully to bed, in time to get right out again with sunup!'

They rode quietly out of town, leaving behind them a waxing clamor. Once clear of town, they left the road and picked stony spots well known to all of them, on which the trail would vanish. They rode fast and separated within the fence of the Y. Sandrock Tom, Three Rivers, and Happy Jack raised their voices in triumphant howl as they raced away to beat the dawn to Monument Rock. Faintly, their long yell came back to the others:

'*Yaaaiiiaaah! Yaaaiiiaaah! Yaaaiiiaaah! Train-robbers from Dead Hawse Crick! Yaaaiiiaaah!*'

Burk, with Turkey and Chihuahua, rode up to the corral and got stiffly down. Burk leaned against Funeral and stared at the dark bulk of the great house. Up there, Myra was asleep. He looked broodingly at her darkened window. He wondered what he thought of her. Blind, stubborn . . . Certainly, she was both. *He* fought the battle of the Y and she trafficked with the enemy, he told himself grimly. Then, his hard mouth softened. After all, it was loyalty that moved her. However misdirected, still it was loyalty. She had always been like that, fiercely partisan. He shrugged at last. For loyalty, steadfastness, were not common enough to be thrown lightly aside, even when wasted on such as Lance Gregg. Her loyalty to Gregg — he had to admit — was a very natural thing. For she had seen nothing but Gregg's best side, and that was a side pleasing enough to have won over some hard-headed men old enough to be her father. And — she was amazingly lovely.

'Odd . . .' he muttered, turning toward the window by which he had left the bungalow and by which he would regain his bed. 'Odd that the two most attractive women I have ever seen should be here in this lonely cow-county, together! Myra wouldn't thank me for bracketing her with Fanny. But ——'

He clambered over the sill. Turkey grunted something before turning away. Burk stopped inside the window.

'What?' he asked.

'I said she has been a right full evenin'. An' me an' Three Rivers, we got the only scratches handed out to our side in that squabble. Yes, sir! Plumb full, she was!'

CHAPTER XXIII

'It was you bushwhacked them robbers!'

Through the open window, Burk saw Lance Gregg riding up toward the Big House. Burk sprawled comfortably in the bed. He was amazingly sore in every muscle as aftermath of that long fast ride. He was very tired, sleepy, yet could not get to sleep. But he was not too sleepy to observe that Lance Gregg, this morning, was not riding his

266

favorite big sorrel. His horse was a long-legged bay — not half the horse the sorrel was . . .

'Now, what the devil brought the Wallop–8 visiting?' Burk asked himself. He lay puzzling that after Gregg had gone on, out of sight. At last, he nodded. It was very clear . . .

He thought that, were he in Gregg's place — if *he* had been leading home a band of successful train-robbers, peacefully possessed of some thousands of perfectly spendable dollars, only to encounter a mysterious line of masked, deadly efficient riders, as Gregg's pack had encountered the Y men ——

'Segur' Miguel! Certainly! He's been racking his brain ever since, trying to put names — other than profane — to us! Trying to determine who held him up! Of course he has! He can't let it hang this way. He *has* to know who's bucking him; who wiped out his bunch; who got the ill-got gains of the robbery! Who ran him like a scared jackrabbit! He can't move a step, after this, with mysterious enemies abroad. He won't dare!'

Burk grinned shadowily. Putting himself in Lance Gregg's place, he knew that *he* would have turned naturally toward the only outfit which had threatned to oppose the One-Gang — toward the Y. But, with the Y's leader a paralytic, what would Gregg think? He would hardly credit Turkey or Chihuahua with getting the information about the robbery; with striking that blow.

'No,' he told himself, 'without undue vanity, I think I can believe that he'd credit it to me or to nobody else, if he believed it came from the Y. So, he has to ride over and have a look; be sure that the "helpless paralytic" is really that!'

So he was not at all suprised to hear approaching the bungalow-door the light, quick footsteps of Myra, with the heavier, more deliberate, tread of a man accompanying.

'Burk,' Myra said from the door, 'Mr. Gregg came to talk about buying some stock from us. I have told him that, under present conditions, he would have to talk to you about mares.'

Burk regarded them steadily as they came into the room. It occurred to him that the weariness, the loss of sleep, suffered from last night's strenuous work, must make him look even more than usual the invalid. It amused him. But he let none of his amusement show. He had his part to play — that of the fractious paralytic.

'Buy!' he muttered thickly. 'Buy! What a strange word — for the Wallop–8! And what does he need with more of our mares? Didn't he steal enough, the day he killed Egbert, to do the Wallop–8? I can't get this straight! Buying is such a departure from his usual methods! Why doesn't he just steal what he wants? Since I've been lying help-less ———'

He looked from Myra's still, tight face to Gregg. He found Gregg's eyes roving narrowly up and down his sheeted bulk. Did Gregg suspect something here? he wondered. Did he chance to suspect the truth? Certainly, he seemed hardly to conceal, now, his attempt to satisfy himself concerning Burk's condition.

'Passing over your poor try at being funny,' Gregg drawled contemptuously, 'I spoke to Myra about a half-dozen head of good brood mares and a stallion.'

He came over closer, so that he stood at the bedside and looked sharply down at Burk. Myra was behind him. He flicked a match-head against thumb-nail, lit his dead cigarette and let his hand sag. Into the palm of Burk's limply extended hand the burning match dropped. Gregg seemed not to notice that. His long, dark-blue eyes were steady on Burk's face. Only by instant and iron

269

self-control did Burk avoid the instinctive jerk that would have flipped the blazing match from his hand — and told Lance Gregg what he wanted to know.

'I wouldn't sell you a head of stock on any terms,' Burk said, stiff-lipped, without letting a muscle twitch under the sear of that blaze in his palm. His eyes were as steadily fixed on Gregg's as the Wallop–8 man's were fixed on his. 'Not at double the price anyone else would pay. For your benefit, Myra, I'll say that we've been stolen blind. We have nothing to sell.'

The girl, moving, suddenly came forward with a little cry. She brushed from Burk's hand the remnant of the match and looked indignantly at Lance Gregg. Gregg's eyes were narrowed faintly. In disappointment, Burk imagined.

'You burned him! You let that match drop on his hand!' Myra cried. 'Did it hurt — but of course, you didn't feel it . . .'

'What?' Burk said with a frown, looking at her. 'Match? What are you talking about, Myra?'

She did not answer. She went to the washstand and came back with a wet cloth and washed the seared palm. Gregg muttered something like an apology. Then he walked to the door. Myra put back the cloth, put her hand for an instant on Burk's, and followed him. Burk lay quiet until their footsteps died away. Then he got quickly up and crossed to the window to look out.

Gregg sat the tall bay under the veranda-rail. Myra was just above him. The bay stood sleepily, head down. Burk watched, then suddenly he grinned and looked about him. On the washstand were two horseshoe nails which Chihuahua had picked up, brought in, laid carelessly down. Burk slipped over and got them. He stood to the side of the window and lifted his arm. Gregg was talking with a sulky movement of big shoulders. Myra watched him, red mouth stubborn-seeming, to Burk's eye.

The horseshoe nail buzzed across the space between window and horse. It struck the bay on the haunch. He jumped, put his head down and bucked violently. Lance Gregg went out of the saddle and struck heavily on head and shoulder. The bay bucked off, grunting, kicking . . . Burk leaned against the window-facing and laughed until he had to put hand to aching side. Not a threat of death could have infuriated the Wallop–8 owner as that piling had done. Gregg was scrambling up to glare around furiously.

Then Turkey came around the corner of

the house. He looked curiously at Gregg, then turned toward the sound of the bucking bay. He stared, then turned back. Upon his grizzled face was the most seraphic joy. But — Burk noted — his hands slid down toward the Colt-butt. Turkey was an experienced soul.

'You — you threw a rock at my horse!' Gregg burst out thickly.

'I did?' Turkey drawled metallically, lifting cocky chin. 'Fella! When I throw somethin' yo' way, 'twon't be at yo' pore hawse! *He* cain't he'p the kind o' company he's in. Still . . . I do' no' about *that,* either! Kind o' looks like mebbe he can!'

He came on past Gregg and toward the bungalow. Chihuahua, too, appeared. He was thirsting for knowledge — Chihuahua. He yelled anxiously to Turkey, who stopped and turned.

'Them pilgrim! She's fall off the horse, ha?'

'Looks like it!' Turkey answered in like loud voice. 'Well, I al'ays did say Montgomery Ward only can go so fur, towards makin' a cowboy! The's got to be something' to hang the clo's on!'

They came inside and fell against each other. Burk was panting on the bed, now. They whooped and beat each other on the back. Burk rolled over and pulled up the sheet. He wiped his eyes with a corner of it. He told them of Gregg's visit to the room.

'I waited and waited for him to mention the robbery, but the low-down cow-thief wouldn't do it,' he said aggrievedly. 'Not even to make social conversation, he wouldn't. And my heart, it's sad within me . . . I was all primed to suggest that it was probably just one part of the gang robbing the others. Barney Settels wasn't in that bunch, so evidently it was just a select few at Lance's heels. So, if I could have injected that note, even the return of the money with the robbers wouldn't have entirely cleared Settels and all others not sticking up the train. But he wouldn't talk about anything but horses.'

'An' he ought've been thinkin' about hawses!' Turkey cried.

Then he and Chihuahua seized each other again and waltzed around the room with coyote-barks that carried very plainly to the Big House — and to anyone close to it.

Noon came and Chihuahua, squatting beside the bed, got up to go to the door. He came back to report visitors. Presently, Aunty Ferguson and Myra ushered in Ma Whittington. Ma came waddling over to the bed, all one vast, optimistic smile. She laid

273

a broad, very capable, hand on Burk's forehead.

'Here! Here! You got to stop this, boy!'
she greeted him. 'The ol' Y, it'll go all to
pieces without you're up runnin' it. A ranch,
now, that ain't like a ho-tel. That's what I
tell Pa, all-time, when he gits restless under
the bit. A woman can run a ho-tel heaps
better'n a man could. But it takes a man
an' a mighty good man to keep a big outfit
like this-here a-goin'! How you feel, son?
Doc' Stevens was sayin' give you time.'

'Better,' Burk said in his 'bedridden voice.'
'We had a little excitement, just awhile back.
It sort of — helped . . .'

Myra made a strangling sound and turned
very red. Chihuahua, squatting now at the
bed's foot, matched the noise. Aunty Ferguson leaned openly upon the head of the bed
and giggled.

'Somethin' — got into — Lance Gregg's
bay!' she gasped. 'Piled Lance — right in
Myra's lap! Then Turkey called him . . .'

She waved to a chair and dabbed at her
eyes.

'Set down! Set down! I ain't be'n to town
in seems like it's a month o' Sundays.
What's new down there?'

'If I never forgot! An' me thinkin' I
couldn't hold in to git here, to tell you-all

about the train-robbers . . . Yessirree, train-robbers! Six of that useless One-Gang stuck up the through train at Dead Hawse bridge at ten last night an' killed the express-messenger an' blowed the way-safe an' got clean off with fo'teen thousand dollars. Well, sir! Nobody ever heard o' anything funnier!

'Feller come ridin' in after midnight; come from Cottonwood to tell the sher'ff to be watchin' for the robbers. An' Judge Amblet come downstairs and plumb fell over the robbers an' the sack o' money! An' on a bar'l, underneath the tow sack o' bills, there was a sign readin', "Here's yo' train-robbers!" It was signed "Riders o' the Night." Now, can you beat that!

'Ed Freeman took that Mexican Chavez a-trailin' the fellers that brung the five dead robbers in an' follered their back-trail to a *motte* o' cottonwoods on Dead Hawse Crick. Found where they'd dry-gulched the robbers. But you couldn't foller the trail away from Yatesville, Ed says.'

'Riders of the Night,' Burk said slowly. 'Reckon it could have been just some of the One-Gang, doublecrossing the others?'

'Well, I swan!' cried Ma Whittington. 'I never thought o' that! But — "dog eat dog!" — it could be. But why would they give back the money?'

275

'*Quíen sabe?*' drawled Burk. 'But that idea is very interesting to me . . .'

'The conductor o' the train identified the robbers. But the big feller that was bossin' the job, the one that shot the messenger, *he* wasn't in the dead ones.'

'That would be Lance Gregg,' Burk said thoughtfully. 'But somebody will get him yet . . .'

Myra regarded him steadily, but said nothing. Instead, with expression guilelessly sweet, she turned to Ma Whittington and asked about Frisco Fanny. Ma looked at her sharply, as did Burk.

'She comes by to see Burk,' Myra explained. At which Ma's sharp eyes came around to Burk, and he knew that he was turning red.

'Well, sir!' cried Ma, 'I never thought I'd have much good to say about ary painted woman, but that Fanny — you know what she's doin'? Supportin' them Carter twins! Been doin' it six months, since Jim an' Alty Carter died o' typhoid inside a hour o' each other. Pays over the money ever' week to Sary Carter. An' Sary — the born idjut! — runnin' to me to ask if she sh'd take money off a loose woman! Well, sir! I give her a piece o' my mind an' about two good yards o' Scriptur' along with it.

'Barney Settels, he's a-cloudin' up these days. Lance Gregg is a-makin' up to Fanny. She ain't ex-actly shoved him off, either. Barney don't like second fiddle none, they do say.'

Burk found himself oddly irritated. Why, he couldn't explain. Fanny was certainly nothing to him — except that she had been strangely friendly, helpful. Or unfriendly to Settels . . .

'But a girl of that sort can hardly shove away any man who comes with money in his hand, can she?' Myra said softly.

'I'd back this girl to shove away any man she didn't want around!' Burk snapped. 'She's different from all the others ——'

'Barney Settels — whoever he may be — will be "clouding up" toward you, as well as toward Mr. Gregg,' Myra said amusedly. 'But you're all alike! A painted lady smiles at you and ——'

She laughed at Burk's black scowl. But it was a brittle sound that drew the eyes of the two elder women to her, then to Burk. Aunty rose a shade hastily and suggested luncheon to Ma. Ma agreed with equal haste.

Burk fidgeted, when they had gone. Chihuahua, squatting imperturbably as for the last half-hour, looked sidelong at Burk:

'You're see them paper under your pillow?' he drawled. 'No? W'y, me, I'm see something there, this morning w'en she's early, w'en you're asleep.'

Burk reached quickly under the pillow and drew out a tightly folded sheet of tablet-paper. He unfolded it and looked for a signature. There was none, but he knew instinctively that the neat, small-lettered writing was Fanny's:

Interesting shipment, tomorrow, from Rhettsboro. Fifty or more good mares, consigned Widburn and Thom, Dugan City. Use enclosure as you choose.

That was all. But to Burk, recalling her hint about the train-robbery, it was more than enough. The mares run off on the day of his fall must be these she referred to . . . Well, he thought grimly, somebody was due for a surprise, tomorrow, in Rhettsboro. Then he looked frowningly at the paper. 'Use enclosure as you choose,' it said. What enclosure? He fished and probed under the pillow, but found nothing.

'You see anything else, another paper?' he asked Chihuahua.

'Paper? More paper?' repeated Chihuahua absently. 'I'm see them paper stick out from

278

them pillow . . .'

He got up and lifted the pillow; shook his head; shrugged helplessly.

'She's not there — them other paper. W'y?'

'This message refers to another paper, or to something enclosed . . . Wonder if she forgot to enclose it?'

'She's mebbe happen so. W'at is it she's say, now?'

'Our mares are due to be shipped out of Rhettsboro tomorrow, consigned to a perfectly honest firm in Dugan City — one we've had business with. Which means that we're going to land on somebody like a ton of brick . . .'

'*You're* not go! She's them daylight job, Burk . . . Turkey an' me, we will go. We will take them Weenchestair. We will walk so-o ni-ice an' soft, down by them loading-pen. We will find, mebbe, them fella Gregg. *Por dios!* We will help him to get sick! But you — no, no, no, *amigo mio!* She's too much chance.'

'Sneak up to the house and tell Aunty Ferguson that I want to see her, alone, as soon as she can get away. Ask her not to let the others know. Just to come out.'

Presently, Aunty bustled in. She looked sharply at Burk. He lay staring up at her

279

thoughtfully, ignoring her anxious question. Chihuahua filled the doorway. Burk suddenly lifted a hand to check Aunty's sharp repetition of the question. He sat up and grinned at her. As for Aunty, she reeled as if she had been struck.

'Burk! Sonny! You — you can move ag'in! Oh ——'

'Sh-h! I've been able to move for a couple of days or more. But I didn't dare spread the news. Now, you've got to help me. I've got to be two places at once tomorrow, in Rhettsboro, clamping down on the One-Gang that's shipping our stolen mares, and right here in this bed, a helpless paralytic: And *you* are the wonder-worker. You've got to get Myra off the place before tomorrow morning and you've got to put up a *No Visitors* sign here — I've had a turn for the worse, or something like that!'

'Le' me get my breath! You could've knocked off my eyes with a pole when you raised your hand at me thataway. Now! You want to go to Rhettsboro without folks knowin' you're not paralyzed. Is that it? But, Burk, won't folks that know you in Rhettsboro spread the news?'

'They won't know me!' Burk said flatly. 'I'll be a shambling, no-'count puncher just looking on. Turkey will stage-manage everything. He can swear to every head of stock in those railroad corrals, I'll guarantee that. He'll officially represent the Y. But I want to be around, to see what happens. We may have to make our plans as we go along. I trust Turkey implicitly. But I want to be there. Can you help me, Aunty? You've never failed me yet!'

'Burk!' she breathed suddenly, ignoring this. ' 'Twas *you* bushwhacked them robbers last night an' put 'em on Amblet's gallery along with the money! I know 'twas! I have studied you too long not to know that's exactly what you'd do! "Riders o' the Night," is it? Burk, I'm right proud that the old Y is runnin' Yates County — an' runnin' it right — ag'in. It's like old times. You bet I'll fix it up. Myra don't know it, but she's halfway to town a'ready. An' if anybody crosses over that threshold tomorrow, before you get back, well, they won't be in shape to tell what they saw, about two seconds after they light!'

Chapter XXIV

'Come see us some time!'

Rhettsboro was very much like another Yatesville. There was one main street, with great cottonwoods shading it; lined with saloons and stores and saloons and more stores; then came rows of residences, badly needing paint, for the most part. At the end of the street, blocking it but for a cross-street, was a white frame building of two stories — the courthouse. Behind the town ran the spur of the railroad, with a red plank station and freight-office. Adjoining this was a line of whitewashed loading-pens.

Paradoxically, it was Burk, who most sought concealment, who left the others of the Y men outside of town and rode in to look things over. He felt perfectly safe, for Turkey and Chihuahua, both very doubtful of the wisdom of his coming, now professed themselves satisfied. Turkey admitted that Burk's mother, if she were still alive, might recognize her son. But, he maintained, it would have to be by that instinct which identifies for a mother-cat her kittens.

He was dressed in faded overalls jumper and pants. His boots were ancient and run-over. The flopping, holey Stetson he wore would have disgraced a tramp. And his saddle was that hung up six years before by Myra's father. As for the rest of him, he had a bristly stubble of beard and his hair was tousled. White dust was thick on him and gone was the military set of his shoulders

282

taught at the military academy. Nor was he riding any horse of the Y. His bony bay was a nondescript plug left at the ranch by a drifting puncher as part payment for a Y mount. It bore a half-dozen vented brands; with a Tin Cup for latest iron — and the Tin Cup was far, far away . . .

Burk rode slowly into Rhettsboro, a long, stoop-shouldered figure too mediocre in every detail of him to draw any curious eyes. It was early. With Turkey, Chihuahua, and the 'Three Mesquiteers,' he had ridden hard during the darkness. Most of the county seat's population was at breakfast. Burk jogged on around the buildings of the main street until he came to the loading-pens. Here he found a peaceful quiet, except for one or two restive animals in the corrals.

The station-agent came to the door of his office. Burk nodded to him and turned an eye apparently incurious upon the mares. One or two he recognized. He moved up closer. He was curious to know how the mares had been rebranded. The agent was a young man, with the pomposity of insect-officialdom.

'What d'you want down there?' he snapped. 'Don't be bothering those mares!'

'Jist wonderin' who was shippin',' Burk drawled in conciliatory tones. 'If they are bein' shipped east an' I can go along, I'd sure like the job.'

'They're going to Widburn and Thom at Dugan City. And they'll have their own men going down with the animals. They're to be sold this morning by the owner, to those buyers.'

But Burk had pushed up close, during the agent's talk. He saw two mares with a Goblet brand and guessed that the others wore the same iron. So old Cactus Gunnell was in on this, was he! He shrugged lazily to the agent and turned the drowsy bay around. Nothing to be gained by further waiting here. He wanted to know, now, who was responsible for the actual shipping. How many of the gang, or its representatives, were in Rhettsboro.

'Nice-lookin' mares,' he said, staring with half-closed eyes at the agent. 'I wouldn't mind tradin' this hawse o' mine, even, fer one of 'em.'

The agent laughed loudly at this. So much stock passed him that he considered himself an authority on both horses and cattle.

'I reckon you would!' he jeered. 'But I don't reckon Barney Settels'd think much of the proposition. He told me he paid a hundred and thirty apiece for the lot. They're breeding-stock. Widburn and Thom will scatter them for five hundred miles.'

Burk grinned lazily and turned away. So it was Barney Settels who posed as owner! And as having purchased from Cactus Gunnell, doubtless, since they were wearing the Goblet brand.

'Interesting! I wonder who came to town with Settels . . .'

As he turned into the main street, he saw Settels's dapper figure. Four men were with him. Two were strangers, but the others he knew well as cowboys on the Goblet — a squat, long-armed, bullet-headed man named Pace; a big, swaggering loudmouth called 'Elbows' for some mysterious cow-country reason.

He passed them without drawing comment. Back with Turkey and the others, he told briefly of his discovery. Chihuahua grinned catlike. Turkey nodded grimly. Sandrock Tom, Three Rivers and Happy Jack merely waited pleasantly.

'Come up the offside of the pens,' Burk told Turkey. 'See how many mares you know. Then — make yourself unpleasant. We'll be in the neighborhood. Do'no' much about Elbows, but Pace is a gun-slinger. Settels is supposed to be hell-on-wheels. He may not buy into it. Don't think the buyers will, either.'

They rode back toward town, separating beyond its outskirts. Burk went straight in, alone. Turkey and Sandrock turned to come from the south at the corrals. Chihuahua and the others went north to converge also upon the loading-pens, but from that side.

Burk posted himself in a tumble-down 'dobe sheltered from view of any on the main street. He was opposite the corrals and a hundred feet or so beyond, to eastward. Between him and the railroad's right-of-way was the breadth of a wide and dusty road. So he could look around the corner and diagonally across at what went on about the corrals.

Presently, he saw Turkey. At the same moment that the squat figure of the foreman appeared on the far side of the corrals, studying the mares, Barney Settels came out of the station-office. With him, in addition to the agent and those four men Burk had seen accompanying him before, was the gnarled figure of old Cactus Gunnel, dressed in shabby, dirty brown ducks.

Then Turkey rounded the corner of the corral afoot. Burk could see Sandrock moving up that way, but behind the corral, along the track. His head slid along the white top-rail of the pens like a wide-hatted bead. Barney Settels was first to observe Turkey, and

Burk, staring narrowly, thought that Settels did not know Turkey. But Cactus Gunnel and his two hands, Pace and Elbows, knew Turkey *quite* well. The old man's astonished jerk was visible to Burk.

'See yuh're figgerin' to ship some mares, Gunnell,' Turkey drawled, quite clearly. 'Happened to be up thisaway an' noticed yo' brand on the bunch . . .'

'Uh — I ain't shippin',' Gunnell's hoarse, sulky voice denied with something like relief in the tone. 'Settels, yere, he's doin' the shippin'.'

'Oh! Yuh sold 'em to him, huh? About fifty-two head . . . Funny! Yuh sellin' him fifty-two head about two weeks after the Y lost fifty-two or -three head . . .'

Sandrock Tom had rounded the station-house. He was noiselessly coming up behind the tense group that stared at Turkey. Burk excepted the agent from knowledge of the real status of affairs. But he watched like a hawk the others. Every one of them must know that the Y foreman had not come up merely to make idle conversation. Even the two men of Widburn and Thom.

'Do'no' nothin' about the Y's affairs!' Cactus Gunnell snarled. 'An', by Godfrey! I ain't takin' nothin' off the Y, neither. Yuh better take yo' foot in yo' hand, Adkins, an' cut stick. Yuh got no call to come hornin' in on our business.'

'I got this much,' Turkey said grimly. 'I'm Ridin' Manager o' the Y, an' I know ever' dam' mare, mighty near, in them corrals. The's a Goblet iron been put on over the Y on ever' last one. Mighty slick job o' brand-blottin', but yuh can't — quite — git — the'! Mr. Settels! Yuh ain't shippin' today!'

'Yuh accusin' me o' rustlin'!' roared Gunnell. 'Why ——'

But his fury had a most artificial sound. Burk, staring keenly with Colt in hand, thought that Gunnell waited to make his howl of outraged virtue until Pace slid over a little way and got a hand up, unobserved of Turkey, to his pistol.

'My Gawd!' cried Turkey. 'Have I been lookin' straight at yuh, Cactus Gunnell, without yo' knowin' who I was talkin' to? Why ——'

Pace's arm jerked. Burk had lifted his own Colt and trained it on the left shoulder-point of the squat puncher. That was all of Pace he could aim at, the cowboy being sheltered by one of the Widburn and Thom men. But before he could fire, he saw Sand-rock Tom's head turn that way. Sandrock whipped up his own weapon and the two Colts roared together.

Turkey leaped sideways and pulled, right-hand and left-hand gun, in a blurred twinkling of movement. Pace sprawled on the ground with pistol still gripped in his out-flung hand. A little wreath of smoke eddied upward from the muzzle. Evidently Sand-rock had shot Pace in time to destroy the point-blank aim the cowboy had held on Turkey. But now, Elbows had pulled a gun — as had Cactus Gunnell.

Burk drove an accurate .45 slug through the vicious, wolf-snarling old rancher. Sand-rock Tom and Turkey both fired at Elbows. But the cowboy got in one shot before they discovered his intent and permanently foiled it. A puff of dust jumped up on Turkey's bagging shirt even as he jerked back the hammers of both guns. But once again, within this two minutes or less, death passed him by with no more than a feathery touch in the passing.

Hoofs drummed by Burk's concealment. Chihuahua, teeth glinting in a feral grin, led Happy Jack and Three Rivers at a mad gallop around the corner of the old adobe. As they came out into the wide street, the agent, the two buyers' men, and Barney Settels — all of whom had ducked hastily out of the line of fire — removed themselves farther. For two men ran around the station, grim-faced bearers of the Winchester.

Burk came out from behind his corner. Being afoot and facing that way, he was perhaps best-prepared for the sudden appearance of these two men. He stopped. It was barely possible that they were peace officers, coming to investigate the row. Deputies, or city officers, were all they could be. But when they hesitated not at all, but jerked up their Winchesters and opened on Chihuahua and his companions, Burk threw doubts to the wind.

He had both Colts out of the shoulder-holsters now. Methodically, as if on the target-range, he set his feet and opened fire. It was impossible to tell, in that haze of powder-smoke and deafening rattle of pistol and rifle shots, who was responsible for a hit. But the two men dropped in something less than thirty seconds. Silence came, so complete that it was as definite a thing as the noise it replaced.

Standing was Turkey. Three Rivers lay flat in the dust with leg pinned under a dead horse. Chihuahua and Happy Jack menaced the street with their pistols, from the saddle. Sandrock Tom was sitting in the street, nursing a bloody hand and cursing terrifically in his deep, bass voice 'that would go a mile on the wind.'

Burk saw men running from all directions. And he recognized the lank six-feet-six inches of Wolf Edwards in their van. So he slid back behind the tumbledown shack and ejected the spent shells from his pistol. Having reloaded, he swung upon the quite unalarmed bay and rode out to the main street. Here, by detouring around the buildings, he came back to the corrals and the station, but in the rear of the packing crowd. Sitting his horse, he could view the activities over their heads.

'What's all this, Turkey?' Wolf Edwards demanded in his low, emotionless voice.

'I found fifty-two Y mares, rebranded Goblet, in the corrals there. I told Cactus Gunnell they was Y stuff. He says he sold 'em to that fella Settels that's been sneakin' around behind the station yonder. An' one o' his men, Pace, tried to shoot me. Nat'rally, Sandrock Tom downed the hairpin. Then Gunnell an' Elbows opened up an' so did me an' Tom. Then the rest o' my boys come up an' so did two friends o' Settels's — or Gunnell's. I do'no'. But the thunder got kind o' gen'ral an' — that is about it, I reckon.'

'I bought those mares from Gunnell,' Settels cried angrily. 'This fellow came horning in, claiming them. Naturally, Gunnell objected. I don't think Pace fired the first shot. This long-legged fellow here fired it from behind us.'

Wolf Edwards regarded Settels steadily. If there was no alteration in his gaunt face, Settels still seemed to find something in the sheriff's flinty regard that did not add to his ease of mind. Abruptly, ignoring the dead man, Edwards moved up to the corral and for three minutes studied the mares. Then he turned back:

'I ain't sayin' a thing in the world, Settels, about how-come you got these mares. But anybody that looks close can see a bunch has been rebranded. More! Happens I was lookin' at stock on the Y two-three months back. An' I see five-six o' them animals on the Y range. Now, you can raise hell, if you want to. But my advice to you is to shut up an' see if that don't make you more'n a holloa would. I knowed Turkey Adkins an' these other boys a long time, an' I take their word.

'Turkey, I reckon them's yo' mares. I ain't goin' to stop you from takin' 'em home. Come on down an' see our county attorney an' we'll take some affidavits about this shootin'. Then, unless Settels gits out a injunction, or somethin', you can cut stick.'

'I've got a sweet chance in this county to

get an injunction!' snarled Settels. 'A sweet chance. I'm letting you get away with this, this time. But I serve warning, Mister Y-boss, that this business is a long way from being settled here!'

'This is shore the Year o' the Big Wind, now, ain't it?' applauded Three Rivers. 'Yuh must come an' see us some time . . .'

CHAPTER XXV

'You let your foot slip!'

They were coming happily home from Rhettsboro — Turkey and Chihuahua and Burk. Somewhere in their rear, Sandrock Tom and Happy Jack and Three Rivers were singing *'Git along, little dogies —'* to fifty-two mares, on which the Y-iron had been covered by a brand now extinct — the Goblet . . . For Cactus Gunnell's passing in the smoke, along with his punchers, had made the Goblet a mere name in the country.

'Settels, he's goin' to need some killin',' Turkey drawled. 'He must be jist about fit to tie, right now. Yuh smacked him in town an' made a untailed monkey out o' him — official, too, you actin' as Boss o' the Y. Now, I come along — official again — as Ridin' Manager o' the Y, an' I take them

293

mares off'n him. What could be sweeter?'

'*Santa Maria!*' snarled Chihuahua abruptly. 'Me, I'm smell them smoke. W'at the hell!'

Somehow, even though their perceptions were not so keen as the breed's, and without the acrid odor of smoke to alarm them, they were tensed. They rammed in the rowels and shot to the crest of the long rise overlooking the Y's dooryard.

'What's afire?' cried Burk, gaping down at the rising pillar of flame that lit the dusky slope below. 'Looks like — no, it's not the Big House. C'm'on!'

They poured down the slope in a compact mass with the horses' nostrils flaring and eyes already glaring white in the flames. It was the manager's bungalow — Burk's sleeping-quarters. And it was a flaring, crackling torch. They reined in with the roar of the flames in their ears and the furnace-like heat on their faces, to stare.

'Find Aunty Ferguson!' cried Burk to Turkey. 'Ask how-come!'

Turkey roweled his mount and went charging around to where the house-servants and the two punchers left there in the bunkhouse were standing helplessly. Burk and Chihuahua came slowly in his wake.

'Just flared up!' Burk heard Aunty Ferguson cry answer to Turkey. 'Fair exploded!'

'An' the Boss in the'!' cried the puncher Sweet. 'We come a-runnin', but the fire was all around. 'Twas burnin' on all walls. Yuh couldn't git near the house. Reckon he — he never had a chancet. God!'

'Ha!' said Chihuahua sinisterly. 'Me, I'm think somebody's do one fi-ine job, Burk. We will hunt them trail, w'at the hell!'

They were joined, presently, by Turkey. He watched Chihuahua flitting like a huge cat from spot to spot, searching for hoof-prints. He and Burk leaned eagerly forward when Chihuahua stood erect and flipped a match away.

'Two men! They're ride like hell — toward them Wallop–8!'

'If we could just beat 'em there . . .' said Burk grimly. 'The low-down murderers! They figured they had me, this time!'

'They'll go the trail, mebbe,' said Turkey. 'If we was to ride like all hell the upper trail . . .'

They went in entire obedience to his grim suggestion. Across the Y range at racing gait, sliding down into Dead Horse Creek with rattle of stones and roweling the cat-clawing horses up the far bank onto the Wallop–8. Here they spurred due west, on the chance that the two practicers of murderous arson would feel safe on Gregg's range and slacken pace.

'Well!' grunted Burk, at last. 'If they haven't made the house already, they'll be coming up this trail soon, now . . . Turkey, you and Chihuahua let me hail 'em. Maybe we can get something out of 'em before they recognize us.'

Minutes passed draggingly as they sat there beside the main trail that led to the Wallop–8 house, four miles away. The spasmodic breathing of their hard-pushed horses eased. Burk began to scowl. It seemed impossible that they should be this far ahead of the pair. He turned in the saddle and glared toward the house where Lance Gregg should be at this moment. What to do? Go on up and confront the One-Gang boss?

They're come!' grunted Chihuahua at this juncture. 'Ha! You're think mebbe-so she's one picnic they come to!'

For it was at a foxtrot that the two men approached. They reined in with sudden explosive gasp that carried clearly. Burk moved forward toward them in the darkness.

'Make it all right?' he grunted. 'This is Gregg!'

'Hell! Yuh scared me plenty!' replied that

puncher Murdock, whom Burk had discharged with the rehiring of his 'Three Mesquiteers.' 'Yeh! We scattered coal oil all around the dam' walls an' her two sides at oncet! Man! Inside a half-minute, she was goin' like a prairie fire. Me 'n' Joe was dustin' the scenery about then. We looked back an' I can tell yuh one thing, Boss! That coyote'll never bother anybody around *these* parts no more!'

'Stick 'em up, Murdock!' snarled Burk. 'You're all wrong! You let your foot slip! There's a rope waiting for you! A long, new Y-rope!'

Warned by the sudden creaking of Murdock's saddle, he jerked up the Colts that he had drawn before riding forward. He had no compunction whatever about letting go the big hammers. These two were no more deserving of thought than rattlesnakes. Behind him, as his own guns roared, flames stabbed out from the Colts of Chihuahua and Turkey. Burk straightened in the saddle and looked tensely toward the pitching animals before him . . .

'Got 'em!' he snapped. Then he swung down and bent over the two still figures in the trail. He lifted his head.

'Reckon it's too far to the house for Gregg or his merry men to have heard the shooting . . . Let's decorate the Wallop–8 doorstep with these sidewinders — no! I've a better idea:

'We're coming to the place where we want a showdown with that Gregg gentleman. Meanwhile, our play is to keep him as worried as may be humanly possible. Now, if he were to come out and find his two little firebugs dead on the step, he'd really be relieved. For he'd figure his job was carried out successfully and the only ones who could actually testify against him were permanently out of court. But — what if the two hairpins just disappear?'

'Ha! She's one dam' fine idee!' Chihuahua grunted. 'Them Gregg, she's pull his dam' hair, *segur' Miguel!* She's wait for them dirty sneak to come, but they're not come — ever!'

'Turkey,' Burk said thoughtfully, 'we can find a good deep cave in the creek-bank and stow these bodies and rock up the cave-mouth. We won't mind their horses going back to the Wallop–8. Chihuahua! You pin a note to Gregg's door — with Murdock's knife for pin, just as a fancy touch. We'll say — let's see . . .

' "Will fire make firebugs talk? *We* think so! Signed: Riders of the Night." '

'That'd worry higher gunies than Lance

Gregg!' Turkey said grimly. 'Let's git goin',
Burk.'

On the dead men's own horses, the three
packed the bodies as they had packed the
dead robbers from Dead Horse Bridge. Chihuahua left them then. They found a cave
that answered their needs and, having
rocked up the entrance, washed the blood
from the saddles and let the horses go with
reins knotted on saddle-horns. They covered
as much of the trail as they could. Before
dawn broke, Chihuahua came back, grinning like a contented cat.

'Me, I'm wipe out them dam' trail after
I'm pin the note to Gregg's door. Now,
w'at?'

'I'll hole up,' Burk decided. 'Turkey, you
two go back. You couldn't trail the firebugs.
You think Gregg's behind the fire. Tonight,
you two come back with whatever news you
have.'

He watched them go, then made himself
comfortable in a *motte* of cottonwoods. With
the old crowbait picketed well inside the
grove, he dozed intermittently through the
day. In waking intervals, he thought of the
whole situation. Where were they getting, in
the campaign against Gregg and the One-
Gang? He had to leave that unanswered.
They had struck Gregg inconveniently hard

a time or two. That much was certain.

'Showdown's bound to be just over the hill,' he thought lazily. 'We can't go on this way indefinitely. How will it end? Man-to-man with Lance Gregg? I'd like that. But — what if he got me? What would it be like to be killed?'

That question, too, he had to leave unanswered. In spite of the deaths he had seen — the deaths he had caused — his own death he could not picture. He let his mind stray to pleasanter paths; to thought of Fanny of the Blue Mouse. He wondered how much truth was behind the story Ma Whittington had repeated. Lance was a big, handsome, free-spending hairpin . . . And — as Myra had said — how could any girl in that position repulse a man who came with money in his hand . . . He shrugged grimly.

'No use playing the sentimental young jack!' he told himself. 'Fanny *is* unusual. She's from some good family. She has fine instincts. But she didn't get into that place, that life, off a springboard; out of a convent in one jump. There's no argument about my liking her. I do! But —— There *is* a but and that seems fatal.'

He lay with hands under his head, watching the sunlight of late afternoon dapple the green leaves of the cottonwoods.

'He has all the luck . . . With women . . . Approaching Myra, I walk in his tracks — and his shadow. Now, it's Fanny. Myra has got to be very much a person; very much an individual. Yet, I hardly seem to know her, any more. Those fool arguments by letter put up a wall between us. Not that I —— Ma Whittington's like every romantic old soul. She has to be match-making. Myra and I are no more suited to each other than ——'

He rolled over. Hoofbeats were sounding, dull on the soft ground beyond the creek. Automatically, his hand went down to Colt-butt. A shoe clinked on a rock. Then Chihuahua appeared.

When he reined in before Burk, his blue eyes were very sad. He twirled the point of black mustache and solemnly shook his head.

'Me,' he meditated aloud, 'I'm w'at's called — sometimes an' some places — one not-so-bad lady-wrangler. But — w'at the hell! By you, Burk, me — *pouf! Nada!* Nothing!'

Burk stared curiously, letting his saddle sag to the ground.

'What might be biting *your* ear?' he inquired.

Chihuahua fished in a pocket and drew out a crumpled scrap of paper. Burk took it and smoothed it out.

'Cactus Gunnell' — the neat, small writing informed him — 'was not the only one to use the Tortugas. There is a box-cañon due north of the Goblet house in which — But does all this make you feel more helpless and more restless?'

Burk shook his head, frowningly. She was beyond him — Fanny. Then it occurred to him that in more than its wording was this a peculiar message. He looked up swiftly at Chihuahua:

'I wonder when Fanny wrote this! Before the town had word of the fire, or — You know, I've suspected that she knew about my being up and around. Does she know, also, that I wasn't in the house when it burned?'

'Me, I'm let you search me!' Chihuahua grinned. 'One small *muchacho* — one Mexican boy — she's bring these paper to Turkey. So, Turkey an' me, we're figure mebbe-so them box-cañon, she's stand one — fine — look. Turkey an' Sandrock Tom an' Happy Jack an' Three Rivers, they're wait, now, southwest of them Goblet house. They're have Funeral for you. Mebbe-so, we're find some *hombres malos,* some most wicked hairpins, in them Tortugas, ha? An' then, *we're* help them to git sick, *por — dios!*'

They rode fast through the dusk — Burk had eaten the sandwiches Chihuahua had brought. Having wiped his hands on his breeches and hitched up crossed cartridge-belts, he looked at the Winchester hanging in the saddle-scabbard and declared that he felt a man again and his *toilette* was complete.

'Me, I'm hear them horse go on ahead of us!' Chihuahua grunted abruptly, some time afterward. 'I'm wonder . . .'

They were over past the Wallop–8 house by now, south and west of it. Chihuahua pulled the deadly little Winchester carbine from its scabbard. He rode leaning forward in the hull. Burk could hear nothing, but he trusted to the Indian-keen ears of the breed.

But they reached the *motte* of cotton-woods in which Turkey and the others should be waiting, without seeing anyone. Turkey's squat figure appeared then. He yelled at them — to come on . . .

'Ha!' said Chihuahua cheerfully, at sight of Sweet sitting with face half-sullen, half-resolute, between Sandrock Tom and Happy Jack. 'Fella, she's one dam' fine life insurance for you, that you're come *fast* ahead of us . . . Me, I'm looking for you all time.'

303

'I'm goin' with yuh-all,' Sweet said flatly. 'I don't see nobody around's got more'n two arms an' two laigs or straddles more'n one hawse. I pack a .45 myself an' I 'low I can use her some. An' none o' yuh-all's workin' for the old Y a speck more'n I am. I knowed yuh was up to somethin' when I see yuh-all sneakin' off one at a time. So I follered. I ——'

Burk had come in range of his vision. Sweet's stubborn blue eyes narrowed at sight of the shabby clothing. But evidently he had better eyesight than they had given him credit for. He cried out:

'It's — it's the Boss. It can't be — but it is!'

'Yuh was dam' thick with Murdock!' Turkey growled at Sweet. 'An' we gi' that slimy snake his powders an' I hear he went right over to Gregg. Kept yuh an' Maguire because I wasn't dead ce'tain about yuh.'

'I was offered a job on the Wallop–8, too,' shrugged the bristly-haired puncher calmly. 'An' dam' me if I wasn't minded to take it, too! For I was right tired o' workin' for a outfit that let its stuff be stole in carload lots. Then things kind o' begun to work under the surface, like. An' I begun to wonder. An' now ——' He looked at Burk and shook his head.

'We have to be hightailing,' said Burk. 'Sweet, we're going up to see if we can't hit the One-Gang another lick on the Y account. I felt about you as Turkey did. But now — well, tonight's your chance to show that you've any business working for an outfit that *won't* let its stuff be stolen — not in one-hair lots!'

'Meanin',' grinned Sweet, 'that we're goin' to take a *pasear* over on Cactus Gunnell's front yard. I don't claim I'll be first man at 'em, if the's trouble. But I will be along about the middle, at the latest!'

Chapter XXVI

'We done hit Gregg a lick!'

Chihuahua scouted the Goblet house like a great ghost. He came back to them and reported it empty. So they passed it and moved due north, with Chihuahua five hundred yards in the lead. It was nerve-racking business, even so. For not a sound came back to them.

'Yuh'd swear that gunie's hawse never had no feet!' grunted Turkey amazedly, after a half-hour or so of this. 'I shore-ly feel heaps better, though, with him out in front. He's one salty hairpin!'

Chihuahua materialized in the darkness, a gigantic shape.

'Them box-cañon, she's straight ahead. An' them dam' rustler, she's build one fire in the mouth an' hide back in them cañon somewhere.'

'Can't get by the firelight, huh?' nodded Burk. 'Any of you-all happen to know this cañon?'

'Been up here oncet,' said Happy Jack. 'The's a li'l' trail along the top, east side. The walls are seventy-eighty feet high an' mostly they bulge toward the top. Hard to shoot down into it — an' hit a man. Do'no' if the's any way out, except at this end.'

'Reckon it's a walking job, then. Turkey, you had better get the horses off to one side. Chihuahua, you and I will have a look-see along the trail Happy spoke of. Keep quiet at this end, unless you hear us shooting, Turkey.'

He led the way quietly to the right. The trail climbed out of the flat which was on a level with the cañon-floor. It was rugged, but not too hard to follow. Up above, they could see the guarding-fire, but not a sign of men. It was a big cañon and evidently a holding-ground used at night. They could hear cattle, and Burk thought there were at least five or six hundred head, from the sounds.

Coming to the end of it, they came, also, to the end of the trail. Burk stared down into the dark depths. In the darkness, Chihuahua eyed him speculatively.

'We're going down into it!' Burk said suddenly. 'Ever climb a rope? It's wonderful exercise, Chihuahua. Back East, they hang ropes in gymnasiums and charge monthly dues for not half the climbing we'll have tonight! I brought along three ropes. They ought to serve.'

'Not me!' declared the breed, most earnestly. He lifted a shoulder-point distastefully as he eyed the unfathomable darkness that filled the cañon-depths. 'Me, I'm fall off. I'm think you're fall off, too!'

'You can beat me with a Winchester,' Burk grinned. 'But this is where I live. I'll go down hand-over-hand and do a standing, back-flip when I get down. Will you go if I lower you?'

'*Um-hmmm!*' said Chihuahua reluctantly. 'But me — I'm lots rather go past them fire, yonder — with one young army shooting at me!'

Burk knotted a bowline-on-a-bight in the end of a lariat, having knotted the three thirty-two-foot ropes together. Chihuahua slipped his legs through the double-loops and looked at Burk, who grinned.

'I'm going to take a turn around this juniper here and let you down slowly. Your job will be to keep off the face of the cliff and make as little noise as possible. When you touch bottom, jerk the rope a couple times and I'll come down.'

He took his turn around the gnarled tree-trunk, then walked out to the edge, where Chihuahua was obviously holding his breath. Burk set in his heels and fairly lifted the squatting breed over the edge. Then he began paying out the rope. It seemed to him that Chihuahua's gasp at the sudden drop must be plain the whole length of the cañon. During an age-long time he paid out the lariats' length, praying that they would not rub any sharp rock-edges on the way down. At last there came a feeble tug on the rope, then a second.

Burk flexed strained arms a moment, then made fast the rope's end and dropped over the cañon-edge. Hand-over-hand, he lowered himself — as so many times he had done for a third of this distance in the gym'. It seemed an endless descent and he was tiring. Abruptly, the fire at the cañon-mouth leaped up. He heard yells. Shots rattled. Almost, he let himself go sliding. But he dared not; he had no idea how far he must drop, yet.

'Quick!' Chihuahua cried — it sounded a mile below him. 'Ah-h!'

Methodically, Burk came on down, hand-over-hand; hand-over-hand. At last his feet touched ground — and with hands gripping the loops which had held Chihuahua, nothing but his toes touched! He let go and almost fell. But to him came the panting sounds of a struggle. He whirled that way and two dark figures reeled toward him, so closely locked together that they made but one enormously thick shape in the gloom.

All along the cañon's length, now, men were crying out to each other in the intervals of firing. Burk leaped upon the embattled pair. He grunted to Chihuahua and, having identified the breed, slipped an arm deftly around the neck of the other man in a back-strangle. Chihuahua slid away and back in again. The man Burk gripped coughed oddly, then collapsed in Burk's arms. An old trick of wrestling. Burk held on the tighter until Chihuahua tapped his arm.

'She's all right,', panted the breed. 'Me, I'm let Señor Bowie talk with him . . .'

They hugged the cañon-wall and edged toward the mouth. The cattle were huddling over against the other side. Presently, they could make out the dim shapes of men behind orange flashes of rifle and pistol fire. There seemed to be at least a dozen of the rustlers. Burk thought that this bunch of cattle was about to be moved. So many men would not be required, otherwise.

'*We're* help them to get sick, ha?' grinned Chihuahua.

He and Burk chose themselves a couple of boulders close in the rear of the hindmost defenders. Then, very swiftly, they fired three shots each, aiming at the flashes of the rustlers' guns. Somebody yelled at them for double-damned fools, shooting too low. But they were an uneasy and a suspicious crew, these herders. Impossible as it must have seemed to them, that they were taken in the rear, they wasted no time in discussing it. An order was given in a yell and bullets began to sing toward them.

It was — Burk admitted absently to himself — an interesting sort of business. He wondered what daylight would reveal — if no slug chanced to put him beyond the appreciation of revelations, before that time. Whom would he see up there in the rôle of cornered rustler? He thought it too much to hope that Lance Gregg would be among those fellows. Lance had never revealed himself as a gentleman who took many chances, or felt any loyalty to those hard cases who rode with him.

'I reckon those train-robbers would have had a word or two to say to him if we'd let any of 'em get away,' Burk thought, driving a bullet toward a form half-seen, half-sensed, fifty yards beyond him. 'He certainly did snatch up a handful of distance and depart high, wide, and handsome, that night we dry-gulched 'em!'

The fight slowed as time passed draggingly. From the mouth of the cañon, Turkey's bunch would blaze away — coming closer to the fire in skirmish-order, it seemed. Each time the rustlers answered with volleys. Chihuahua and Burk whanged away, firing at anything they thought they could hit. Then would come a pause, in which small sounds of the night became loud sounds. Then another rattle of shots.

At last, there was the graying of the sky, coming after pitch-darkness, to foretell the dawn.

Burk lay behind his boulder. Over to his left he could hear the sounds of someone moving. Evidently, he thought, Chihuahua had grown cramped. The rustling noises were suddenly drowned by another outburst of firing. Burk moved, to see what was doing. Out of the corner of his eye, he glimpsed a squat, dark shape — rearing like a sinister phantom above him. He stared at it.

'Hell! *That's* not Chihuahua!' one half of his mind remarked wonderingly, even as the other half was rolling him over on his back, jerking up his feet.

He pulled knees up under his chin, then shot his feet upward to catch the towering figure in its face.

His assailant was caught midway in his drop toward Burk. He was momentarily straightened. Something tinkled with the sound of breaking glass as it struck the boulder beside Burk.

Burk dropped his feet. Without taking time to try getting up, he shot the man.

A noiseless figure streaked across, to take the swaying man in the rear. But he crashed downward before Chihuahua had reached him. The light increased. They stared down at him and saw that he was a Mexican in cowboy ducks, a stocky, muscular figure. A long and slender-bladed knife lay on the ground.

'Thought he was you,' grunted Burk. 'Then he reared up and was coming down on me with that toothpick and I gave him both heels in the face, then drilled him.'

'*Por dios!* Me, I'm think some things from

them school back East will be good for these cow-country,' grinned Chihuahua.

'Ha!' he snapped regretfully, peeping around the boulder. 'I'm wish for my Weenchestair . . . *I* would help them rustler to get sick!'

'Let's walk up on 'em — rock to rock!' proposed Burk grimly. 'We can trust Turkey to follow our lead. I figure that we just have six-seven, at most, to deal with. There couldn't have been more than a dozen in the beginning. If none of our boys have collected lead out there with Turkey, we ought to be even-steven . . .'

They slid around the boulder on its two sides and wriggled along to the shelter of another. Silence hung thick in the cañon now. No sign of men ahead of them. They crawled ten feet farther. Chihuahua's Colt flipped up. Then he shook his head and lowered it.

'Not sense to kill 'em twice,' he said with a grim smile.

Burk, too, could see figures sprawling behind rocks and in tiny gullies, three or four of them. But none with life . . . He wondered if the rustlers could have got away. He lifted his head above the rock that sheltered them and a bullet rang on the stone. Splinters stung his neck. He collapsed, cursing fervently.

Chihuahua had fired at the puff of smoke down-cañon. There came a defiant yell in answer, and at the sound Burk shook his head disgustedly. He cried out for Happy Jack and there came quick answer.

'That's Turkey's outfit! They have got into the cañon!' he grinned at Chihuahua. 'We're shootin' at each other. Turkey! Oh-h, Turkey! Can you see anybody between us?'

'Nary soul! Yuh reckon them dam' hounds has Injuned off?'

'Look!' Chihuahua cried suddenly. His eyes had been roving. 'One side-passage! Them fellas — we're not see 'em again, quick!'

A narrow opening showed in the east wall, a thin crack still dusky in the dawn-light. Evidently, the holders of the cañon had used it, for withdrawing from a hopeless fight. Chihuahua went to explore it. He came back to say that it was empty — and that the remnant of their enemy had gone that way.

'Well!' Turkey nodded grimly, as he and Burk moved about, surveying the battle-ground. 'Anyhow, we shore-ly hit them Sticky Loopers a lick! Yessirree! We done hit Gregg a lick! Five-six dead right yere. An' yuh said Chihuahua got one back yander when yuh-all first come down. Well? No use tryin' to foller 'em, I reckon. How many was the', Chihuahua?'

'Three, *no más,*' said Chihuahua. 'They're head for them Wallop–8, mebbe-so?'

'Possibly,' Burk nodded absently. 'Even probably. We'd better haze this bunch of sorefeet back over to Y range. I don't think we'll be bothered. Gregg can't have more than a couple of men with him. We about halved his bunch when we wiped out Murdock and Joe. Even with those three, he'd hardly try to stop us. We'll cut south and head around Wallop–8 range. As for this bunch, that's a nice, handy-limbed cottonwood up there at the cañon-mouth . . . We'll decorate it with these fellows. Leave a *Riders of the Night* note on 'em.

'Then, afterward, *we* don't know a thing about any battle, here. We just found a bunch of strayed Y-stuff, over south of the Goblet range, while we happened to be wandering around in that neighborhood. We naturally choused 'em home. Who wouldn't?'

Chapter XXVII

'A hot time ——'

Chihuahua laughed suddenly. Burk turned in the saddle to peer through the darkness at his friend. Yatesville's lights had just bobbed into sight as they topped a ridge.

'Porqué?' Burk inquired. 'Why this sudden mirth and unseemly laughter?'

'Porque se — because it is, my friend!' Chihuahua grinned. 'In these long, many times most tiresome, life, w'y will we ask *porqué?* If we're laugh — good! Make them laugh quick. For in one moment more, mebbe-so we're not feel like making the laugh, ha?'

'In other words, it doesn't please you to say.'

They jogged on toward town and another thought came to Burk:

'You said that Myra came out, then went away,' he drawled, trying to keep his voice level — though why it shouldn't be level he had no idea. 'What'd she have to say? Besides her natural expressions of grief over my untimely and impossible-to-fully-evaluate taking-off? Did she give Turkey a bunch of powders for the running of the Y, as coming from the Y's Entire and Unhampered Boss?'

'Oh, she's one fine girl,' Chihuahua said solemnly. 'She's tell us it's very sad an' she's wish you're lead them better life an' be more prepare an' mebbe-so she's for them best —— An' she's tell Turkey to go ahead an' make w'at powders she's like for the Y. Then she's ride for them Wagon-Wheel.'

'What for? What's the Wagon-Wheel got to do with it?'

'*Nada!* Nothing! But she's tell one girl on them Wagon-Wheel she's come see her sometime. So — she's go.'

'*Amor de dios!*' Burk gasped. 'If that isn't ice-box coolness for you! Why —— Why —— It's too bad I was burned to death, but she couldn't disappoint Marjory Williams —— Well ——'

He rode on, nursing sulky and indignant amazement. He had pleasantly expected to hear from Chihuahua of Myra, white-faced, wet-eyed, grief-stricken, collapsing under Aunty Ferguson's care and — and all that proper and decent sort of thing. Instead, she had spoken like a hired mourner and traipsed off to pay a long-delayed visit to Marjory Williams on the Wagon-Wheel!

'Uh — did she happen to be eating an apple?' he asked acidly. When Chihuahua grunted in puzzled tone, he explained —

317

bitterly: 'You see, Myra's very fond of apples. I thought maybe she ate an apple and told Turkey how sorry she was. That would sort of mix business with pleasure, you see. I'd hate to think that she'd been put out. If she had an apple, it's all right.'

'Me, I'm not see them apple,' Chihuahua decided gravely. 'Mebbe-so she's have them apple in her pocket. No . . . she's not eat any apple. She's have one *fried pie* w'en I'm see her. Mebbe she's apple pie?'

Presently, with nearer approach to Yatesville, he broke in upon Burk's savage meditations:

'Turkey, she would say we're two dam' fool, coming for Yatesville, tonight. Well . . . me . . . I'm never own them paper w'at will say I'm have the much sense!'

In a Mexican's corral on the edge of town, they swung off and, reaching for the *latigos,* suddenly stopped. Burk looked at Chihuahua, Chihuahua looked at Burk. Their hands dropped.

'Better leave the kaks on,' said Burk. 'Might be better.'

As on that other night, the light from the Blue Mouse shone in a yellow rectangle across the sidewalk. From the dance-hall came the jiggling music of fiddle and accordion. Feet stamped.

'Hi, there! Ol' Joe Clark!
Hi, there! Betsy Brown —'

Chihuahua moved into the dance-hall by plan. Burk went down the sidewalk to the bar-room door and shambled in and across. He had never changed clothing, had neither shaved nor bathed, since Rhettsboro. With shoulders sagging, with dragging feet, he was a sad scarecrow. The fiddles were still squealing:

'Hi, there! Ol' Joe Clark!
Is you leavin' town?'

In the wide arched opening between bar-room and dance-hall, he stopped to look around. Chihuahua had already scooped his favored blonde into the curve of a long arm. He grinned down.

For a moment Burk's stupid-seeming stare failed to find Frisco Fanny. His eyes roved from dancers to tables. And he looked straight into her gray eyes.

She wore the short-skirted, *décolleté* Spanish costume that so suited her. Small head was crowned by high comb. He wondered if she recognized him. It seemed to him that she did not, for her eyes went boredly about the dance-hall. Then he speculated concerning the notes she had

319

sent him; particularly he considered the note telling of the box-cañon in the Tortugas. Did she guess that he had been up and riding, while others believed him helpless abed? Did she guess that now he was out and eager to strike at Lance Gregg's One-Gang, instead of entombed in the ashes of the burned house on the Y?

But this speculation got him nothing. His dulled eyes began to shine a little; faintly, his mouth-corners lifted. An interesting and amusing idea had come to him. Why stand here wondering, why not go over to her and risk everything on one play — put himself in her hands by unmasking for her? Dance-hall girl — boss dance-hall girl — she might be; indubitably was. But there was nothing about her of the sordidness that clung about the prettiest of these others. Instead, there was an atmosphere of cleanliness and of straightforwardness that ——

'Oh, hell!' Burk said helplessly to himself. 'Trying to figure her is going to get me down with a cramp. I'll be dizzily cock-eyed in any language including the Scandihoovian. So ——'

As he straightened, to slouch over to her table, she got up. One might almost have thought, Burk said to himself, that she had sensed his purpose and stood to prevent it.

But at this moment Lance Gregg came threading his way through the dancers on the margin of the floor. Many a girl's eyes turned to his big swaggering figure.

He was dressed as immaculately as usual, in white silk shirt with neckerchief of blue silk knotted artfully about strong brown throat; with, tonight, silvery gray whipcord trousers drawn down over the legs of alligator hide boots. His wide-rimmed white Stetson was pushed back upon brown hair. Neither spurs nor cartridge-belt he wore. Burk's eyes searched for tell-tale bulges — and found evidence of a pair of derringers in Gregg's trousers-pockets.

Straight back to Frisco Fanny he went and she seemed to be waiting for him. She looked up at him and he smiled, then jerked his head toward the rear of the hall, where half-walled booths replaced tables for those who desired greater privacy in their drinking. Gregg slipped an arm about the slender waist and they went toward the booths. Burk, frowning, suddenly grew narrow of eyes. For Fanny turned and he could have sworn that she looked him straight in the face! That the high comb bobbed a bit, with a sort of vaguely beckoning motion of her head!

He slouched across the floor, skirting the

shifting mass of the dancers. They had hesitated at the first booth, but had gone on past it — Burk thought because they had seen it occupied — into the adjoining booth. But when he glanced mechanically into that first booth, it was empty. So he slid into it without making any sound that could be heard above the noise in the dance-hall. He adjusted his chair so that he could lean backward, with head almost against the thin partition between the first and second booths.

'Missed me, honey?' he heard Lance Gregg say tenderly. And her low admission of the fact, in reply.

He had to concede her, here and now, even more of skill than he had before. Somehow she managed, as she went on talking to Gregg, to make her voice low and intimate-seeming, as if not a word were to be overheard by any soul in the world save him. And still, Burk could hear everything that was said.

'You're staying away a great deal,' she told him. 'I'm not exactly blind or deaf. . . . And — isn't it going to be over pretty soon? Can't you bring your — let's call them problems — to a head, then settle them all with one stroke?'

'Suppose I do?' Gregg's deep voice — to

Burk's ear — shook a little. 'Let's suppose I do just that — quickly. What then? Is this at-arm's-length business going to stop then?'

'Why,' she laughed, 'I'll tell you — then . . . I'm peculiarly constituted, Lance. That's merely a statement of fact, without any explanation or apology. I *do* like to pick winners. Not particularly because of their winnings, either. But because I like the type of man who wins. The biggest man in any given group.'

One could have thought that she was merely thinking aloud . . .

'It sounds odd, doesn't it? Coming from Frisco Fanny, the boss dance-hall girl! But when I decided to come to Yatesville, because I was tired to death of Dallas, it was quickly plain to me that something was going on under the surface, around here. I looked to see who was responsible. And the terms of the problem itself revealed to me the name of — the man most interested in bringing about a certain result.'

'You're damned clever!' grunted Gregg, and there was admiration, honest-sounding to Burk, in his voice.

'Perhaps! But merely learning that it was to *your* interest to wreck the Y so that its owners couldn't patch it up; so that it would fall into your hands through a sale at a dime on the large dollar — that was not enough to know. Not for — Frisco Fanny! For after I knew that *you* were head of the mysterious, all-powerful ——'

'*Don't say that!*' he snapped — but more in warning than in anger.

'— Organization,' she went on calmly, 'I wondered if you could ride the whirlwind you were starting. You left Laredo —'

'Who told you I had been in Laredo?' he demanded gratingly.

Burk leaned a little forward. *That* had somehow got under Lance Gregg's hide! There was a mixture of alarm, savage anger, attempt at nonchalance, all blended in the eight words.

'A little bird!' Fanny laughed. 'You came here with nothing. You needed — and you need now — both the Y and a great deal of money to repair the damage you have done and will do to it. You've had to pass on to your men a good deal of what has been — well, received. Lance, you've no choice! Somehow, you have to strike a blow that will achieve that. After you've done that, you have to prove yourself able to dominate those whom *you* consider subordinates, but who consider themselves ——'

'Settels,' he said quietly. 'And — Fanny! I

never met a woman like you! I've been crazy about you — you know that. I've not been able to keep it from you, even if I had wanted to. But if you aren't a mind-reader ——'

'A woman can do wonders when — when' — her voice broke for an instant — 'when she loves a man. Don't, Lance! Sit still, or I'll go!'

'You've called the turn straight down the line,' Gregg said slowly. 'I haven't enough. But I am going to have it! I'll smack these folk for a stake that will be remembered for fifty years! And nobody will be able to say that I had anything to do with it! I've had it in mind for some time. But that cub of the Y —— He worried me. He had fool's luck in forestalling me. I admit it. He — almost worries me, now . . .'

'Why?' Her surprise was perfectly done. 'He's certainly —— Well, I'm sure he won't bother you now.'

'Because —' His habitual, wolf-like caution seemed to grip him. Burk grinned sardonically. He knew what Fanny was not supposed to know; that Murdock and the other practicer of arson were worrying Lance Gregg. The fear of their turning up in court; the 'Riders of the Night' activities and Gregg's uncertainty as to the personnel

325

of the 'Riders,' were preying on him.

'He was about certain,' Burk thought, 'that it was the Y bushwhacking him after the train-robbery. So he planned to burn me to death. Then the "Riders of the Night" do away with Murdock and Joe Will — and he can't be *sure* they're dead. Then the "Riders" recover those sorefeet over at Gunnell's. It must begin to seem to him that he's in a split stick. For if he got me in the fire, then I wasn't bossing this gang which has been smacking him! And if I am not responsible — who is? He'll be wondering if some of those subordinates Fanny's rawhiding him about are taller — and trickier! — than he figured. It's getting right pleasant.'

'I've got the scheme!' Gregg said abruptly. 'It's of such a nature that — well, my dear, you won't have to miss me . . .'

Burk listened admiringly to her deft, innocent-seeming attempts to make Lance Gregg say more. But Gregg seemed suddenly to have turned cautious. As if — Burk thought — having found that she knew so much more than he had guessed she knew, he would be sure that one thing was a secret from her.

Burk edged toward the booth's door. He must get out of there before Gregg saw him. Through Fanny's stage-management, he had learned things which had been surmise before. He was that much forwarder. Too, there seemed little hope of learning more. He did not want to face Gregg tonight. There was possibility of being recognized. Which would be virtual assurance — here, tonight — that he would never use the information he had gained.

He slipped noiselessly out. Chihuahua was still dancing. As Burk stood looking over the floor and the dancers, he saw Barney Settels staring in his direction. Burk had no more desire to face the One-Gang's first lieutenant than he had owned to meet Gregg himself. So he shambled across the end of the dance-floor, moving with aimless manner toward the door he saw — a door which must lead to the back of the building.

Opening that door, he found himself in a dark passage. The ill-fitting door failed by an inch to close. Burk stole down the passage with left hand extended before him, exploring the darkness. From under his shirt, he had drawn a triggerless .45 — drawn it in instinctive obedience to some warning emotion. Suddenly, the door behind him was jerked open with a crash. Burk whirled catlike, knowing that the light from the dance-hall must show him clearly. But

— so did it silhouette Barney Settels in its rectangle.

'Got you!' Barney Settels cried triumphantly. His hands hurled flame in orange blasts, down the passage. Ghostly fingers seemed to pick, pick, pick at Burk's shirt.

Burk had ended his spinning about with back to the wall of the passage. Automatically, the hammer of his Colt was lifting, falling, lifting, falling again, under his thumb. It seemed impossible that either of them could get out of this four-foot-wide hall — alive. There was nothing to do but try to kill as he was being killed. No time for anything else.

But when his firing-pin clicked on an empty sixth chamber, he had not felt a bullet. And Barney Settels still stood erect, with the door sagging to behind him, darkening the hall. Burk leaped for the door that must close the rear of this passage. His hand fell upon a latch. He jerked and saw starlit sky. He was out, still hardly believing that no further bellowing of Colts had sounded, no lead had torn into him.

He ran up the rear of the line of buildings, stumbling over tin cans and bottles. Presently he stopped and looked back. It was too dark to see anything, but he heard the muttering of many voices. He had turned instinctively in the direction of that corral which held the saddled horses. Now, he went as quickly as possible onward and into the corral. There was nobody there, so he swung up on his mount and, leaving Chihuahua's, rode outside to wait.

Time went on, in its passing made the more interesting by the turmoil that now rose from the sidewalk before the Blue Mouse. Burk watched the moving figures up there. They seemed to be hunting him. He wondered if they knew whom they sought; if Settels had merely streaked after him without saying anything to others of the gang.

Chihuahua materialized with his normal silence; he grunted humorously and went in the corral.

'She's dam' funny!' he grinned to Burk, coming out mounted. 'Them fella, they're look for one man w'at's kill Barney Settels. One very tall, short man, w'at's very thin — an' fat . . .'

'Oh!' said Burk. 'Who helped 'em identify this fellow?'

'W'y,' said Chihuahua aggrievedly, 'me, I'm wish for to tell 'em w'at kind of man must be found. Will I let them murderers get free? W'at the hell!'

CHAPTER XXVIII

'Yuh dam' fools'll git killed ——'

Up to the line-camp came a sweat-streaked horse. Burk, squatting with tin cup of coffee in one hand, looked up and first disclaimed acquaintance with the horse, then with the rider — a fellow who rode as if he were all joints, flopping this way and that in the saddle.

Turkey and Chihuahua, with the 'Three Mesquiteers,' were also staring. The fellow sawed away with both hands and the tough-mouth nag broke into a lumbering trot, then to a walk. At last, he stopped.

'Hell's poppin' in town, fellers!' cried the pallid man in the saddle, panting as heavily as his horse. 'Fanny told me to come out to the Y an' pass the news to you folks. They told me up at the house you-all was here an' ——'

'What's happened in town?' Burk snapped. 'Talk, man! Talk!'

'Masked gang — One-Gang, mebbe; I do'no' — blowed the whole dam' back-wall out o' the both banks. Reckon they'd have got clean off, too, but somebody passed the word along sudden, an' folks turned out in their boots an' shirt-tails an' opened up.

330

They been fightin' back an' forth since three o'clock this mawnin'. The town folks, they're like the fella had the bear by the tail — they got this gang in between 'em, but da's'n't git up close. Fanny says you-all'd want to know . . .'

'We — do!' said Burk. 'It's half-after five . . . C'm'on, boys! We'll pick up Maguire and Sweet and the new cook, going. It's our chance!'

They were saddled and going hell-for-leather with a promptness that made the messenger gasp. He flung up his hands when Burk called to him to come with them. So they rode away from him and, on a rise, saw Maguire and Sweet working with the cattle recovered in the Tortugas. Burk jerked his six-shooter in the air and fired five shots. He waved to Maguire, who was nearest, beckoning him.

The two punchers set spurs to their animals and came racing, but the six did not wait. They went through the Y dooryard pell-mell, quirts licking fore and aft. Burk slid to a halt before the cookhouse door and the new cook, a lean, waspish little man, popped into the opening.

'Want a fight?' snapped Burk. 'Grab yourself a horse and follow us to town — but file off your front sight and throw your spurs away, if you come with us today!'

The cook flung his saucepan of dried apples over-shoulder in a single smooth motion. He was gone like a coachwhip snake for the corrals. Burk grinned briefly. The dirty sugar-sack apron the cook had jerked off had covered a low-swung Colt. Evidently, this *cocinero* was a man ready to meet all complaints and complainants halfway.

Pounding down the white trail they went. Burk looked 'under his arm' once and his mouth tightened at sight of those lean, brown, intent faces following him. A salty crew; a salty, salty crew! He only hoped that the townsfolk had kept the One-Gang engaged.

To them, above the pounding of the hoofs on soft dust, came presently the rolling sound of gunfire. They heard it long before they could glimpse the town itself, from that ridge where first Yatesville became visible. To Burk there was no room for speculation concerning the source of the warning which had brought Yatesville swarming out to smash Lance Gregg's master *coup* — that of which he had hinted the week before, in the Blue Mouse.

Fanny . . . Frisco Fanny . . . How she must

have hated Gregg! thought Burk. He could give no other reason for her detective-work and her notes to him, whom she knew to be Gregg's bitterest enemy.

The town popped into view. It presented the aspect of a minor battlefield. Up and down the length of Main Street, puffs of gray smoke rose at intervals very brief, indeed, from store and saloon and dwelling-house. The front of Rufe Redden's store and that of the Congress Saloon were focal points for the heaviest blossoming of smoke spirals. It required no mind-reading to decide them the headquarters of the conflicting factions.

But from the shelter of corrals; of freighters' wagons; even of low plank sidewalks; the townspeople of Yatesville were sending lead into ——

'Ah-ha!' said Burk. 'Some gentlemen have had to come out into the open and take sides at last! Turkey! Look at that bunch inching up on Rufe Redden's place — and on the Municipal Hotel. Reckon Pa Whittington is emancipated at last — for the day. If that wasn't his old buffalo gun that belched just then, I never heard it — and I have. We can scatter those gunies acting so discourteously toward Rufe and Pa Whittington. Le's — go!'

He roweled Funeral and the black squealed furiously. Down the slope he tore. Behind Burk the *thuddah-thud — thuddah-thud* of pounding hoofbeats became the frantic hammering of a war-drum. And from Sandrock Tom, whose bass voice would 'carry a mile on the wind,' came a wild roar that was picked up instantly by the others —

'YeeeeO WWW! Yip-yip-yip-yip!'

Before that terrific battle-yell; before the compact burst of wild-eyed, foam-flecked, and straining horses; before the grim riders who ignored reins — using both hands to hold long-barreled Colts; the sympathizers of the One-Gang thought it life insurance to wheel and fly. Not all of them succeeded . . . Bullet-caught, in the very apex of their leaps, men crashed flat into the dust. But not a warrior of Burk's was left in the open behind that mad charge. On past Rufe Redden's store; past the front of the Municipal Hotel, where Pa Whittington's .50 Sharps' bellowed like a buffalo-bull; so Burk led his crew, with Maguire and Sweet now tailing it.

He wheeled in the shelter of a cottonwood-log corral at that end of the street and surveyed the scene of battle. There was the tawny flash of a buckskin horse coming around the corner of the corral, to join them. The waspish cook lifted himself from where he lay across the saddle-horn. He spat bitterly. He had a Colt in his right hand, in his left the long carving-knife from the Y kitchen.

'Yuh dam' fools'll git *killed,* doin' stunts like that!' he snarled. 'Yuh like to got *me* killed, a-follerin' yuh!'

The corral was in position commanding three posts of the enemy — or parts of them. A 'dobe shack that offered shelter to attackers of the Municipal Hotel had two windows facing the Y men. Nobody could leave the Congress Saloon by the rear, without coming under their fire. Nor could another street attack be made on either the Municipal or Redden's store, except under the cross-fire of those in the corral.

The rear wall of the bank was just beyond the Congress's rear wall. Back of it was a bunch of horses. Burk eyed these sharply. If the One-Gang should give over its attempt to whip the whole town, here it would likely burst forth, going for those fifteen-sixteen head of saddlers. He saw something like a tow sack on the ground, between building rears and horses. But never had he seen a tow sack moving like a snake.

Chihuahua's rifle whanged at his side. The tow sack reared erect, then fell limply back.

Chihuahua slapped another .44 into the sack, for assurance, but without drawing movement. Then the nine of them settled down, to throw lead at whatever target offered.

Still, those horses fascinated Burk. If the One-Gang had secured its loot from the banks, what Lance Gregg would want was escape. Then those horses would be the point at which he would strike. There was the possibility that the banks had not been stripped before Yatesville waked and descended on the gang. If that were so, Gregg would try to fight until he had opportunity to scoop up the money.

But still, Burk watched hawklike, while the others played Winchester music for the benefit of the outlaws in the Congress Saloon and the 'dobe shack covering the Municipal Hotel, and buildings beyond. Suddenly, four men sprang out in full view, racing with heads down for the horses. Chihuahua saw, from the corner of his eye. He and Burk pumped bullets into those faint-hearts as fast as they could work the levers of the Winchesters. A man fell; another; a third turned to run back to the shelter of the buildings. The fourth seemed to bear a charmed life. He got to a horse and sprang on it.

'*Sangre de Cristo!*' snarled Chihuahua furiously. He seemed to relax, holding carbine limply. He took one long breath and up came the deadly brown barrel. Almost negligently, it seemed, he squeezed trigger. And down from the horse, like a man changing his mind, slid the fugitive. He lay like a heap of old clothes in the dust.

'Hell! I'm going to go see life!' Burk grunted, to the others. 'Keep those hairpins in the 'dobe from punctuating me while I trot to interview Rufe Redden.'

'Yuh crazy nitwit!' roared Turkey 'The's no chance, o' gittin' by that shack, an' to the hotel. We'll all go!'

'Nope! You're the li'l' lookouts at this end. If you move, they can break out. Open up on the shack so I can get past.'

He was gone, and behind him came trotting the waspish cook, Colt in one hand, butcher-knife in the other. They were almost sheltered by the corner of the hotel before the defenders in the shack discovered them. They skipped around the corner with bullets burning the air behind them and Burk lost an inch of skin to a grazing bullet on his shoulder-point.

He burst into the rear of the hotel and found Ma Whittington stoking a fire in the kitchen stove. A huge boiler of water was sizzling on it. She greeted Burk with a smile of a Valkyrie and nodded toward the boiler.

'Goin' to run 'em out o' the shack next door! Pour this down from our second-floor window. Looks like the One-Gang's goin' to git theirs this time, Burk. An' serves 'em right! Tryin' to burn you up was about the last straw! Aunty told me all about it!'

'How's tricks in front?' yelled Burk, over the din of shooting from the front. 'Need any help?'

'Reckon not. The's Pa an' a half-dozen or so. I was the', till Pa run me out. He says *this* ain't hotel-managin' an' he chased me!'

'I'm goin' to see Rufe Redden, then.'

Burk and the cook were nearly shot at the back of Redden's store by a guard there. Only by the speed of their drop and the volume of their yells did they make this earnest citizen recognize them as allies. Past him, they shouldered on up to where Rufe Redden stood at an improvised loophole. Rufe turned at Burk's touch — and nearly dropped his rifle.

'No, I wasn't in the house and so I'm not dead,' grinned Burk. 'I am not paralyzed, either — though I really was. How's the war, here?'

'Not so good; not so bad! They're doublin' up some on us. We shoot at the Congress an' the bank an' the Blue Mouse, then they shoot from the house next door to the dance-hall — about two of 'em. Tryin' to catch us at the loopholes, of course.'

'I think I'll have a look at the back of the other side of the street,' Burk said grimly. 'Are the — the girls still over there in the dance-hall?'

'Do'no.' Hope not. For the Blue Mouse is goin' to look like Ma's ol' colander, 'fore this business is done. But I reckon, for them as is alive when this is over, Yates County's goin' to be a better place to live.'

With the cook trailing still, Burk went up the back of the buildings and spoke briefly to those citizens covering this end of the main street. They agreed that, if he could get across, alive, he could liven the war from closer quarters. Old Jim Hull, the freight contractor, spat and grinned at Burk.

'Reckon, though, if yuh can git out o' bein' burned to death, the way yuh done, yuh'll be likelier'n most to *git* across, Burk.'

Obligingly, Hull's command sprayed the buildings opposite with a leaden hail, while Burk and the snarling, complaining little cook raced across. Flat against the end wall of a building, they stopped to breathe. There was a big corral directly behind this building, but it seemed unoccupied by the One-Gang. But as Burk edged toward the rear corner of the building, the saddle-horses which had been in the rear of the Congress came calmly down and entered the corral.

Burk looked around the corner very cautiously. He placed the rear door of that house adjoining the Blue Mouse. The house from which, according to Rufe Redden, two good shots were annoying those in Redden's store. It seemed to Burk that, if he and the cook took this house, it would be doing something worth-while. The cook agreed, sourly.

They inched along the building's rear, half-expecting to have a blast of fire in their faces, any minute. But when they came without event to that door they sought, it was open and there was silence inside. Burk peered in. Dusky interior revealed nothing of the back room.

He slid in and heard the rasp of the cook's feet behind him. To the door of the next room, standing ajar. He looked through the crack and saw Frisco Fanny sitting on a cot, staring straight ahead with far-away expression, arms locked about her knees. She was very pale.

He stepped inside the door and she looked up at him mechanically. Then the gray eyes widened. She was on her feet in a single smooth movement and on her pallid face was horror. She made a sort of strangling sound. Burk stared. There was no sound, anywhere, to explain her alarm.

'What's the matter?' he demanded. 'Think I'm a ghost? I — thought you knew . . .'

'Look out, Burk!' she screamed — and lurched toward him with arms outflung.

Burk whirled.

'So!' said Lance Gregg. He had come soundlessly to the door that opened into the front room. At his shoulder showed the fade of Bob Tetter, whom Burk had wounded in the street once before.

'So!' said Gregg, again. His blue eyes had flashed from Fanny's twisted face, back to Burk's. 'This explains everything.'

Tetter fired with upward jerk of the gun already in his hand; fired before Burk could move. Then Gregg, whirling sideways, fired twice in drumming succession. His first shot was at Fanny, the second at Burk whose bullet — missing Gregg, its real target — caught Tetter in the face.

To Burk, even in that split-second when he was watching the girl sway dizzily, there was time for thought. It seemed to him that the cook, who had been at his heels all this time, had crashed his pistol-barrel down upon his skull. The room seemed to swell tremendously, then as flashingly it contracted, to swallow him, where he stood with crimson constellations swimming before his eyes.

Chapter XXIX

'He's .45 softened!'

He seemed to struggle back to consciousness through a thick black fog. He was conscious of a weight across his body. Dully, he opened his eyes and blinked around. There were the walls of the room, just as he had seen them last — ages ago, it seemed to him. Nothing else to see.

His hand, moving, brushed something soft and limp, that lay across his breast. With terrific effort he moved so that he could see. His head threatened to split. He was facing Fanny, whose face was upon his shoulder.

Then he came back to the present with a convulsive jerk, recalling everything. Gregg had shot her. He sat up, putting his hand with rough gentleness under her head. She was paper-white. Her shadowed eyelids were down. But they fluttered as he moved her slowly. She looked up at him; smiled weakly. He saw her lips moving and bent his head to listen.

'He knew — then — that I'd been the traitor. So, being Lance Gregg — he wanted to kill us — both. That man — behind you — saved your life. He — threw a knife — that struck Gregg's arm — spoiled his aim. You got only — a scalp-wound. Gregg — has gone.'

The eyelids sagged again; she was limp on his arm. He got up, holding her steadily. He put her upon the cot. He drew off the silk waist and found a hole in her right side that made him gasp. But the slug seemed to have gone straight through and out without touching so much as a lower rib.

He ripped a sheet into bandages and bound up the wound with a thick pad to stop bleeding. Then he stood straight, to listen. As he stood there, a sudden savage burst of firing came, that for intensity topped anything he had heard during the whole battle. He ran to the back door, passing with no more than a glance the body of that grim little rooster, the cook.

Out at that corral into which the horses had gone was a thick press of men now. As they crowded toward the corral's gate, they dropped, one and two at a time. But twelve to fifteen of them got inside. Out they came again, quickly, still pelted by the fire from the buildings they had quitted. They scattered like frightened quail. One glimpse, Burk had, of Lance Gregg's tall figure in the van. Then they were gone in swirling dust.

Men appeared as by magic, from every hand. They fired at the retreating outlaws. Burk saw two saddles emptied. But Lance Gregg was far ahead now. Burk saw the tall sorrel drawing farther and farther ahead of his followers. Then Turkey and Chihuahua, with the others of the Y contingent, popped around a corner of the Congress Saloon. They came running down, separating to look sharply into each doorway. Then they saw Burk.

'Yuh crazy nitwit!' Turkey greeted him. 'Where yuh been?'

'Sweet! Get the doctor — and quick!' Burk snapped. 'There's a girl badly hurt, in here. She gets first attention.'

Sweet nodded and went racing off to preëmpt the services of Doctor Stevens's new assistant. For there was plenty of doctoring to do, now, in Yatesville.

Men were swinging up on their horses, putting out after the running thieves. Turkey grunted his idea that they should join the chase. Burk nodded. They went at a slinging trot for their horses. They got them, swung up and rode out of town to westward, heading for Dead Horse Creek.

But not at once could they overtake Yatesville a-horseback, Yatesville aroused, Yatesville paying off an old, sore score! A limp figure they saw, first, sprawled on the ground with a horse grazing near by and dragging a leg. Sandrock Tom leaned from the saddle to look at the dead man's face. He straightened.

'One o' them hard cases from Prester. He's .45 softened.'

They reached the cottonwoods that fringed Dead Horse Creek and Chihuahua jerked a thumb toward one giant whose long limb had sprouted strange fruit. They looked up as they passed, then spurred on. Three of the dangling men were strangers. But, in his own county, his fellow citizens had taken and hanged Bill Grimm, nor had troubled even to remove from his gaping vest the ball-pointed deputy sheriff's star.

They slid down into the rocky creek-bed and topped clawingly up above the other bank. Well ahead, just popping over a ridge, they saw the dark mass of the posse — or a part of it, perhaps those efficient souls who had been first and, with halting to save Yates County the cost of trials and ropes, were now last. They were south of the Wallop–8 now. But still the riders — pursuers and pursued — were heading west.

'Hey!' Burk yelled, reining in with hand jerked aloft. 'I think there's something funny about this. Why is Lance Gregg going right past his own place this way? It looks to me logical that he'd try salvaging whatever he has in his own house if he's hightailing out of the country — as he must be!'

For an instant he scowled after the now-vanished posse-men, then turned in the saddle, toward the north.

'Maybe I'm all wrong. But I want a look at his house!'

He spurred Funeral and at racking gallop they came toward the south side of the long, low Wallop–8 house. There was no smoke, no sign of life, about the place. Sinister, it lay a squat shape in the little hollow of a sort of basin in the rolling foothills of the Tortugas. They spread out fanwise, then the ends of the fan moved forward to become the horns of a crescent.

At fifty yards' distance Burk stopped them. They studied the house, then went slowly forward. Chihuahua spurred up. He listened.

'Somebody in them house,' he said with sea-blue eyes narrowed intently, 'she's groan like the hell!'

'We'll take a chance! Rush it!' Burk decided.

With his hand-jerk, they sent the horses scuttering across the remaining distance. They flung themselves out of the saddles. To the small windows and the door they ran, Colts or Winchesters up and ready. Chihuahua and Burk made the door. Chihuahua grunted. Burk stared into the long, almost-bare front room.

Across the flagstone hearth a gaunt and egg-bald man sprawled, the center of a widening puddle of blood. His mouth was open and he was groaning dismally. Burk looked quickly from old Booboo Emerick of the Axe to the dusky corners of the room. But Emerick seemed to be alone.

Burk jumped inside the door with gun in each hand. But he could find sign of no other presence than the groaning Emerick. He crossed to the hearth quickly and bent over the Axe owner. Emerick's eyes opened feebly; glared up at Burk.

'Lance Gregg — he downed me!' he mumbled. 'But I never figgered — I was dead already. I thought when yuh was dead, yuh never hurt no more. Only thing I hope is — Gregg comes along, now, to join up with us. An' if Ol' Devil, he don't step ag'in' me, I'm goin' to make — Gregg wish — he hadn't never got killed an' come to hell!'

Turkey came across to look down. Emerick's mouth sagged as he gaped up at Turkey.

'Adkins, too, huh? Who killed yuh, Turkey? In town?'

Then Burk understood.

'He's out of his head. He thinks he's dead, because he believed I was burned to death. He's about gone, looks like.'

He shook old Booboo Emerick gently.

'Tell us about Gregg. Where's he? Why'd he shoot you? You want him for a neighbor? Then tell me where to find him!'

'Do'no' — where he went. I lost him — when he outrode us comin' from town. I sneaked off to the side, like he done. Come yere. He was before me. Packin' up — money hid on the place. He wouldn't — le' me come along. Wouldn't — gi' me a nickel — gitaway money. I went for — m' hawglaig — he beat me — to it — git his skelp!'

'See if you can cut Gregg's trail, will you, Chihuahua!' Burk called to the breed. 'He can't be so far ahead.'

Emerick was dying. Burk shrugged and went out. After all, if that flagged hearth made a hard death-bed, Booboo Emerick had made it for himself. And *he* had no time to waste.

Outside, he mounted. The others were waiting for him. Chihuahua, afoot, was trotting in a circle that radiated about the house, with face close to the ground and constantly widening his circuit. At last he straightened with a war-whoop and came running for his pinto. He went into the saddle like a cat.

'East!' was all he said.

Straight for Dead Horse Creek the trail led. Gregg had been pushing his mount! Riding at a gallop, still they could see in the soft places the deep-struck hoofprints. Down into the creek's bed and up the other bank the trail pointed. On the flat beyond the water, still Greg's horse had pointed due east. Straight past and north of the Y house it went. But Burk began to be oppressed by dread that he could not name. The farther they went, the greater his uneasiness became. At last, he could bear it no longer.

'You-all go on, following this!' he yelled. 'I'm going to cut southeast and see what's at the house.'

He left them at a tearing gait that no horse there could match. Funeral had covered many a mile that day, but now he settled down under Burk and unreeled the miles behind him like ribbon from a spool. Burk could state his fears, now, and his face was grim and grimmer as they raced toward the Y.

'If he cut south and came back for the house — and Myra happened to be there — knowing nothing of our business in town ____'

It pounded in his mind, over and over, set to the drumming tempo of Funeral's flying hoofs. Burk's mouth was a tight line. He could see Myra, now, plainer than ever he had seen her in the flesh. All the arguments and the quarrels of the past slipped away. They were of no importance. He forgot how she had defended Lance Gregg against every charge of his.

Yellow-haired, blue-eyed, red-mouthed — she was the loveliest thing he had ever seen. He knew that now. No . . . he had known it all the time. But he had stubbornly refused to admit it. Perhaps Lance Gregg was already at the Y, where not a man remained. Perhaps the same big hands which had turned the Colts on Fanny were gripping Myra now. He fowled Funeral savagely and the outraged black grunted and threw into his pace the extra spurt he had not known he possessed.

Chapter XXX

'Shall I count three?'

So Burk came pounding into the Y door-yard. He flung the big horse back upon its haunches and dropped off. With Colt in each hand — they had been drawn at the moment he left the others — he raced across the big veranda and to the door.

That, if Gregg had really come here, he would surely be waiting with ready gun, Burk forgot. Rather, it did not occur to him. He whipped inside the great door. In the hallway he glared about him. The house was strangely still, it seemed to him. Deathly still. He took a slow step toward the stair.

Then Myra appeared at the stair-head and bent to look down. He gaped stupidly up at her. She took the first step downward. He went toward the foot of the stairs, not conscious of walking. She was perfectly calm, but between her brows a small frown showed — puzzlement, it seemed. She looked — he thought absently — as if she had never dreamed, certainly did not dream now, that such things as killing were in the same world with her.

'Myra!' he said thickly. 'Myra! You — are you all right?'

351

'All right?' she repeated curiously, stopping halfway down to stare at him. 'Why, of course! Why shouldn't I be? Why do you ask — and look at me that way? And, what in the world have you been doing, Burk? You look like the veriest tramp and ——'

'Why, yes, I suppose I do,' he nodded vaguely, looking down at himself. 'I haven't had time to clean up a lot, lately. But — I just came to — to see if you were all right ——'

Suddenly, it came to him that this sudden reappearance of his made no more apparent difference to her than had his supposed death in the ashes of the manager's bungalow — as Chihuahua had reported her reaction to that supposed death.

He shook his head vaguely. He turned and stumbled across the hall and out of the door. He was at the steps, leading into the yard, when reaction came. He clung to the rail, there, and began to laugh. He laughed until he was weak; then went out to Funeral, tears streaming from his eye-corners and running down his beard-stubbled cheeks, cutting muddy channels in the dust that caked his face.

'You couldn't beat it!' he told himself gaspingly. 'No, sir! You couldn't beat it! Old boy!' he said to Funeral, 'you and I are two dam' fools. But probably I'm both of the two.'

He thought — without any particular emotion or interest — that he had better go after Turkey and the others. Lance Gregg was gone. Burk could not see how Turkey's party could overtake Gregg. Yates County was done with him, anyway.

He led Funeral over to the corral. He looked through the rails and mentally picked the chunky black which Chihuahua had once ridden. He got his rope from the saddle and shook out a small loop; went in and tossed it over the black's head. He brought it out and unsaddled Funeral; turned the weary horse in. The black laid back his ears as he felt the swellfork drop down upon him. Burk pulled the *cinchas* tight, then grinned.

'Going to unwind, maybe?' he grunted.

He gathered up bridle-reins and caught the horn, rammed foot into stirrup and went up with mechanical speed and sureness. The black horse unwound as he found the off-stirrup. For thirty seconds he gave an exhibition second only to that the luckless Eel had staged here. Burk kept his hat, this time, nor lost a stirrup. But his guns flew out of open-topped holsters as he rode this chunky horse to a standstill.

He rode back toward the corral, stooped and picked up his rope. He knotted the tassel-end on the horn and began to coil it. Lance Gregg rode around the corner of the house and pulled in, ten feet away, with a big hand holding a Colt on the saddle-horn. Burk stiffened in the saddle, staring incredulously. He had so thoroughly convinced himself that Gregg had ridden straight out of the country that seeing him was unbelievable. Mechanically, he shook his head, frowning.

'I reckon *this* is wind-up,' Gregg said — and grinned. 'I will give you one thing, though: you have lasted longer than anyone else who ever bucked my play. Partly, of course, because I was too much occupied to really devote efforts in your direction. But, today, you've come to the end of the trail.'

He looked significantly at the empty holsters on Burk's belts; let blue eye roll to the fallen Colts. Burk sat frowning, moveless. He hardly saw how Lance Gregg could miss at that bare ten feet of distance. It seemed that Gregg had called the business — this *was* wind-up, trail's end.

'Yes . . . trail's end. For you,' Gregg said pleasantly. 'For me — for us, that is — if the future isn't precisely what I'd decided to make it, it still seems quite livable. Quite! I have a small matter of forty thousand in my saddle-bags here. And as much more on deposit in a San Antonio bank. We can manage on that, nicely. Even travel a bit! Texas isn't the only place!'

'We?' Burk said stiffly. 'What do you mean — we?'

'Myra — of course, is the other half,' Gregg grinned. 'I think she may not care to go. But after she's gone — she'll be glad to stay. Myra has a lot of pride, you know. Don't look so — so hopeful — so — expectant! I killed my trail on Piedras Hill. Those Diamond Dicks will use up a lot of time, there. Well! I warned you, in Yatesville, long ago. You yapped defiance — as a puppy would. Now ——'

Slowly, very slowly, the hand lifted from the saddlehorn. The blue eyes were smoky; the full mouth curled. If he understood nothing else about Lance Gregg, Burk understood that here was a killer who enjoyed killing; enjoyed watching a doomed man wait for death. And it was death. Certainly it was nothing but death that awaited him. The carbine in its sheath could not be jerked out before Gregg fired a half-dozen shots. If he spurred and ran for it, even if Gregg missed his first shot, he would still overtake and shoot him down. And there was no sound anywhere to tell of help coming — if help could come before that curling finger tightened the last fraction of an inch.

'Shall I count three?' Gregg inquired, with mock-politeness.

Then the idea came. It was a wild, desperate thought. It had not one chance in a thousand of succeeding. But he could find no other. He jerked his head sideways and let his mouth sag amazedly. He was facing the empty veranda. Gregg's head jerked, too, involuntary — and he stopped the movement almost instantly, seeing through the ruse. But in that instant of stopped motion, Burk had moved his feet. The rowels dug into the black.

The horse moved flashingly — jumping straight at Gregg's big sorrel. Burk heard the Colt's roar; heard it roar again; felt pain. But up snapped his right hand, with the rope. The loop darted snakily across the two yards separating them. It fell over Gregg and certainly that third shot went wild as the black spun and darted off to the left.

It happened in a twinkling. The rope twanged as the slack was taken up. Gregg was whipped out of his saddle with a force that staggered the tall sorrel. Burk dared not slacken the lariat. Gregg had another gun; doubtless it was loaded. The loop must hold his arms to his side. He rammed in the hooks and the black surged on. He saw Gregg bumping at the rope's end.

He saw the pistol fall from Gregg's hand. The other hand was empty. He flung himself out of the saddle and ran up the rope as on a thrown calf. He watched the big hands closely until he stopped over Gregg. Then he stiffened and stared. For the loop was not about Gregg's arms, above the elbows. It had caught his neck. It was drawn incredibly small . . .

Burk bent quickly and, with one hand holding the rope, the other on Gregg's shoulder, moved the limp body a little. He tugged at the *hondo,* with difficulty loosened the constricting noose and pulled it over Gregg's head. He noticed that the head rolled slackly in his hand.

He squatted there, beside Gregg, frowning. He put his hand on the shirt-front, over Gregg's heart. He could detect no beat. Nor could he find a pulse in the thick wrist. Slowly, grimly, he shook his head.

'And I *have* said, out of the fullness of my youthful knowledge, that Fate is something writers have manufactured,' he mumbled. 'He had a rope coming to him, the gift of any honest jury in the world! And, instead of adding one more murder to his string, he got the rope — and died with a broken neck!'

He stood up and looked toward the house. It occurred to him that even so calm and uninterested a person as Myra might reasonably be expected to investigate pistol-shots, since they had sounded in the door-yard. He went back toward the house. No sign of Myra. He went up the veranda steps and across. He stopped in the doorway and looked in.

Myra lay at the foot of the stairs, face down, one arm under her, one arm out-flung, as if she had fainted while holding hand to heart. Aunty Ferguson appeared at the top of the stairs, now, rubbing her eyes, calling to Myra.

'She's fainted,' Burk called, from where he knelt with Myra in his arms. 'I'll bring her up to you, Aunty.'

'Fainted! Fainted!' Aunty cried. 'Why —— What happened? Burk! Did — did I really hear shootin'? I was asleep —'

'You did,' Burk said, climbing the stairs. Myra lay limp in his arms, a light burden, and — now that he knew that he meant nothing at all to her; that his living or dying could not move her — somehow the most precious burden he had dreamed of — ever.

'I just killed Lance Gregg,' he finished curtly, going past Aunty to put Myra on the bed in her room. 'He shot at me, but I roped him — I was gunless at the minute. I — broke his neck.'

He went downstairs and, as he crossed the hall to the door, he heard hoofbeats — many horses' hoofs. He came out into the light in time to see Turkey jumping from his horse to pick up a dropped pistol. All of the Y party was there. So were riders from the town; riders who had followed the gang out of town.

'Gregg's hawse! An' Gregg!' Turkey was crying. 'An' yere's Burk's gun — an' his other gun! I ——'

'It's the wind-up,' Burk said, and they whirled toward him.

He came out, to stand and tell grimly, quietly, of Gregg's death. Turkey made a savage sound of satisfaction. The citizens nodded quietly, satisfiedly. It was the wind-up, they agreed.

They told Burk that eleven good men and true of Yatesville had gone to Boot Hill, along with sixteen citizens whose going would be noted only with relief, and with eight members of the One-Gang. Adding these casualties to those the outlaws had suffered in their run from town, there couldn't be many left.

'Jim Hull an' some more was headin' for Prester,' Pa Whittington drawled thoughtfully. 'Thank God! Ed Freeman had gone to Rhettsboro! Wasn't a thing to cramp our style as we come up to our gents. An' nothin' to hender Jim Hull in Prester. Yuh know, I'd hate to be a right-down dyed-in-the-wool Violent Villager when Jim's posse hits the' an' unrolls its bale o' manila.'

'Any of you happen to know how Fanny is? The girl at the Blue Mouse whom Gregg shot?' Burk asked.

'Yeh! She'll be a' right. Doc' says likely yuh saved her life, Burk,' Pa grunted. ' 'Tain't a bad wownd an' the way yuh bandaged it, she'll be a' right.'

They jingled off, on the chance that some stragglers of the One-Gang might be found. For, as Pa said, they had plenty ropes. Burk looked at Turkey; looked at Chihuahua; shrugged and turned wearily toward the house. At the stair's foot, Myra stood.

'I'm glad Fanny is going to get better,' she said evenly. 'It would have been terrible — Lance Gregg killing her — I — Burk . . . Do you still want the whole Y? I'm willing to sell and go away. I — was wrong all the way, it develops. I have known for a good

360